Don't Break *My* Rice Bowl

Robert H. Dodd

with
Patricia Rykiel (née Dodd) and Beth Jackson

Book Cover and Illustrations
by Justine Rykiel

Cataloguing in Publishing Data: a catalogue record of this book is available in the British Library.

This first edition published in 2022

by Holey Jumper Press

Hardback ISBN 978-1-7396155-0-5
Paperback ISBN 978-1-7396155-1-2
eBook ISBN 978-1-7396155-2-9

'What a brilliant, moving and vivid "through the looking glass" book this is. An irresistible read; beautiful, cover to cover.'

—Gareth J. Mitchell, Presenter, BBC World Service

'From the fundamentals of getting food on the table, to the role and impact of fathers, from ambitions to benevolence, not to mention a "Godless" war, there is something for everyone. If I were back in the classroom, I'd teach this book in a heartbeat. It would encourage a plethora of classroom conversation!'

—Nicholas M. Guarracino, Editor and former English Teacher

'To the thousands of histories, memoirs, and novels of America's Vietnam Experience, this is a laudable addition, a descriptive, fast-paced story told from the point of view, not of a combatant, journalist or citizen, but by a civilian agricultural expert inspired by the miracle of rice. Eddie represents the America and the Americans who really wanted to make life better for the Vietnamese. This thought-provoking book deserves a place in the light (not in a dark drawer from where it came!). It is about survival, and so much more than a story of war.'

—Dr Peter J. Woolley, American Political Scientist

To the grandchildren

'The question is not what you look at, but what you see.'
—Henry David Thoreau, *Thoreau's Journal*, 5 August 1851

THE WHITE HOUSE

WASHINGTON

July 12, 1966

Dear Mr. Dodd:

I am pleased that you have volunteered to help the people of South Vietnam.

You and seven other young men are a new kind of pioneer. As on-the-farm advisers to Vietnamese peasants and agricultural workers, you will play an indispensable role in carrying out your country's pledge of aid to Vietnam in a second-front war on hunger and poverty.

I am hopeful and confident that others, encouraged by your example, will want to become one of you.

The Vietnamese people in the provinces and villages are eager to modernize their farming methods, to speed up land reform, to build schools for their children, and to improve health facilities. They need advice and assistance. You and your colleagues will help them to adapt and learn to use U.S. technical and practical farming knowledge and to obtain the supplies and services they need.

Your work and that of other Americans in the villages and on the farms can contribute in an important way to shortening the war and saving the lives and resources of both Americans and Vietnamese.

I extend my personal commendation for your bold and patriotic desire to help a courageous people struggling for freedom and human dignity.

Sincerely,

Mr. Robert H. Dodd
County Agricultural Agent
Old Court House
Fonda, New York 12068

Contents

Foreword........1
Prologue: The Jog........9

PART ONE........17
Hearts and Minds........19
RICE........28
Divinia and Rosita........39

PART TWO........57
Saigon, 'the Pearl of the Far East'........59
The Docks........70
Colonel Horst........83
The Orphanage........91
The Cooperative........102
Ted........113
Dynamo Will........125
Very Big Luck........135
Zoom........146
The VIPs........155
Carl........170
Village Piglets........179
Marshmallow and Cricket........188
House Party........195

PART THREE........209
Lunar New Year, 1968........211
Deadly Believers........218
The Weed Killers........230
Evil Machine........238
Broken Rice Bowls........245
Face-Off........252
Love Song........260

Afterword..265

APPENDIX..271
A Vietnam Vet's Book Review....................................272
Character List 274
Writer Inspiration...276
Robert H. Dodd, Overseas Assignment Life.............280
Acknowledgements and Thanks 286
Book Club Questions..289
The DBMRB Team Bios 290

Foreword

'It's like magic!' Dad marvelled, deleting and inserting text with enthusiasm. He was enthralled with the pleasures of his Osborne portable computer, having recently discovered the ease of editing his words. It was 1983. I was 17 and on a summer trip to the States, standing behind him as he typed, when his manuscript 'Don't Break My Rice Bowl' first came to my attention. That year a draft was completed and printed. However, quite unlike him, as he tended to get on with things in a full-steam-ahead style, he put his work aside, coming close but never finishing it.

His no-warning death in New York City a few years later meant the manuscript remained tucked away, left incomplete. Whenever I moved, my copy always came with me, but the manuscript sat in my drawer for 35 years – as the world moved on (and went digital!). It took the quiet days of the 2020 Covid-19 pandemic for me to appreciate the writing as a link to the past, too good to ignore. As I settled in my reading spot on one of those strangely calm lockdown days, time stood still as I entered the worldly adventures created by Robert 'Bob' Dodd.

This novel, while fictional, includes many autobiographical elements. But it is through the eyes of an agricultural advisor named Eddie that the story is told. The narrative's focus is the intertwining lives of people connected with rice – and rice science and agricultural production were areas in which my dad, Robert, was an expert. The plot has scientists, farmers, villagers and rice paddies in the foreground, with the Vietnam War lurking in the background, just as he had experienced in a chapter of his own life.

He was that rare breed: accomplished in science and science communication with a stand-out flair for the arts. He kept story ideas in pocket-sized notebooks, wrote poetry on various hotel letterheads, made sketches too. Over the years, neatly inked letters and postcards would appear through my childhood letterbox, creatively describing his life far away. Indonesia and Swaziland were the places I heard about most. He made his words count for something, with a playful tone – like signing off with 'Satsuma!' just because he thought it was a funny word to say, or 'Trebor', his name spelled backwards.

Family life for Dad was sprinkled between his work assignments abroad, working as an International Agricultural Consultant. For over 20 years he worked across the world, gone for months to years at a time. The fork in the road moment away from traditional family life happened when I was an infant. Our mother astonished family on both sides of the Atlantic by dramatically taking my sisters and me from New York State back to her homeland in the South of England. Our father never followed, despite hearsay it was the plan. Instead, he acted dramatically too, heading to Vietnam months later to work as an agricultural advisor, joining President Johnson's 'Hearts and Minds' campaign.

Over the years there were various visits to our house and holidays where we reunited, despite my parents' divorce which was quietly finalised. Around him routines were turned on their head. He packed his parenting into compact chunks; it seemed as if there was no time to waste.

Encouraging the arts was a running theme, including taking us all out to try our hand at landscape painting. For a numeracy boost, he produced a neat stack of homemade times table flashcards (he must have had a fondness for this teaching tool as flashcards are mentioned in his opening sentence).

He also rushed us to become worldly, projecting his 35mm assignment slides of sometimes smiling, sometimes malnourished, but always beautifully brown children onto a bare spot on our lounge wall. We learned that life could be less comfortable in other parts of the world. Kwashiorkor, a severe protein malnutrition causing a child's stomach to distend, was just one slideshow revelation.

My cousin Debbie told me he was called 'Tidy Bob' in her house. It made sense. Surprise bedroom inspections (with a ten-minute warning), navy style, with my sisters and me standing to attention by our beds, were carried out with pretend seriousness from him and giggles from us. When he looked under my lumpy quilt and saw all my bedroom junk under there, his expression was a priceless *Gotcha!* one.

Around age nine, I helped him reseed an area of lawn, and acting slapdash was not an option. Soil preparation, taking methodical care, was expected by my over-qualified teacher. And his 'how to pack a light suitcase' lesson (where all the clothes are rolled) was something that, at the time, I never imagined would be useful. I was wrong there! 'Tidy Bob' characteristics were present back then, just as they are evident in the story ahead. The characters he created who got things done without a big fuss – those who valued producing over consuming – were the types he liked in life and who, you will see, get commendation in this book.

When I was 11, he stayed with us from August to January, the longest stretch it had ever been. I came home from school those autumn and winter days to roaring fires that warmed the house right through, and rib-sticking chowders and chilli con carne simmering in large pots. He replaced our old portable record player with a stereo unit and chunky wall-mounted speakers. On Christmas Day he gave us each a record – mine was *Strauss Waltzes*. Dad brought in a wider world – noticing pretty-shaped, ruby-red beans in my dinner bowl was just further evidence. The earthy scent of his pipe, an after breakfast 'things are going well' birdsong whistle, the crinkling and folding of a flapping newspaper – there was a lot to take in, including the headline: 'Elvis is dead.'

The classical music, the hands-on buzz about the place came to a hard stop not long into January. Dad took his efficiently packed bag and left us. Someone else's gain on the international agricultural scene was his daughters' crushing loss. I cycled to school with puffy eyes, feeling a shell creep over me, trying to thicken my skin. The house vibe was akin to broken biscuits, in fragile bits and pieces, like those left at the bottom of the tin. He was not forgotten as the all-female, laissez-faire routines – reminiscent of the *Little Women* coming of age – once again resumed. Time healed, but the wound ran deep.

In *Don't Break My Rice Bowl,* you will see how he reveals a father's perspective on these grown-up matters, creating a character who discusses the ripple effect of divorce and losing influence over his children, while the custodial parent increases her sphere of influence. Reading Dad's words in 2020 triggered a tearful realisation of his side of my childhood story. Problems back home are a small rumbling theme in the novel, but for me, it was the part that had a scraping-off-a-scab effect. I knew his words had uncovered my Achilles heel when I read a section aloud to my husband one night and became choked up, left unable to speak. Dad seemed to have a no-go zone for discussing his absent days, and yet, in his fiction, he lays out his pain for the reader to see.

Philosophical chats, I remember, were more natural to him compared to the 'heavy emotional stuff' (a phrase I've borrowed from his manuscript). He spoke of 'going to the woods to live deliberately', to 'suck out the marrow of life', as Thoreau wrote. At 15, I joined Dad and his second wife Beth, along with my sisters, for our Great Lakes camping holiday where we set up base in the 'rustic', woodsy side of camp. I pointed out to him the sign for the shower block over in the 'non-rustic' side, and he said with a little smile mixed with exaggerated concern, 'There are men over there blow-drying their hair. We're not going there!' He gave us a bar of soap and pointed us towards the obvious place for ablutions: the glistening lake that neighboured our tent.

A couple of years later, a quick stop-off coffee break at a Quebec café turned into another 'classic' Dad moment. He noticed a funeral was about to start at the church opposite, making me look in the same direction just as the coffin was coming into view. 'Hey kiddo, that's how it ends,' he casually mentioned, followed by comments to the effect of Chaucer's 'Time and tide wait for no man', so don't dilly-dally. Despite the 'Hey kiddo', it was a bit heavy for a 17-year-old to be sipping her hot chocolate, contemplating the body in the box.

Dad died at New York's La Guardia Airport on 15 May 1987. By extraordinary chance we met at the airport in the late afternoon with the intention of flying to Maine together – a plan that was changed the day before. It should have been an exciting reunion after 20 months apart, but in an airport lounge scene that scarcely seemed real, his heart went into cardiac arrest. After resuscitation efforts from airport to hospital, the urgency and energy to try and bring him back to life shifted to dignified silence. A nurse handed me his wallet and watch, having a chilling, 'this is really happening' effect. Lingering in a chair pulled close, stunned and tearless, I held his hand and his ticking watch, and at age 21, heard heartbreakingly familiar words in my head: *That's how it ends, kiddo.*

His bright-light life, aged 50, ended in an instant, and the fragility of life became his parting lesson. But with this book we get a little more of him. His writing reminds us that aspirations are important, challenging the 'get in line' approach to life where you plod along on a predictable course. In *Don't Break My Rice Bowl,* he also struggles with the realisation that ambitions can be flattened by a reality sometimes out of our control. The book's title has significance in Vietnamese culture – no spoilers here as Dad explains the meaning eloquently himself.

How significant it felt one lockdown night in 2020 when I watched the musical *Hamilton* on the small screen, absorbed in its emotive tale. *Forgiveness. Legacy. Grief.* During the closing minutes of the performance, listening to the song 'Who Lives, Who Dies, Who Tells Your Story', I knew at that moment the manuscript would not be returning to the drawer.

I asked Beth if she would like to help bring Dad's work to life by creating a book. As a recently retired editor and librarian, and always generous with her time, she was the perfect choice to be working with the words. Our starting point was my crumpled dot-matrix printout; the digital version from the Osborne computer was lost long ago. My daughter, Justine, impressive in the arts like her grandfather, was the obvious choice for creating the book cover and illustrations. And if the Foreword and the Afterword are the 'bookends' to a story, nothing seems more appropriate than to close out with words from Beth, including a 'behind the curtain' peek at our editing process.

My lockdown walks during this project became immersive strolls with Dad. The robotic 'read aloud' voice of the book file playing in my ears somehow became *his* voice. When I heard, 'You shit!', I felt it. When I listened to the amusing lines – such as the one about a 'white sweater stretched under great pressure' – I put them on repeat. Dad and the characters were coming alive. And it got stranger... While typing his words late one night, reading sections aloud for the entertainment, I felt the urge to turn around and look at the couch. What was this? A spirited waltz? *Kiddo, you're reading my book!*

If life had not been cut short, Dad would be in his 80s now. He missed the older years to open up, maybe explain. But the Robert Dodd spirit fills the pages ahead. There's a red thread of music scattered throughout, just as he liked in life. A 'dad' humorous touch too. In the thoughts and dialogue, it's *him* I hear.

Put the kettle on as now is the moment to sink into your comfy reading chair, to experience Eddie's Asian adventure, in a time before social media and smartphones, in a place where conversations (and handwritten letters) were king. And when you have met all the players, not overlooking the 'small' characters, you may like to ask the question I kept asking myself: who are you rooting for?

I did dilly-dally – so sorry about that. But Dad, perhaps time was needed; and we both know, timing is everything.

I now see your writing desk was your place to open up, a healing space. How many of Eddie's footsteps were yours too? If only I had asked about Eddie. If only... But after nearly 40 years, we have reached a moment where Beth and I can finally say on your behalf: '*Don't Break My Rice Bowl* by Robert Hamilton Dodd is now complete.'

Patricia (Trish)

Robert with daughter Patricia on a landscape painting outing, 1976

Prologue: The Jog

Conventional and conservative and common... the 'c' words flipped before my eyes like printed flashcards. Cautious and careful... I was stuck. A large shaggy dog was sniffing at a lamp post across the street. 'And castrated, you and me, buddy, if we don't watch out!' I shouted as he turned, scowled distrustfully and backed away.

It felt good to be outside, away from the suffocating blankets and damp female heat of the bed. How appropriate to be out running early on this skeleton of a morning rather than warm indoors. 'Just love to punish yourself, hey Eddie?' I muttered to the frozen juniper bushes along the sidewalk as I exhaled a plume of white steam which blew back into my face and ringed the fur hat I wore for winter jogging.

My 'Russian Hat', some neighbours called it. And because of it, I'm sure they thought me a little odd, perhaps even a confirmed communist. Not your real American... certainly not a decent, conservative, New England Yankee kind of American, at any rate. Not the type to be trusted with town affairs, serve as usher and pass the plate at the Congregational Church...

I pulled the hat down over my ears and settled it low across my forehead. It felt snug and warm, but the absolute pleasure was in knowing the fur hat gave the neighbours – especially the widow, Mrs Elliot, who evidently slept little and made it a point of honour to station herself behind her lace curtains to keep an eye on me – something to cackle about. Of course, since that morning just before I went overseas when I was feeling high-spirited and trotted up onto Mrs Elliot's porch, pressed my nose against her parlour window and cheerfully wished her good morning, I didn't expect to be able to detect where she was hiding. That was going to take some of the fun out of my morning runs.

I had been home about three weeks before I got this urge to start jogging again. As I thought of it now, it seemed strange I hadn't done any jogging while I'd been away; hadn't even thought of it. Didn't need it. But now I felt the need deeply, and it wasn't to be put off.

Bare maple trees were silhouetted black against the palely lit sky as I trotted by. I loved the bite in the air, loved the frozen bleakness of the little New Hampshire town, the winter starkness that emphasised the basic form of things rather than hiding it away beneath superficial colouring and the dash of summer. The houses hugged themselves in defence against the cold. Why white, I wondered. Why do they invariably paint a house white in such a cold climate? Orange or yellow would be warmer, brighter, maybe cheer people up a bit during the winter. I slammed my hands together… then smiled. Sure, pal, where've you been, said another voice in my head. Ever hear of tradition?

Nothing had changed; it felt like I'd never been away. Somehow I had expected things to be different after my return. And yet, I knew, nothing changes. A week, a month later, everyone's life is exactly the same – no more, no less than before. I remembered the grand thoughts I'd had too: about taking charge of my life, about personal growth, expanding horizons, my marriage to Jean… all the sociological rubbish in the slim paperback books that spread like a fungus in one corner of our little bookstore. As I picked up the pace slightly on the flat stretch at the foot of the hill, I wondered what I had expected. After all, nine years of marriage, a settled home with an easily handled mortgage, an established career as a produce inspector with the state government... what was going to change?

Rounding the corner, that sense of pleasure at simply pushing one leg ahead of the other and letting my mind wander freely came over me. The thick mittens Jean had knitted from an old Vermont pattern in one of the Sunday papers kept my hands comfortable; only my face felt the sting of the dry, cold air. A traffic light flashed yellow as I crossed the street.

'Yellow... proceed with caution,' I mumbled as I hopped the kerb, bent my head down and went along in an easy lope towards the river road. Caution? Hadn't that been a big part of my problem? 'What the hell good has being cautious ever done anyone?' I couldn't help saying it aloud, the words jiggling out of my mouth and slipping across my shoulder in an airy whoosh.

Caution, yes, and this half-life in this sleepy town – this pinched, fretted- and fussed-over little life. My mind raced ahead. And what about my humdrum, dead-end job that I could see stretching on before me interminably... to what? 'Retirement!' I shouted to my fur-capped, crazy-eyed reflection flashing along mechanically in the plate glass fronting the hardware store, like one of those fake rabbits at the dog races.

Retirement. I suddenly saw myself at the centre of a little gathering, a party around 3 pm on my last Friday at work, with the few people who hadn't managed to sneak out of the office early. 'Jesus!' A cake... with a candle! Some words from my division chief – a recent political appointee who'd only just learned where the men's room was and who thought old Mrs Walsh, the grey-haired statistician, was the one retiring. And there I stand, my heart knocking against my ribs, my new teeth clicking, tufts of white hair sprouting from my ears. Jean is beside me, playing the role of the dutiful wife, yet both of us know our minds are on winters in Florida – pedalling our three-wheeled bikes to the grocery store to get in on the one-cent sales.

'...and, ah, Eddie's... ah, faithful service to the people of New Hampshire...' dribbling from the chief's lips, his arm placed fondly around my shoulder. Then, embarrassed fussing with a hastily gift-wrapped box. Oh dear, a watch! A pocket watch. Gee, need one. Inscribed? My name and dates of service? Really? 'Hey, that's really, really nice...!'

I let out a loud yell, a sort of hog-calling whoop along the street. Then I noticed Sam Findley getting set to haul the morning papers inside his news and tobacco shop. 'You've misspelled my name, you fool – on the inscription!' I shouted towards Sam, knowing the old man was hard of hearing. He turned and nodded pleasantly as I glided past.

I turned right off the main street and slowed down my pace as the cold and the ache in my legs began to get to me. The road followed the river, now sheathed in ice, silent. So, Eddie old boy, that's your future all laid out for you, straight and direct, like the railway line across the great Australian desert... the Nullarbor Plain! You can't miss, just stay low, do your thing... On second thoughts, do the thing they have decided is your thing, and you'll make it. Make what, that nagging voice asked. Well, get by; you know, get along just fine.

And Jean, how do I get along just fine with her? Surely that's no problem; an easy one for you to handle, came the answer in that smooth, persuasive tone of the well-adjusted. Easy to say, buster, but it's a problem... And I realised more clearly than ever that behind my decision to go to Vietnam was our situation, our messed-up relationship. Not bad, not fighting and hating and saying things that could never be taken back, none of that. Just no heat. There it was... just no damn heat!

The surface was broken up badly on the river road by the truck traffic to and from the sewage plant, so I had to watch my footing. I thought about how Jean and I carried on together, accepting the rules, the roles, but I knew it was an empty business. Wife, husband – the ready-made tags; just put one on and act accordingly. Who needs spark?

At a huge white pine, with its graceful, horizontal branches reaching out 20 feet from the scaly trunk, I turned and headed back towards town.

But I couldn't convince myself that life without the spark was any good. The thought nagged at me like a rock in my shoe. At Houston's Plumbing, I prepared for the uphill grind – 'the slog to windward' I called this part of the run; how far I got without having to walk determined my fitness. I thought about my recent time in South Korea and tried to figure out why I had felt so different there. Four months; they had whizzed by, and here I was again. It had been a great opportunity. I knew I should be feeling good about what I had accomplished, and I did, but it was too short, too fleeting. My chest was heaving and hurting from the cold and exertion as I topped the ridge. The last punishing climb would have to be walked.

I'd enjoyed every minute away; not often anyone can say that about anything. That's why the time flew. The excitement of a new, totally different culture; yes, that was a big part of it. But also the work: helping to set up a produce marketing system. That was meaningful. Why? Why is it more meaningful in a crowded, bustling Asian country than here in comfortable New Hampshire?

I stopped suddenly, out of breath; my legs felt wobbly. I turned on the hill and looked down over the town. Novelty? Sure, but something more. The people? Yes, definitely. I liked the Koreans, admired their cheerful energy, their Asian doggedness. I remembered how sympathetic I'd felt, about their problems, their lives; I could get excited about trying to make things better. That was it… it was just being able to get excited about something. How the hell can I get excited about making things better in New Hampshire, I wondered. I mean, what's the problem here? Maybe it was the feeling of urgency in a place like South Korea, the need to do something about the basics: food and water. Or did it have to do with the people's acceptance of what little they had while trying to improve things? I didn't know.

I was out of shape, that I knew. I tried to concentrate on breathing correctly but couldn't. I thought about the letter from Fred Bolling. Fred, who I had met at the Department of Agriculture when I came back to Washington, and who had asked me if I would be interested in hearing about any other overseas assignments. Sure, I had answered offhandedly, feeling full of myself – a big-time foreign agricultural advisor, after only four months' experience – and figuring Fred was just being pleasant, giving me a compliment about my work overseas. I didn't expect to hear from him again.

And now the letter, about agriculturalists being recruited to spend at least 18 months as advisors in Vietnam. Was I interested in being considered? Interested?! What an opportunity to change everything, to get away and find some meaning… but could it make any difference, really? Does this sort of thing ever help anyone?

Is it fair to Jean for me to just break away and go off after… after what? What could be done in the middle of a war? I'd been glad enough to be past draft age when troops started heading over a couple of years ago, and now I'd be signing up to go voluntarily! Who stands to gain… Vietnamese villagers? Or me, is it me who benefits? Do I care? Hey, easy man. One step at a time. Get your balance. You can make a contribution; stop at that. Yes, sure, but at the bottom of it all I knew deciding to go to Vietnam, for me, had a lot to do with escape.

I stopped to catch my breath. 'Damn!' I panted, wanting to wish away the next few months of waiting for security clearances and other necessary paperwork if I was going to go. Then I started off at little more than a walk. As I shuffled forward, thinking, words I had seen so many times before jumped out at me from the licence plate of a car parked by the kerb – the New Hampshire motto: LIVE FREE OR DIE. 'No kidding,' I muttered. My bitterness surprised me; it surged from the core of my being and expressed my frustration. Crossroads: go right, carry on to more of the same and be done with it. Forget it; settle down, accept this whole damn useless mess and, at the end, die and get out of the way. Or go left, and…

I stumbled on, recalling words and phrases from unpleasant conversations with Jean during recent weeks. 'So, what does it mean?' she'd asked when the letter came from Washington about the possible Vietnam assignment.

'The East, the excitement of doing something meaningful, the sense of being involved in…'

'Fighting off mosquitoes; living by open sewers!' she'd countered sourly.

'Well, perhaps, but…'

'We'll always have poverty, you realise?' Her curled fingers twitched methodically as she rapidly purled a row along the hairy scarf. I shuddered. Like a huge spider…

'What?' I asked.

'Human nature, Edward. I'm talking about human nature. There will always be poor people, and war and injustice. You do see that, I suppose?' said in a steely, patronising voice.

'Do you think nothing can be done then?'

'Probably not,' from her bent over head, the needles clicking. Click, click, clickety-click.

'Goddamn annoying!'

'No need to swear, nor be annoyed. If everyone would just mind their own business, perhaps the world would be…'

'I mean the clicking of those damn needles!'

'Oh, Edward, what's the use? You refuse to be rational.'

'Fuck rationality!'

Then the exasperated but self-controlled, ever-so-superior look, and silence. Silence for hours, days.

As I approached Mrs Elliot's house I looked for her but couldn't tell if she was watching from behind the curtains. 'I'm back, my dear,' I called out to her front window, then waved. 'But not for long.'

I fell up my porch steps and stumbled into the house. I was going to be sore for several days; I knew that. It seemed stuffy and hot now. The kitchen light was on; I could hear Jean making breakfast. I took off the fur hat and jacket and hung them on the rack by the door.

'Well, Jean, it's only for 18 months, then I'll be back to settle in for good,' I said weakly from the hallway, but not really giving a damn. No answer came from the silent kitchen. Oh God, no tears, I prayed; please spare me that.

'Jean?' I called from the hallway.

'What?'

'I'm going.'

Silence… I leaned my head against the wall and waited and listened.

'You shit!'

PART ONE

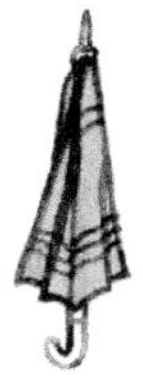

Hearts and Minds

We sat in a sawdust-littered bar on upper Powell Street in San Francisco, drinking draft beer and snapping peanuts. The musicians had returned to the low platform and while Ted topped up the glasses, the six-piece Dixieland band blasted off with another lively number; the bright brassy notes surging across the smoky room as the players, quickly getting into their stride, wove improvisations around the familiar melody.

I settled back as Ted propped his elbows on the table and cupped his head in his upturned hands to enjoy the music as we gradually let go and relaxed on this last evening in the States before our flight to the Philippines. The slightly muffled, half-off-key plunking of the piano led the group through the transitions, then, paced by the sharp, acid bite of the trumpet, the players came to the final deep breath and the clamorous finish. 'Great!' I yelled and, along with everyone else in the place, clapped my appreciation.

A slim-waisted waitress placed another pitcher of beer on the table and turned towards the bar. We watched as she skilfully swivel-hipped her way past the tables and chairs, a serving tray balanced precariously over her head.

'They're not like boys, you know, Ted.'

'What?'

'They are not just soft boys who dance backwards.'

'Who?'

'Girls, you nit!'

'Hey, what's this "nit" business?'

'Just a little something I picked up during my worldly travels, old cock!' I said, laying on the English accent.

'You're a strange one, you know, Eddie,' he shouted over the pounding music. 'Who the hell are you, anyway? What makes you tick?'

'What makes any of us tick?' I responded, speaking more to myself than Ted since he'd turned to look at the band. I didn't know for sure, about myself or anyone else. Like a lot of people, I knew what I didn't want or like, but I had only the vaguest idea of what I needed or should aim for.

Ted turned back to face me. 'Are you going to Vietnam to get away from something?' he asked.

'Maybe to find something.'

'Well, I doubt if it's there.'

'Bad luck!' I said and smiled at his serious face. 'Come on, let's keep it light on our last night.' I reached over to fill his glass while he just stared at me.

Ted and I got on well. We'd quickly become friends right at the start when we met in Washington. I'd hit the ground running like a bloodhound dropped to the scent, except in my case, all the senses were atwitter. Washington did that: brought on a feeling of excitement at participating in the nation's, even the world's, business. It could become addictive. Along with the rest of the hot-eyed people on the streets, I found myself caught up in the swirl, the barely controlled make-important-of-trivia hysteria that swept back and forth across the throbbing city like a hot wind. In a pale blue seersucker suit and carrying my pointed, black umbrella – even though the heat blistered the tar on the streets and there was no hint of rain in the shimmering sky – I was ready.

About half the men had arrived by the time I got from the airport to the government hostel on Connecticut Avenue. That's when I learned, from a news release posted on the bulletin board, that we were the first group of agriculturalists to answer President Johnson's call for civilian advisors to go to Vietnam to help 'win the hearts and minds' of the peasant farmers and villagers. Great stuff; had a nice ring to it. 'Hearts and Minds', and – as Ted later added in Saigon while we admired the lovely, slim Vietnamese girls – 'arms and legs and...'

There were 14 of us in the group, ranging from about 25 to over 50 years of age, from all over the US. Ted and I shared a room. He was a sandy-haired young-looking guy in his late 20s who had been serving as the agricultural agent in one of those poor, empty counties in northern Pennsylvania nobody had ever heard of. He'd arrived in town a few days earlier and was all settled in when I showed up.

'Why the suit?' Ted asked. We were sitting on the little veranda overlooking the gardens and the tennis court drinking a couple of beers he'd stashed away in the communal kitchen.

'Oh, just my travelling gear,' I answered.

'Looking the part?'

'What part?'

'The international agricultural development expert,' Ted said as he sprawled comfortably on the deckchair wearing a pair of ragged shorts and a well-worn t-shirt with 'ABC World of Sports' splashed across the front.

'Well, I've worked in South Korea,' I said, looking at this tight-lipped guy.

'Really? Why the umbrella – expecting rain?' he asked, his face expressionless.

'Never know. Actually, it's something I picked up in England; spent a year there enjoying the maritime climate after I got out of the navy. Great time,' I said, suddenly wondering why I was bothering to explain. Ted was like that, at least during those first few weeks. He had a way of getting me to talk about myself even though he didn't seem very interested in what I said and gave away nothing of himself.

We all quickly settled into a routine, travelling to the State Department each day for the training sessions: discussions about the people and history of Southeast Asia, language lessons with three shy Vietnamese women, and sensitivity training. Some of the men didn't think much of the Washington training and wanted to get straight out to Vietnam and go to work. I didn't mind at all – nothing could bother me. I was on a high just being away from home and on this new adventure.

Learning to handle the Vietnamese language – mainly getting the hang of the different voice tones which changed the meaning of a word – was the most challenging part of the training for all of us. In some ways it was like learning a lot of new songs; the tone was the thing and had to be absolutely correct. Slowly, however, we made progress and began to believe that just possibly we might be able to communicate in Vietnamese one day.

Sensitivity sessions were the most enjoyable part of the training. Dr Leitz, an affable psychologist, came in a few times a week to lead the group. He was keen to get us talking about ourselves and 'interacting' with each other. The idea of the group was all the rage. To be a 'team player,' Dr Leitz explained, his eyes brimming with affection for his latest 'group', 'is to be an effective player.' Naturally, he didn't think much of the comment that people choosing to work in Vietnam were probably misfits and damn poor team players! I had to laugh at that one. We certainly were misfits!

'Not so,' Dr Leitz countered in his firm but friendly way. 'You men were selected because you've been successful in your careers,' he said, puffing us up to bursting point. 'And you've been successful because of your ability to function effectively with other people: colleagues, supervisors…' He talked that way, usually looking smug and knowledgeable, like a television commercial doctor who's just calmed a distraught person with some sound advice about a gently effective laxative.

'Or we've been selected because other people weren't fools enough to apply!' Ted put in sarcastically.

One of Dr Leitz's pet themes concerned the reasons we had put ourselves forward to serve in Vietnam, considering the dangers of war, the hardships to be expected and all. This interested me since my own reasons weren't very clear. For all the pleasure I got in being away from the things at home that bothered me, I still felt guilty about leaving.

At one session, Dr Leitz tried to get some of us to open up more and talk about our reasons for volunteering. He looked at me and nodded. I guess I was ready to start exploring these things. Anyway, I began to explain how I wanted my life to count, to add up to something meaningful.

'What does that mean to you, Eddie?' Dr Leitz asked.

'I know this sounds corny, but I want to do what little I can for those people so they can have a chance for a decent life,' I heard myself responding, sounding trite and holier-than-thou. I went on about America's responsibility to help Vietnam with its social and economic problems and not only with the war-related stuff. I could almost see Jean giving me that damn smug look of hers, reserved for when I got on my soapbox. Even so, I was beginning to realise Vietnam was going to be more than a lark; things unspoken so far, buried in my subconscious, were lumping up, taking shape. I stopped talking abruptly and looked down. The room was quiet for a moment, then Dr Leitz, always supportive, said a few words about the need for all of us to reflect on our motives and be honest with ourselves about the Vietnam assignment. He then announced the end of the session.

Ted and I went for a cup of coffee at the cafeteria where he asked about the heavy emotional stuff. 'Well, Ted, I think I believe everything I said in there; I really do feel what we're getting ready for in Vietnam is important.'

'Sure, no argument,' he said lightly.

'I did get carried away a bit, though, and forgot to mention the good salary, as well as the chance going to Vietnam gives me to escape from my troubles at home and be considered a hero to boot! I don't think Dr Leitz wanted to hear that!'

'You're becoming Asian already,' Ted observed.

'How do you mean?'

'Saying things you think other people want to hear.'

'No, not entirely,' I responded, unable to say if I was becoming more like an Asian, as he said, but feeling in the future I could be more truthful with myself.

'Hey, wake up, Eddie,' Ted nudged, snapping me back to the San Francisco bar.

'Oh, just reliving the training…'

'Forget it. Glad it's over. If I'd known we had to go through all that guff, I might have thought differently about this job.'

'Nah, you wouldn't.'

'You're right,' he said, grinning. 'It's tailor-made for a couple of flakes like us!'

'Careful, huh? That hurts!' I said, then settled back to enjoy the music. The bar was full of people now, and the band, responding to the noise and excitement of the crowd, was substituting loudness for artistry.

I'd been thinking of calling my brother Carl to say goodbye and decided to see if there was a phone in the bar.

In a narrow hallway next to the toilets, I found the phone, dug out some coins and dialled the number. As I waited for the connection, a soft-looking blond guy bumped against me on his way to the men's room.

'Hi, sweets,' he said and ran his hand lightly over my shoulder.

'Cuban Embassy, 'ello, who you want?' a strange voice said on the phone.

'F-off, pal!' I said and pushed at the blond guy.

'*Ay, Caramba!*' the weird voice gasped over the background clatter made by the angrily slapping teletype.

'Oh, such language! You're a naughty…' the blond guy was saying.

'What the hell! I want…' I was confused by the strange voice. I twisted around to see where the blond guy was. He stood in the men's room doorway smiling at me. Then I heard the phone bang hard against something and scuffling noises and shouting. '…a leetle joke, Senor…' the strange Spanish voice, now quite faint, trailed off as the phone was handled and I heard someone breathing.

'Hello?'

'Carl?'

'Yes'

'Eddie here. What the hell is going on there?'

'Hey, hello Eddie. Christ, what a racket! Where are you? I'm sure glad you're not the publisher. That was our new photographer. Peace Corps kid; spent time in Central America; thinks he's a Latino; guess his mama didn't teach him anything about professional phone etiquette. Doesn't give a damn, but good sense of humour.' Carl was laughing. The band was blasting away. I held one hand over my ear to try to block out the noise.

'Sounds like your kind of guy,' I said, glad to be in touch with my whacky older brother again.

'He is, takes great pictures; no inhibitions, you know? Sure livens up this place. How you doin'? Where are you?'

'I'm in a bar in San Francisco, the band is going crazy, and there's a guy watching me from the doorway of the men's toilet.'

'Sure sounds like fun!'

'Yeah. Well, I'm leaving tomorrow, just calling to say goodbye.' The blond guy had disappeared into the toilet.

'You know, I've been thinking. Maybe I'll try to come out to visit you once you get settled in, if I can get the skinflint who owns this rag to kick in a few bucks for a ticket – if I promise to write up a story or two.'

'Sure, that would be swell! Plan on it. I'll let you know when's the best time later.'

'OK. Do you know what you'll be doing yet?' Carl asked. The blond guy was back, standing against the wall as though he was waiting to use the phone.

'Advising in one of the provinces, working with the agricultural people; that's all we know.'

'Sounds good, Eddie,' Carl said as I strained to catch the words. 'I guess you realise there's a name for your condition?'

'What condition?'

'Male menopause.'

'Male menopause!' I shouted down the line, then remembered the blond and looked over at him.

'Tee hee,' he said distinctly as he lounged against the wall picking his yellow teeth.

'Yep, you're at that age, man,' Carl went on. 'Last chance to make your mark in the world; do something meaningful. According to the books, it has to do with your sense of impending mortality.'

'You sound very wise and knowing. The big 4-0 really agrees with you!'

'Been reading up. By the way, you don't expect to come back 18 months from now and drop into the old slot, do you?'

'Oh, I don't know.'

'Look, don't worry about it. You're lucky to have this chance. Don't miss it. People will say you're mad, but don't let it bother you. Just remember, they're jealous because they can't escape from the big…'

'Shit sandwich?' I laughed, completing Carl's line. It was one of his favourite terms for what he considered the whole ratbag of tension and pressure, and consumption-orientated claptrap we called our high standard of living. I looked over at the blond guy. He stared at me for a second, then silently mouthed the words 'shit sandwich?', a questioning look on his face.

'Yeah, that,' Carl said. 'And don't get confused and start to think you're going to make any changes in the world. Hell, look at this photographer of ours. To hear him, he spent two years smoking quality pot and chasing the *senoritas*. Just enjoy the chance to escape, the adventure.'

'OK, Carl, take care and thanks for that terrific advice. Don't know what I'll do without you! Gotta go now.' The blond guy quickly straightened himself up and walked back into the crowded bar.

'Of course, what's a brother for? *Adios*!'

RICE

Manila, glinting white and hot beneath the tropical sun, pulsed with activity as the minibus rattled through the streets on our way to the rice training centre 40 miles south of the city. I forced the rusted window down a few inches and craned my head around to see the sights. The smells of lush vegetation and flowering trees, of engine smoke and human waste flooded through the window; a nose-twitching blend of dampness, sweetish decomposition and various rank, unfamiliar odours. Jean's comment about the open sewers came back to me as the bus travelled beside a canal oozing with chocolate-coloured slime and lazy brown water creeping towards the sea. I told you so, I could hear her say. I had to laugh. If she could see me now, she'd be convinced I'd gone mad and was in need of her sympathy.

'Why you chuckling, Eddie?' an older fellow nicknamed Shoop said from the seat behind.

'Huh? Oh, just thinking how great all this is,' I said over my shoulder.

'This? Great? It's the pits, man. You're mad… and there must be something wrong with your nose!'

'Working fine,' I said and turned back to the window. Now, at last, I thought as I settled myself to enjoy the sights, we are on our way! First to the countryside for intensive rice training, then back to Manila from where we would be taking field trips to some nearby farming areas, and finally on to Vietnam. It was all happening; I felt great!

The bus moved slowly along the road, closely watched by a group of field workers, their heads shaded by large cone-shaped straw hats, their feet and legs planted in the soft, ankle-deep mud. Shimmering light reflected from the wind-ruffled surfaces of the rice paddies, the acres of flooded fields looking like huge dazzling mirrors. The area was a patchwork of vivid colour: rich reddish-brown of the soil in bare unflooded paddies, pale lemon of recently transplanted rice seedlings, and intense blue-green of mature plants that gradually graded to a golden hue as the grain ripened.

After we left the bus we were shown into a small auditorium. A thickset man stepped to the front of the room. 'Welcome to the International Rice Research Institute,' he said when we'd settled down. 'We call it IRRI for short, pronounced just like the town in Pennsylvania. You can call me Stubbs. I'm the senior training officer here.' He had a pleasant, deep voice and spoke in the nondescript accent of an American who has lived abroad for many years. His arms and face were tanned; his curly, grey-flecked hair cropped close to his head. 'We're going to make rice experts out of you guys in two weeks!'

'Hey, out of sight!' someone in the back called, obviously glad to be out of the bus.

'Out of sight, indeed,' Stubbs echoed as he set his face in a rough approximation of a smile, folded his arms across his chest and took a look at us. He must have sensed our restlessness and moved to finish his introductory remarks. 'But it won't be easy,' he continued. 'Not terribly difficult for experienced agriculturalists like yourselves, but you'll have to work.' Stubbs paused briefly, took a big pipe from his pocket and started to stuff it with tobacco, then added, 'I'm a Corn Belt man myself. When I arrived here some years ago, all I knew about rice was it went into rice pudding!' He began to chuckle at his own humour.

'You mean there's more to it than that?' someone joked.

'Please be quiet over there!' Shoop said with exaggerated politeness, like a high school librarian hushing a cheeky, boisterous kid.

'Come on, you guys, knock it off,' Ted said firmly.

'Now, where were we? Ah, yes, there is so much more to rice than creamy rice pudding,' Stubbs continued, trying another of his crooked smiles. His expression then went flat.

'Naturally, we're going to work your tails off. But, if you put the time in, if you work at it in the fields and greenhouses, and if you keep your eyes open and ask questions when you don't understand something, you'll go to Vietnam knowing more about the rice plant and how to make it respond than any farmer you'll ever meet.' He sucked at his pipe for a few seconds, scanned the faces in the room and continued.

'Let me tell you something else. In a country like Vietnam, the average rice yield is about 1½ tons of grain per hectare. We will show you how to grow at least 4 tons per hectare, season after season, without fail. You guys are going to be shock troops for the Green Revolution! You're lucky to be in the right place at the right time.'

'Hey, you should rename this place RICE – the Rice International Centre for Excellence!' I called out.

'I like it! That's way catchier,' Shoop agreed.

'Bueno!' Julio, an attentive guy from Puerto Rico, said and whistled to indicate his approval.

'All right. I get the picture,' Stubbs said pleasantly. 'I see we have some spirited fellows in the group. No problem. We'll work it out of you in the fields. For now, let's go over to the dormitory and get you guys checked in. Then we'll have some dinner. We start first thing tomorrow morning so I suggest you have an early night. OK, follow me.'

Stubbs was right when he said it wouldn't be easy. From early in the morning until late evening, we worked in the fields or attended lectures given by IRRI staff specialists. Along with Stubbs, these experts gave us a comprehensive course in modern rice growing, from seed treatment to planting, harvesting and storing the grain.

The basic idea was to have each person perform all the tasks associated with growing a crop of rice – a sequence that usually takes four months – in just two weeks. This was possible because, at the Institute, rice was at every stage of growth in one field or another, and we shifted to the successive stages as we studied each task in the crop sequence.

On the second day, after getting some seed soaking, we went out to the fields to prepare beds where the pre-soaked seed would be planted the following day. After that, teams were formed to start the ploughing of the main paddy.

Water buffaloes, known in the Philippines as carabaos, were used in the flooded fields to pull the simple, hand-held ploughs. Each two-man team was assigned an animal, and with the help of a Filipino farmhand, we all took turns learning how to get the lumbering, large buffalo to ease the plough through the soil. The objective was to turn the soil over and form a level slurry of fine mud into which seedlings would be transplanted.

Usually docile, the carabaos could become intractable in the hands of novices, we soon learned. Just after Shoop took over from the Filipino fellow, his animal took a swipe at him with its thick, curved horns. Shoop very gingerly urged the grey-black, mud-splattered animal across the field on his first try.

At the far side of the paddy, Ted was having trouble. 'Whoa!' he shouted, his buffalo beginning to pick up speed as it approached a tricky corner manoeuvre. 'Damn it, slow down, old boy!' Ted bellowed as he saw the animal getting closer to the dyke at the end of the run. Not sure the carabao wouldn't just crash across the dyke and keep on going, pulling him after it, he let go of the plough and yanked hard on the reins. The animal stopped short. Ted paused to get his breath, then picked up the plough, cradled it to his chest, lunged forward through the mud and dropped the plough in front of the startled animal.

The buffalo was dumbfounded by this move; such behaviour was totally outside of its experience. By this time, muttering to himself, Ted had settled the plough into the soil for the return run and was trying to get the animal to turn around. The water buffalo was so put out and confused by the fact it was looking at and was not in front of the plough that it refused to budge. The animal's large doleful eyes searched the face of this crazy white man who now waved and shouted for it to do something. Quite a sight! I had to laugh at poor Ted's predicament.

Within an hour we were covered in mud, top to bottom; it oozed between our toes, slopped at our legs and got inside our shorts. The buffaloes flicked water and flecks of mud from their tails into our eyes and hair. All over the field, men were yelling and cursing as they tried to manipulate the animals and slippery ploughs into position to turn some reasonably straight furrows.

Stubbs arrived to see how we were progressing; he was shocked. 'This looks awful,' he announced. 'Look there, you haven't touched that piece… that's not ploughed!' In one corner, great lumps of clay were pitched up, making little islands in the field. 'That should be perfectly level,' he said, clearly disappointed. 'You can't irrigate a rice paddy with high spots – they'll dry out, your plants will die.' We stood beside our animals or on the dykes looking at the appalling mess we'd made.

'You guys don't know how to handle those animals. Why, hell, any peasant farmer in Asia can do a better job of ploughing than that; and you guys are college grads!' Stubbs groaned. 'I'll tell you something about carabaos: you have to let them know you like them! Carabaos won't do a damn thing for you unless they know you care! Now come on, get in there and do it properly.'

'They're hard to love, Stubbs,' Ted shouted breathlessly as he was dragged past by his determined-looking buffalo.

'They're not. They're beautiful, sweet-natured creatures!' Stubbs yelled after him.

'OK, you guys, let's see some affection over there!' I called from across the field as I got my animal into position for a pass at one of the high spots.

'Heya, love that critter!' shouted Shoop from the dyke. 'Pat him on the ass!'

'Yahoo…!' a thin, stalk-like guy named Larry yelled as his carabao broke into a trot and pulled him off his feet. He dropped the plough, fell over to one side and sank to his knees in the sloppy mud while the huge buffalo, incensed by the improper handling of his reins, charged forward, sending the plough skidding and jumping along the surface of the field.

Arms akimbo, Stubbs shook his head in pure disgust. 'Get this mess cleared up. I'll see you guys at dinner,' he growled sourly and stamped off.

We were settled back in the lecture room while Stubbs warmed up to his favourite topic: rice. 'Well, as you can see, we are well funded and have some of the most respected scientists doing work here. IRRI is a tremendous long-term investment in facilities and people. The goal is to provide the farmers of Asia the best possible seed and the most productive ways to grow that seed in the different climatic zones and soils of the region. And where has all this gotten us?' Stubbs asked, without pausing for an answer. 'After many years of plant breeding and selecting, we are ready to recommend a couple of high-yielding rice varieties for planting by farmers. You men are at IRRI at a time when we are releasing our first varieties, called IR-5 and IR-8.'

'Hey, how about that!' someone said as Stubbs paused to measure the effect of his little speech.

'The old technological fix!' said Steve, an unusually quiet man from the Midwest who, when he did rouse himself, often was the spokesman for the few men in the group who seemed more concerned about the religious implications of our work in Vietnam than the food problems. I hadn't heard the phrase before and I wasn't sure what Steve was getting at.

'Of course,' Stubbs said coolly. 'After all, we are scientists. You can criticise the...'

'A technological answer for every problem,' Steve broke in. 'The American, or Western, ideal of a...'

'No, not every problem, but for some, yes,' Stubbs responded calmly as though he'd been through this argument many times before and had resolved it to his satisfaction. Still, it made me think. Steve had a point. Throwing money at problems; manipulating, creating technologies to make things better. Better? Always? How? I wondered.

'Solutions which usually lead to the need for more solutions...' Steve spoke up again but then seemed to lose interest as his words trailed off.

'Often that's true,' Stubbs said. 'But don't forget most of us are here because of what you call the "technological fix". We, or our ancestors, would have been eliminated by famine or disease had it not been for science and technology.'

'So, Stubbs,' Ted butted in, 'what's the chance of us taking the new seed to Vietnam?'

'We knew you fellows would ask that. At the moment you won't be able to take any seed with you, not because we object, but because an official request first must be received from the Vietnamese government.'

'Hell, that could take years. They might not even know about the new varieties,' Ted responded.

'Oh, they know. We've had some of their top agricultural people here. They've seen the results in the fields and have gone home with all the research information. That was months ago.' Stubbs shrugged his shoulders. 'Don't ask me what goes on over there.'

'What's being done about it?' I asked, glancing up from sketching my very best amiable-looking carabao.

'Nothing. There might be good reasons they have delayed; we don't know,' answered Stubbs. 'What I do know is one of your main jobs in Vietnam will be to encourage the government to introduce the improved rice varieties and help their technicians and farmers properly grow them. You men are going to be very heavily involved in rice farming for the next few years. In fact, that's why you were sent here for training.'

Stubbs had the hint of a smile on his face. 'You know, many of our Filipino farmers call the new rice "miracle rice" because of its high yield. I just thought of something – you guys will be the "Miracle Workers" of Vietnam!' Stubb's face broke into a full smile, making a slight cackling noise and then he thought of something else. 'It's a damn miracle none of you got trampled by an irate carabao out there.' Tears started in his eyes as he tried to control his amusement. He turned to the blackboard, packed tobacco into his pipe, lit up, and began writing with his head wreathed in a cloud of white smoke.

It was during the rice training that Ted and I became good friends with Shoop. He was something of a loner, preferring to read or write letters rather than join the other men in the evening. Sometimes we three would meet in Shoop's room for a drink to 'reinforce' each other, as Dr Leitz would have said.

Shoop had only one reason for going to Vietnam: money. With him it was all very simple. He had a leave of absence from his job near Albany, New York, and after his tour of duty he would return to his work and family. With a house full of kids, a couple now finishing high school, Shoop's only interest was getting ahead on the mortgage, putting aside a little money for the extra expenses he could see coming as his kids began attending college. Uncomplicated and easy-going, Shoop knew himself well. He was comfortable with the decision he'd made to sign up for work in Vietnam and was enjoying the change of pace and the peace of his single room after his hectic, noisy home. He was amused by the soul-searching, the doubts and confusion expressed by some in the group. He had little to say during the sensitivity sessions except for one short speech. Prodded by Dr Leitz, Shoop openly described his situation, explained his motives, and ended by saying he couldn't understand what all the fuss was about. 'You sign up for a job in Vietnam, you go and do the job, and you return home… no big production,' is how Shoop had put it.

One evening, after Stubbs had kept us out in a large paddy most of the afternoon hand picking weeds, Ted and I went along to Shoop's room. That's when I started kidding him about his drinking habits.

'You shouldn't drink up here all alone, Shoop. It's not good. You are becoming a closet drinker, first step to becoming an alcoholic,' I said sternly, as though I knew all about the perils of solo drinking.

'A quiet drink or two does no harm, and a man needs a little privacy away from all these young kids, Eddie,' he responded quickly, likely buzzed from an earlier drink.

'You mean me or Ted?'

'Ha, you're no kid, Eddie, but you could use time for reflection after the heat of the day. Does a man good.' Shoop was reaching for his big bottle of whiskey.

'Shoop's right. If he wants to sit up here and drink by himself, that's his business,' Ted said.

'So, there you are, Eddie. Baby Sandy knows,' Shoop announced loudly.

'Baby Sandy?' Ted asked, puzzled.

'Yeah. Look, isn't that Baby Sandy?'

I didn't know what to think and smiled at Ted. Shoop, who never really smiled except with his eyes, busied himself with the glasses.

'That's him all right,' Shoop went on. 'Just picture him in his little blue and white sailor suit, tripping along the lane… what a darling!' I laughed, faintly recalling an early character from the funnies page, or was it a child movie star called Baby something? It must be Sandy. Shoop would know about such things.

'What are you guys going on about?' Ted demanded, obviously irritated at being the object of a joke he did not understand.

'Hey, Eddie,' Shoop called as he came out of the bathroom with a towel and two extra glasses he'd just rinsed. 'Baby Sandy goes to school!'

'Baby Sandy gets a horse!' I said in a cute, lilting voice, picking up on the idea.

'Who the hell is Baby Sandy, you mugs?!' Ted insisted.

Ted's annoyance added to my amusement. Shoop just stood holding his big bottle of cheap whiskey, his eyes flashing merrily, the alcohol taking over.

'Ah, screw you two!' Ted said.

'Baby Sandy gets laid!' I blurted out.

'Baby Sandy gets his dork dunked by a Da Nang dolly,' Shoop croaked.

By now Shoop's face was brick red, his eyes blazing with delight. We clasped arms, then started marching around the room as Shoop began to chuckle. He had the towel tucked under his belt and was still hanging onto his whiskey bottle.

We took turns declaring Baby Sandy this, Baby Sandy that, then shifted to a clumsy tarantella step; Shoop's towel flapped madly, his bottle held high, as I whirled him around.

I was laughing as we flopped on the couch, gasping for air. Ted was grinning at us: two crazy, red-faced fools giggling where we'd dropped. He walked over, took the bottle of whiskey from Shoop and fixed three stiff drinks.

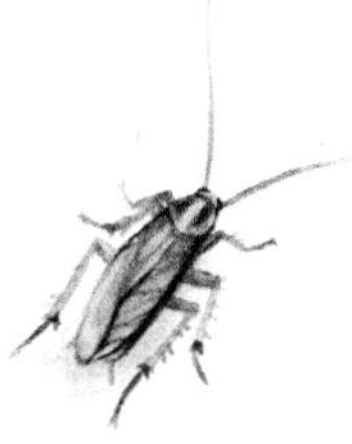

Divinia and Rosita

We were staying in Manila for a few weeks while making daily trips to outlying farming districts for additional experience before going on to Vietnam. The Philippines was ideal for training because many of the farming problems the country faced were similar to those in Vietnam, and the tropical climate much the same.

Each morning, we stuffed ourselves into the tiny bus and set off to look at irrigation schemes, farms and agricultural projects in the countryside around Manila. We were guided by Warren, a rural development specialist who had worked with US foreign assistance programmes for over 20 years – the past six in the Philippines. Worn and dried like old saddle leather, Warren no longer believed in foreign aid. From his field experience in a number of poor, overcrowded countries, and because of his underlying pessimism, he'd concluded development assistance didn't work, or at least made little difference in the lives of the people at the bottom of the economic order: the rural poor. Although counting the days until his retirement, Warren understood the kinds of problems we would face in Vietnam and counselled us about what to expect. I didn't share his cynicism, but I liked him and appreciated his practical, if usually negative, insights.

'The trouble with introducing better seed and fertiliser is these improvements often disrupt the society you're trying to help,' Warren was saying in his slow, thoughtful way to some of us sitting in the back of the bus as it lurched along a country road on one of the trips. He'd been droning on for over an hour since our last stop at a government farm-credit office. I was fighting to stay awake. 'The new ways often will benefit the already better-off farmers more than the poorer ones and, even if culturally acceptable, the improvements can cause the gap between the poor and the rest of the society to get wider…'

'It reminds me of an old Billie Holiday number,' I interrupted, pulling myself up, trying to shake off the sombre mood brought on by Warren's words. I started to sing: 'Them that's got shall get…'

'Hey, knock it off, Eddie!' somebody shouted from the gin rummy game in progress at the front of the bus.

'Yes, I know that tune, Eddie,' Warren said, smiling wanly. 'You're going to find a lot of that in these countries, and being flippant is no answer,' he added a bit irritably. I settled down in the seat and remained quiet while Warren continued. I knew he was right, but still couldn't see the need to be so serious when discussing the problems of the poorer countries.

Sometimes we got off the bus in a village and wandered around talking to the people, asking about the crops and living conditions. Regardless of the language difficulties, the villagers were always friendly and full of fun. It brought back memories of South Korea. Those with the least of the world's goods seemed to be the best-natured, more accepting and willing to let time pass to exchange a word, a thought, a laugh. I felt more at ease, closer to these simple people here in a dusty village than back home at a pot-luck dinner or an office party. It was easier to touch another's life here. Why, I wondered, as the experience was repeated in the villages; why that impenetrable shell around people in one culture and the apparently easily bridged gap between people here?

Even Warren was relaxed in the villages. He brightened up and enjoyed the easy banter that went on between our group and the villagers. Because he knew the local language well, Warren helped translate. He was in his element, sitting on a low wooden stool on the bamboo floor in one of the tiny pole-houses, talking about crops and the weather, occasionally picking up a wide-eyed, shiny brown toddler who wandered close, and propping the child up on his bony knees. Warren told us no people on earth were more friendly than the Filipino peasants. And as we sat among their bright, laughing faces, answering questions and swapping stories, I knew they were indeed special.

Naturally, visiting farms and listening to Warren's pessimistic view of life didn't take up all our time. Ted and I strolled the city streets trying out the local foods and entertainment, hitting a few bars to get the flavour of the place. We soon discovered Manila was two cities. Behind the facade of gleaming, modern office buildings and hotels fronting tree-lined Roxas Boulevard and beautiful Manila Bay – the business and classy tourist sections of the city – nearby streets like Mabini and Del Pilar were walled with nightclubs, day clubs, massage parlours, steam baths and seedy bars catering to every human desire and kinky aberration. Here in car-jammed, smoky streets and alleys, the deals were made; the pimps and hookers netted their prey.

It was a bright Saturday afternoon. Ted and I were picking our way past the piles of trash along one of the back streets, carefully avoiding spots in the crumbling pavement where missing concrete slabs exposed the deep, jagged storm drains now loaded with trash. Young men clutched at our arms, trying to entice us into a peep show or other diversion. 'Participatory sports!' Ted said with a laugh about this other, long list of activities being proposed as we dodged our way up the street.

Bargirls in thin, cheap dresses sat on folding chairs and little stools yakking among themselves or showing a bit of thigh and sputtering suggestive remarks in the staccato Filipino English as we passed by. At corners, we were surrounded by wafts of blue-white smoke from the food sellers' carts as they busied themselves with pans of sizzling chicken and fish. Flattened, splayed squid were stretched on tall racks against building walls while bargirls squatted by the charcoal braziers to await their piece of the strong-smelling, yellowish, charred flesh.

In front of the Blue Moon – indistinguishable from all the other bars except for the name painted crudely in yellow on a pale blue board – we met Divinia and Rosita.

'Why not?' I said, feeling up for a drink and ready to quit the hot streets. 'Let's have a quiet drink with these two lovelies!'

Ted agreed with a nod and we followed the girls inside. The room was cool and dark after the intense glare outside. It smelled sour, like a dirty mop, of stale beer and cigarette smoke. When my eyes became accustomed to the dull reddish light, I discovered the Blue Moon, like the few other bars we'd been in, had booths against one wall and a long, linoleum-covered low counter along the other side. Throbbing rock music, its primitive beat vibrating the floor, blared from a jukebox at the rear of the narrow room. A couple of San Miguel beers, some mouldy nuts wrapped in a small paper cone, and two tiny glasses of unsavoury-looking, amber-coloured liquid appeared on the bar. Rosita saw my surprised look.

'It's just tea,' she said. 'Cold tea.'

'Tea… why tea?' I asked, sniffing the glass.

'It's what we drink. It's not expensive.'

'Not expensive for you?' Ted asked innocently.

'No, of course not, for you,' said Divinia, indicating with a giggle just what rubes she thought we were.

'You mean we pay for your tea?'

'Of course,' Rosita answered, sounding surprised.

'What do you get out of that?'

'Half the price; half goes to the bar, for running the business, for the decorations…' Rosita waved her arm around the room as if to show off the exquisite decor. I followed the motion of her arm and saw torn plastic seat covers, cracked or missing floor tiles, a damp-looking ceiling and grubby, threadbare curtains at the window.

'Pretty obvious a small bomb has recently exploded in here,' I said.

'Ha, you are funny,' Rosita said with a laugh and snuggled against my arm.

'Nice,' said Ted in that terse, dry way of his.

'And what do we get out of this tea business?' I asked.

'Our pleasant company, of course,' said Rosita sweetly. I was trying to think of something clever to say about her pleasant company when Ted jumped up.

'Ugh, shit!' he hissed in disgust, pushing back from the bar. 'A damn cockroach!' On the rim of his glass, a sizeable, reddish-brown cockroach was dipping its antennae into his beer. The veined, folded wings looked enamelled, faintly glossy in the dull light. The insect methodically arched one, then the other of its long feelers into the beer and swept them past its mouth; its spiny legs gripped the glass. Divinia reached over and expertly flicked the cockroach off the rim of the glass with her finger. It hit the bar, shot to the edge and disappeared beneath the counter.

'Damn roaches,' Ted said, pulling his seat up and looking uneasily along the bar top.

'Yep, they're survivors,' I said, remembering I'd read cockroaches have been around for a couple of hundred thousand years. 'One day there'll be nothing left but roaches, they'll be crawling…'

'Would you like to see the lions?' Rosita asked suddenly.

Ted was sipping his beer. He choked slightly and coughed. 'What lions?' he said, speaking in a cracked voice.

'They're just up the street in a bar.'

'Up the street in a bar! Lions are up the street in a bar?!' he asked incredulously. Suddenly Ted didn't look so damn smug. I started to grin at his expression.

'They're in cages. They have monkeys too.'

'Monkeys?!' Ted stammered. 'What the hell...'

'Sure'

'Well, let's see them!' I said.

We walked along the sidewalk past cluttered gift shops with lamps and trinkets made from mother-of-pearl; past stuffy little tailor shops displaying square-bottomed Philippine shirts made from a local fibre called ramie; past smelly sidewalk food stalls and the many bars and massage parlours. After a couple of blocks, Divinia and Rosita led us into a dingy-looking bar and walked directly to the rear, where they stepped aside and motioned for us to push open a frail wooden door and go into the back room. The girls made it clear they wouldn't be going in.

I pushed the door back and stepped inside with Ted close behind me. The room was small with stained, bare concrete walls. A dirty bulb, suspended on a cord from the sagging cobwebbed ceiling, cast an eerie, pale light over the trash-strewn floor and the boxes, cages and rolled-up gunnysacks. Clumps of wet shredded paper and musty straw lay in the dark corners. A rat scurried along the slimy floor and scratched its way to cover behind some smashed crates and piles of rubbish. The air was stifling – a heavy, sticky, evil brew.

A mangy, half-grown lion was flopped the full length of a small wire-netting cage. Three screeching monkeys, hoping for food – with crazed eyes, scabby, raw rumps; their gorgets dirty grey – rattled and banged the sides of another cage. My skin crawled as I stood halfway into the filthy room. The damp foul air, the overpowering feral smell of urine and rotten meat, choked me. Ted looked sick and just stood shaking his head in disbelief.

'What a-fuck-ing-mess!' he said disgustedly.

'Help feed the animals!' shouted a fat boy in filthy shorts and a sweat-blotched shirt who waddled into the tiny room.

'He looks after the animals,' Divinia said, poking her head around the door. She was holding her nose. 'Give him some money and come out now.'

We were glad to escape. Thrusting some money at the boy, we backed out quickly and headed for a breath of air on the street. Divinia was amused by our reactions. 'Did you enjoy it?' she asked.

'Oh, sure,' I replied casually after a couple of deep gulps of air. 'Like a trip to Central Park Zoo!'

'Just like home,' Ted added.

'Yes?' Divinia responded pleasantly. She and Ted linked arms and fell in step behind Rosita and me as we walked back up the noisy, crowded street.

We were sitting with Rosita and Divinia in the upstairs room of the Blue Moon one afternoon, having returned early from one of the field trips about halfway through our stay in Manila. It was even darker than the main bar on the ground floor. An ancient jukebox and a small space for dancing took up one end. Dark booths lined each wall. 'It's just like a train carriage,' Divinia said brightly. Ted and Divinia selected some of the slower-paced songs and danced now and then while Rosita and I sat in a booth chatting. When a drink was needed, one of the girls hammered her shoe on the floor and a boy appeared at the top of the back steps to take the order. At one point, I called for another beer and asked Rosita if she wanted anything.

'No thanks, Eddie.'

'What, no tea? No tea, no profit!'

'No, I don't feel well.' Rosita was holding her hands to her belly.

'Hey, what's wrong?'

'Sick.'

She pulled herself out of the booth and trudged to the toilet in the back of the room. When she returned, she dropped heavily onto the seat and sat scrunched up in the corner of the booth.

'Rosita, what's wrong?' I asked again, but she just moaned and leaned her head down against her pulled-up knees. Turning to Ted, I shouted over the music, 'Rosita's sick!'

'What's wrong?'

'Don't know.'

'An ulcer,' said Divinia, 'she has an ulcer.'

Ted came over. 'Is that true?' he asked Rosita.

'Yes,' she answered meekly.

'Have you seen a doctor?'

'Not recently.'

'Why are you working in a joint like this?' he asked. 'You drink that lousy tea all day and half the night; you eat greasy food from the sellers on the street…'

'There are no other jobs,' Divinia interrupted him.

'You should have medicine and special food,' I said.

'Ha, you don't understand,' Rosita said bitterly. 'I have no skills, no schooling, nobody to help. I live with my younger sister in one room. I have to support us; she goes to school. I have no money for doctors or medicine. I can't afford good foods.'

'Where is the doctor?' Ted asked.

'There's one a few blocks away,' said Divinia.

'Come on, Rosita. Let's go there now,' I urged, feeling sorry for her, but at the same time thinking what bad luck to pick, out of all the bargirls in Manila, one who's ill. 'Selfish bastard,' I mumbled under my breath.

Rosita nodded her head. As she dragged herself from the booth a sudden spasm of pain doubled her over; her face twisted as she bent low and pushed both hands against her middle.

Divinia stayed at the bar while Ted and I escorted Rosita to the doctor's office. She was embarrassed and totally miserable walking between the two of us, past the groups of girls standing around outside the bars shouting vulgar comments as we passed.

The waiting room was depressing: the walls painted a dingy brown, some battered old chairs lining the otherwise bare room. I went to the small window and told the nurse that Rosita needed to see the doctor. In the corner, a young pregnant woman waited quietly; her rough hands folded placidly over her bulging, coarse cotton dress. Finally, Rosita was called in.

'Eddie, please come in here.' Rosita was at the door. 'The doctor wants to talk to you,' she whispered as I came over from my seat.

'Me? What for?'

'I don't know.'

The doctor was in his mid-60s, with thinning Brylcreemed hair combed over in a weak attempt at hiding a bald spot. He wore a well-worn lab coat, ink-stained around the top pocket, over a white shirt and striped tie. He sat at his desk and motioned for me to take a seat.

'What is it, Doctor?'

'Just a moment, please,' he said and asked Rosita to wait outside.

'Say, Doc, she's the patient, not me. Don't send her out.'

'Well,' the doctor said, 'I just want a word with you alone. Your friend appears to be quite ill; she needs proper care and treatment. I wanted to know your relationship to her.'

'My relationship? I met her in a bar, Doctor. That is the relationship.'

'I see.'

'Perhaps you don't see. I have known Rosita for a week or so; I've had a few drinks with her; we are friends. We don't sleep together.'

'Ah...'

'Ah, what?'

'I just wondered about that.'

'Look, Doctor, this girl looks ill, acts ill; you say she is ill. Never mind about my relationship. What about her and the treatment?'

'Little can be done.'

'Why?'

'Money.'

'Money?'

'Yes, she has none, she must work, she does what she can; she has drinks with people like you. Your girlfriend needs to change her life completely, she needs proper food, rest and medicine, perhaps an operation. How is that possible?'

'What are you saying?'

'I'm saying, except for some tablets I can prescribe, there's nothing practical anybody can do for your friend. Like so many of the girls who work the bars, she is beyond proper help. What these girls need – a home, security, a paying day job, good food and some money beyond bare existence – no one can provide. These girls are the victims of the system; they are used by people like you. Do you understand what I am saying?'

'Yes. Well, perhaps. But what can I do?' I said, trying to keep my mind focused on the immediate problem, Rosita's problem, unwilling to face the larger issue: the general exploitation of so many people in a country like the Philippines. I wasn't ready for that. I just wanted a little fun…

'You haven't understood… you can do nothing.' The doctor stood up. As I reached out, felt the dry, firm grip of the doctor's hand, I looked into his black eyes and glimpsed a deep sadness in the man. 'Here, give this prescription to your friend. Pay the clerk at the window for the office visit. Good luck,' the doctor said as he turned back to the papers on his desk.

Ted and I sat glumly in the hotel dining room with time running out. It was our last day in the Philippines; we were flying to Saigon in the morning, and if anything was to be done to help Rosita, as we'd been discussing, it would have to be done within the next few hours.

'Look, we can sit here sucking up coffee and moaning about how tough Rosita has it, or we can get off our asses and do something about it,' Ted said wearily, apparently as exasperated as I was at going over the same old points: would it do any good for Rosita? Would she ever really be able to quit the bar and get herself a decent job? We were fat-cat Americans face to face with the realities of the Third World. We had good intentions but were pretty damn naive. I was tired of the wavering, the talking, the options and the doubts.

'Well, let's get going,' I said abruptly. 'To hell with all the niceties and the talk. Let's just do it!' The frustration of not doing anything was harder on me than almost any action I might take. What's that phrase? Act in haste, repent at leisure? That was me, all right. We pushed the chairs away from the table and quickly headed for the door.

A taxi took us over to the main business district of the city, where we got out in front of a tall modern building, a branch office of the Bank of the Philippines. Inside the plush, quiet lobby, Ted and I approached a smartly dressed middle-aged woman who sat at a desk off to one side of the cashiers' counters.

'Good morning,' I said.

'Good afternoon,' the woman replied. She surveyed us coolly over the top of her reading glasses.

'Ah, yes, afternoon,' I corrected myself. 'Anyway, we want to open a savings account for someone else, a... friend, a girl,' I said clumsily. The woman's blank stare unnerved me.

'You are American?'

'Yes.'

'And your friend?'

'He's American, too,' I said, 'but I can't see what difference that...'

'I mean your other friend, the girl,' she said stonily. She removed her small glasses and placed them on the desk, looking up at me for an answer.

'She is Filipino.'

'And her name?'

'Rosita, Rosita Cruz.'

'Address?'

'What? Oh, I don't know,' I said and looked at Ted. He shrugged his shoulders.

'Where does your friend work?'

'Well, I'll be serving as an agricultural...' Ted started saying facetiously, his eyes twinkling.

'Aw, come on, Ted, don't clown around,' I said, cutting him off. He smiled at his little joke. The woman's eyes brightened slightly.

'She works in a, a lounge... a sort of restaurant,' I said.

'Name?'

'Rosita. Oh, the place? I, er, forgot,' I stammered stupidly. I was feeling hot and uncomfortable as the woman continued to stare with unflinching eyes. 'Do you know, Ted?'

'Nope,' he responded calmly, obviously agreeing it was none of this woman's business that Rosita worked at a dive called the Blue Moon. Funny how quickly we had become protective, I thought.

'Is she a waitress, a cook, a cashier?' the woman asked. I was sure she was toying with me, having a bit of fun. Probably a pretty dull job; she has to get her kicks where she can...

'She's a waitress,' Ted answered.

'Your friend will have to sign the signature cards. Is that all right?'

I thought the woman was implying Rosita couldn't sign her name. Hell, for all I knew, she couldn't. 'Sure, of course it's all right. If you'll stop asking all these silly questions and just give them to me,' I said irritably as I leaned over her desk and stared straight into her dark expressionless eyes.

'Look,' she said briskly, 'don't get yourself upset. This might surprise you, but I have opened this kind of account before.'

'What kind?' asked Ted, enjoying himself.

'The kind American men open for "friends" of theirs,' she answered, beginning to relax, a smile starting at the corners of her thin lips. Ted grinned at the woman. I was still too upset to join in the fun. 'Your name is Ted,' she said, returning his smile. 'What is your name?' She turned to look at me.

'Lady, you sure have a lot of questions. My name is Eddie, OK?'

'OK, Eddie. All you have to do is get Rosita to fill out these cards and sign them, then bring them back here and we will take care of everything. How much do you want to put into the account?'

'Two hundred dollars from each of us,' I answered and looked at Ted who had a broad smile on his face. 'What the hell's so funny?!'

'Hmm,' she teased and glanced at me, and stood to shake my hand. Then she took Ted's hand and said to him quietly, 'You better get your friend Eddie a drink after this is all over!'

'I will,' he replied and rolled his eyes at the woman. She smiled and waved as he turned to leave the bank. I was already heading out of the building.

'Hey, wait up. The lady said I should get you a drink!'

'Stuff your drink, and your lady too!' I growled.

'Nice lady, huh, Eddie?' Ted said as I waved for a taxi.

The Blue Moon was almost empty at this hour. A couple of girls jumped up when we entered the bar but dropped back into their seats when they recognised us. Rosita called out as she hurried from a booth in the rear of the room. 'Eddie, Ted, why are you here now?' She was excited as she took my hand. 'Good news! I have good news!' she bubbled. 'Some friends of ours, some boys from Divinia's home village, are going to play and sing at the Hilton starting tonight. They're very good; it's their big break! Do you want to see them?'

'Yes, sure, Rosita, we can go to the Hilton. But right now we haven't got much time; we have to go to the bank,' I said quickly.

'What for?'

'To open an account for you,' I said and pulled out the signature cards.

'For me! Why?'

'Rosita, we want to help. Will you use the money to go to the dressmaking school and get yourself a sewing job after you finish?' I asked as we sat down in one of the booths.

She looked nervous and uncomfortable. She kept her head down. 'Why do you want to do this, Eddie?' she whispered.

'We're both doing it,' I said. 'We want you to get out of this bar and look after yourself properly.'

'You are leaving tomorrow, no?'

'Yes. Now come on, Rosita, just fill in these cards and we'll take them to the bank,' Ted said and pushed the cards towards her and got out a pen. She filled in her name and address and signed the bottom. She then kissed each of us lightly on the cheek. She folded her hands on the table and put her head down, saying nothing. Rosita appeared small and rumpled. I looked at her dandruff-flaked hair and shuddered. I felt lousy, for her, for us, because of the whole damn mess: our manipulating and pushing to get what we thought was best for her. I touched her hand and wondered if the loss of dignity wasn't harder for her to bear than doing without the help.

After delivering the signature cards to the woman at the bank and making the deposit in Rosita's name, Ted and I went to a small restaurant.

'That was painful,' I sighed as we took our seats.

'Yes, it was,' Ted agreed.

'Perhaps she will use the money to go to sewing and dressmaking school. Who knows, maybe she will get on just fine, start a new life,' I said, wanting to convince myself that what I said would actually happen.

'Maybe,' Ted said. 'It's pretty damn foolish all the same.'

'Ah, hell, Ted, come on. That's what my wife would say: "We'll always have poor people, Edward." It's done now. Of course it's damn foolish, so are most things any of us do in this crazy world… take getting married, for example!'

'In some ways, Eddie, it was just a quick way to ease a guilty conscience. You run into a problem, it's bigger than you can handle, and you buy your way out.'

'Of course you do! Perfectly rational behaviour!' I said blithely, no longer willing to be depressed. 'Rosita needs help and we provide it. Luckily, Divinia has her family to fall back on, or we'd probably have done something for her as well. That's life… you just plug along, do what you can. Does your conscience bother you?'

'In a way, yes.'

'Ah, the dilemmas, the dilemmas!' I started to grin. 'Why don't we order some food – so as not to do this on an empty stomach – and try to get to the bottom of this serious moral issue?' I suggested puckishly, refusing to give in to Ted's gloomy thoughts.

'OK,' Ted agreed, finally relaxing. He knew the subject was closed. He looked across the table and smiled. 'OK, pal, let's have some food, but instead of more of this talk, why don't you tell me that story about the armadillo? You never finished it, you know.'

'Well, of course,' I said expansively. 'You see, I had caught this frisky armadillo while on vacation in Florida and had it in one of those sports bags, you know, the kind with the zipper top, at the airport coffee shop in Fort Myers while I waited for my flight north. I hung the bag on a coat rack just behind a table where a couple of old dears came to sit…'

Rosita met me at my hotel to go over to the Hilton. When I came out of the elevator, she was waiting. My heart knotted. She wore a poorly fitting faded red dress, thick cotton stockings and a pair of old, cream-coloured, high-heeled shoes. She had a death grip on a small white beaded bag. Rosita looked over-painted and cheap.

'Rosita, you look great!' I swallowed the words and took her hand as the hotel guests pushed past us into the elevator. At her request, I wore my seersucker suit and black shoes. Suddenly my collar was too tight; I felt hot and over-dressed.

'Let's catch a taxi,' I said and guided Rosita through the lobby to the hotel exit. She kept her head down. I wondered how the hell I had got myself into this. When the taxi arrived at the Hilton, a young man dressed in a maroon suit with gold buttons and wearing a tasselled fez on his head pulled the car door open and welcomed us.

'Good evening, madam, sir. The wedding reception is in the Mindoro Room, second floor.' The little bastard! He knows damn well we aren't going to any wedding!

'Thanks, buddy,' I said too casually as I took Rosita's arm and guided her through the revolving door. Inside, in the main lobby, 30 or more of Manila's beautiful people were chatting and laughing as they greeted each other. They were having cocktails before going up to the wedding party. The women wore gorgeous pastel-coloured diaphanous gowns and were strung with jewellery. Rosita, looking tawdry and embarrassed, shuffled along beside me as we threaded our way through the crowd.

'Come on, Rosita, cheer up,' I said, my voice sounding hollow. 'What the hell do we care!'

Ted and Divinia were settled into a large stuffed sofa in front of a table near the bandstand. It was early evening; the richly decorated room was nearly empty. Rosita dropped onto the sofa and buried her head in Divinia's lap. Her bony shoulders jerked as she started to cry.

'Damn, I see you ran into that obscene mob out there,' Ted said.

I settled into a seat across from Ted. 'We did,' I sighed. 'I need a drink.'

When the trio arrived, the young men were surprised but very happy to see Rosita and Divinia and greeted them warmly. They seemed pleased to have Ted and me there as well to hear them on their opening night. Soon the group was ready to start; the lead singer asked Rosita if she had any special request for their first number. She dabbed at her face with a crumpled handkerchief; mascara was smudged around her puffy eyes. She looked wounded, vulnerable. She pulled herself up and clutched Divinia's hand.

'Sing me a love song,' she sobbed.

Next morning, when I checked out of my room, I left the seersucker suit on the bed for the room boy. Somehow I knew I would never want it or need it again.

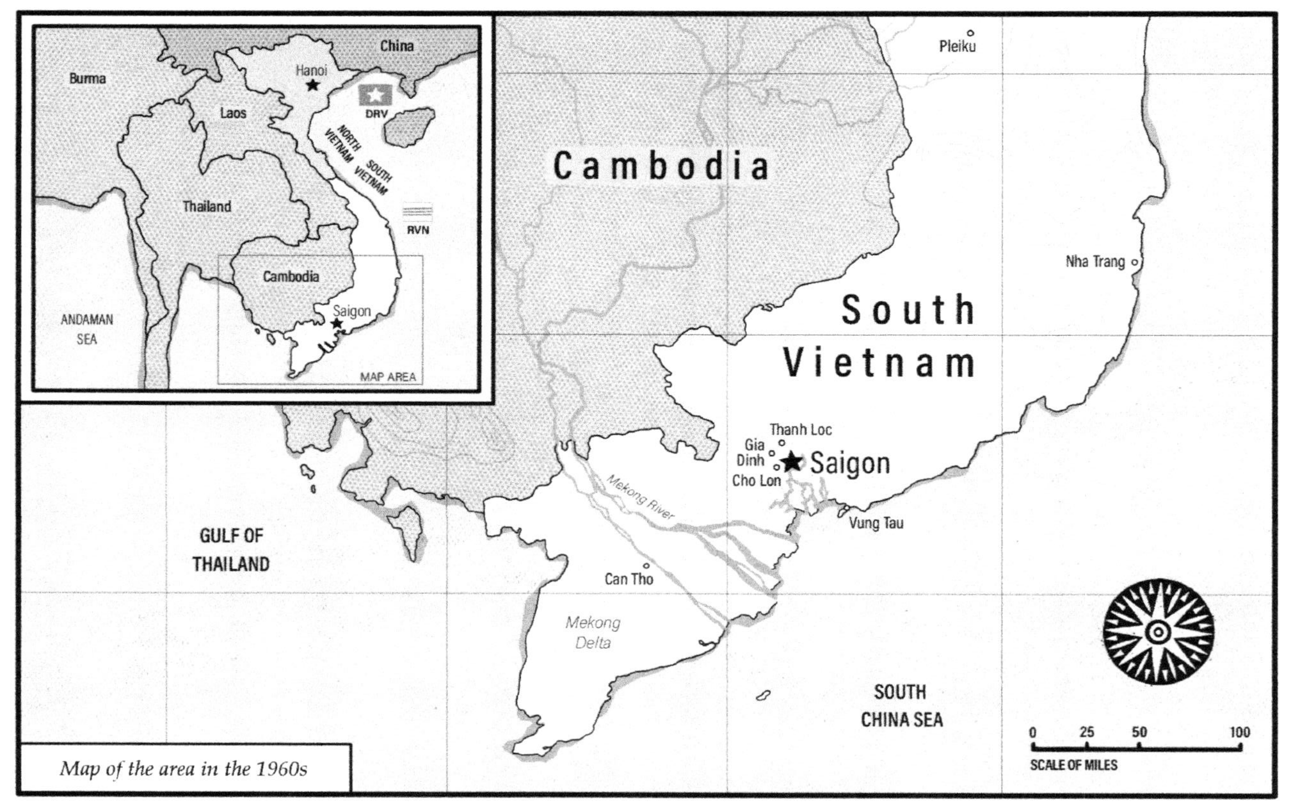

Map of the area in the 1960s

PART TWO

Saigon, 'the Pearl of the Far East'

Even after Manila, Saigon was a shocker; a stinking, noisy, unbelievably crowded and filthy city steaming under the morning sun. Thousands of unmuffled engines on cars, trucks, motorcycles and motorised rickshaws created a constant, ear-shattering roar as upright bikes wiggled daringly in and out. Thick smoke from the engines and countless rubbish fires cast a dense, acrid smog over the streets. As our bus thumped in starts and stops towards the downtown section, the stench of crowded humanity and rotting garbage accumulating at the open markets and stalls of the sidewalk vendors turned my stomach. To breathe in Saigon was to hurt.

The city was in decay. From what I'd read, Saigon had been a quiet, tree-lined, elegant city, known for years as 'the Pearl of the Far East'. I don't know what I'd expected, but this was no exquisite pearl! Obviously, Saigon had fallen from grace, condemned by ancient Vietnamese gods to choke on its own putrid excretions.

The military dominated the scene. Large numbers of South Vietnamese Army troops, the ARVN, were stationed at critical points throughout the city. In addition, grey-clad, armed national police closely controlled the flow of traffic and people at all major intersections. Soldiers of nations allied with South Vietnam – South Korea, Australia, the Philippines and the United States – wandered the streets and filled the shoddy bars.

Barbed wire enclosures, heavy cement ramparts and sandbags protected sensitive or exposed military and civilian compounds. Traffic was blocked off from certain key streets where a police or army post might be vulnerable to a hand-grenade thrown from a passing motorcycle or some other kind of attack from communist-led Viet Cong.

Within this squalid setting, throngs of civilians bustled and shoved to glean a frugal living or, as we soon learned, to attend to their respective, profitable trades as pimps, whores, black market operators or dope dealers. For the latter group, business was brisk as constantly increasing numbers of foreign troops and civilians flooded into the city. On this day, the 14 of us, fresh from rice production training in the Philippines, were added to the city's population.

'This is where you men will stay for a week or so until you receive your provincial assignments,' said George, an agricultural officer from the USAID Mission who had met us at the airport. The government bus had stopped outside the Eden Roc Hotel on the lower end of Tu Do Street in the heart of the girlie-bar district. 'Except for the cockroaches that lick the glue off your stamps and move the furniture around while you sleep, it's not such a bad place, and there's plenty of action along the street for your recreation!' he said with an ugly leer. A couple of the guys looked like they could quite easily have gone straight back to the airport.

The Eden Roc, a relic of an earlier and more genteel time, was a narrow, solidly built, five-storey building jammed into a tight row of what must have been attractive shops and restaurants. We walked into the cramped entranceway; a small circular stairway on the left led up to the second-floor lobby and reception area and the guest rooms above. An old-fashioned, small French elevator rumbled noisily through the centre of the spiralling stairwell. On the right, what had been the main hotel dining room now was a large nightclub and bar. Loud music blared from the open door as a couple of scantily clad hustlers gathered at the entrance to look over the arrival of the fresh meat.

We checked in at the registration desk, paired off and received keys. The two young receptionists behind the desk, dressed smartly in white blouses and dark skirts, had looked overwhelmed as we came trampling up the steps to the tiny lobby. Still, with some good-natured chatter and a few tentative Vietnamese words, we had them laughing and promising to show us some of the local sights… 'later'.

Ted and I dropped off our bags, then returned to the street to wait for the other men and the drive to the AID building. In front of the shop next door, some older women in long, faded wraps and cone-shaped hats busily swept the yellow-tiled sidewalk with long-handled straw witches' brooms. Across the street, squat three-wheeled carts carrying blazing charcoal braziers offered steaming soup and fried foods to school kids and shoppers. Vendors at tiny sidewalk stores, or with their glittering wares spread on cloths on the pavement, displayed watches, lighters, jewellery and other items. At the far corner, where cars were backed up waiting to turn into the clotted traffic of the main boulevard, a man was gesturing frantically, hoping to interest passers-by in a number of large crude paintings done on black velvet.

Well, here you are, Eddie, my boy, I thought as I stood on the hot tiles watching the activity on the street. Vietnam at last! Much like the Philippines and South Korea, only more intense. Asia seems to have some common elements!

The AID building, formerly a large apartment house, was a glaring white, massive concrete box surrounded by high wire fencing and sandbags. We entered through heavy double doors, past the US Marine sentry and trudged up the back stairs to the Agricultural Division located on the fifth floor. We had a quick look around and got some coffee from a large pot on a table next to a roomful of Vietnamese quietly scribbling translations before George called us into the conference room.

'OK, fellows,' he said as we settled around the table, 'we've a lot to do today – getting you guys checked in and letting you meet some of the staff here so you can learn about our programmes. This afternoon you'll meet Mr Tam, Director-General for Agriculture, over at the ministry.'

'When do you think we'll get our province assignments?' somebody asked.

'We've been working on that and should be ready to say who goes where in a couple of days. We've picked the key areas where your help is needed most. In some cases you'll be assigned to a province where an army officer has been acting as the agricultural advisor. It will be your task to take over from these officers and really get the programmes moving.'

Cool, crisp, efficient – that was George. I had to wonder how often he got out of this rabbit warren to see any farming. Relax, what difference does it make to you, I reminded myself. I was no doubt restless, now I was finally here.

'When exactly do we go to the field? This city scares the hell out of a country boy like me,' one of the guys asked.

'Well, you men should start moving out to your posts about the middle of next week. For now, don't be bothered by this place. It's noisy and dirty and crowded, but at least the VC can't operate here quite as openly as they do where some of you will be stationed.'

'Hey, what do you mean?' asked Shoop, sounding worried. 'Do the VC move around freely out in the countryside, shooting at any foreigners they run into?'

'No, it's not quite like that,' George answered casually. 'But you must always remember there's a war going on. It's not like your regular war, where a front line exists, and our guys are here and the other side is there; everybody is mixed in together. The VC often look like the average villager.'

'You mean they don't wear green uniforms that say "VC" or wave a red flag around?' one of the guys joked.

'Well, don't worry about all that. Some soldiers said the VC are a superstitious bunch, and the way to scare them away is to flash 'em an ace of spades. It brings them bad luck. So, guys, have a couple of aces in your wallet, tucked behind your expired condoms, you know, for your protection!' Steve chimed in, chuckling at his own quick wit.

George wasn't amused. 'In most cases you'll be living in secure areas, perhaps even inside an army compound. There are plenty of friendly troops out there; you won't be alone, and you probably won't see an honest-to-goodness VC the whole time you're in Vietnam,' he said, ignoring the attempts at humour. 'Except for one or two of you who will stay here in Saigon, each of you will be assigned to a provincial advisory team made up of all sorts of Americans, including the military people, police advisors, counter-insurgency types and civilian specialists like yourselves in such fields as health, education, refugee affairs and so on. Don't worry, you won't be dropped out in the middle of some farming district to go it alone.'

'It sounds like we're just about to join the army, fellas,' I said.

'No way, man! I did my time,' Shoop snapped angrily. I looked over at him. He seemed to be getting tense and worried about this. What's going on with him?

'Well, not quite,' George said, turning to look at Shoop. 'While you will be part of a team that includes a lot of military people, and you'll be working closely with the army, you are civilians and will report back to this office. I guess in about half the provinces the senior American is a military officer, but that shouldn't bother anyone.'

'I won't carry a gun,' Shoop said darkly. God, he's getting his dander up – not the Shoop we've seen so far.

'You won't have to. You might change your mind later on; you certainly won't have to go armed,' George continued.

'I won't change my mind,' Shoop muttered stubbornly.

'OK, look, let's discuss what we feel should be your priorities when you get to the field,' George said, trying to move on. He outlined the relative importance of the various projects and said rice production must be a very high priority because the country was now forced to import large amounts of this essential food.

'Vietnam used to be a major exporter of rice to other Asian countries; now it imports thousands of tons every year because of war-related disturbances in the production areas…' George was saying.

'Like the village chief being shot!' Ted piped up.

Ha, Ted; precious!

'That can happen,' George said, looking a bit surprised. 'What I'm saying is, a lot of rice is imported into this country at a very high cost. Much of it comes from Louisiana, in fact.'

'You're kidding?!' I blurted out, finding that impossible to believe.

'Yes indeed. Can you believe Vietnam, with its vast Mekong Delta and thousands of hectares of the best rice-producing land in the world, must import Louisiana rice? Can you imagine what that costs?'

'No, I can't believe it. And who pays for it?' I asked.

'We do, the US government.'

'Why?'

'Because the Vietnamese government has no money, quite simply.' Quite simply. I hated that. So goddamned smug… quite simply!

'What about introducing the high-yielding varieties from the Philippines?' Ted asked.

'Well, we knew when we scheduled your training at IRRI you guys would be hot to bring the IR varieties to Vietnam. At the moment the people over at the ministry are studying it, trying to decide if the new varieties would cause any problems here, perhaps displace some of the high-quality local varieties. We are working with them on what might be the best way to introduce the IR rice into the country if they decide they want to have it here.'

'The IR varieties produce four or more tons per hectare while the...' someone started to say. I wanted to ask about that 'if they decide they want to' line, but couldn't break in.

'Yes, I know. I've been to IRRI a number of times,' George sniffed like the snooty kid on the block with a new bike.

'So, what's the hold up?' I wanted to know.

'The bureaucratic wheels, the politicians, the ministry people,' George answered. 'Also, as you might guess, there's a pretty powerful lobby group from the rice-producing states at home. They don't want to lose this very profitable market for their rice.' Oh, goodness, no. Wouldn't want to lose the vote of the honourable senator from Louisiana, now would we?

'While the American taxpayer foots the bill for the imported rice, the local nobs discuss whether they should permit the use of the high-yielding varieties here and lobby groups at home push for continued exports of US rice to Vietnam... what the hell?!' Ted interjected. Yeah, what gives, George? I echoed in my mind.

'Yep. Sounds unreal, doesn't it?' George answered calmly. 'That's politics, baby! Besides, remember, this is a sovereign country, not an American colony. Their government has the right and the responsibility to decide what's in their national interest. You guys better get used to it. There are things going on in this country that are hard to understand... you've got an education coming.'

'Well, George, how do you think it will settle out?' asked Julio. Probably got a rice farm in Puerto Rico, wants to get in on the action. Sly one, that Julio...

'Oh, I expect you will be heavily involved in the effort to import and grow the high-yielding rice, but I can't say how soon that will be. For now, when you get to your posts, concentrate on what can be done to improve the production of the local varieties. Also, take a look at how to increase maize and sorghum for livestock feed, look at ways to get more fruits and vegetables from the small home gardens every family grows. Check on local fish production as well. Inland, there is a need for inexpensive, high-protein foods; freshwater fishponds could help here.' Sure, George, and maybe we can pave some of the roads, and cut timber, and pick blueberries, and volunteer for neighbourhood night guard duty. No problem, buddy!

After lunch, George accompanied us across town to meet Mr Tam, Director-General for Agriculture at the ministry headquarters. His office was in one of three thick-walled buildings set around a wide, tree-lined courtyard opening onto a relatively quiet residential street. Unlike the AID building, it looked part of the landscape, civilised, with less tension and frenetic activity. The low, whitewashed structures, vestiges of the French colonial administration, had sharply canted red-tiled roofs, tall louvred windows, high ceilings and cool stone floors. Make a great courtyard painting, I thought. A study of shape and light; high tone palette…

The director-general looked surprisingly youthful – a wiry man in his early 40s with pale olive skin and warm brown eyes set deeply into his wide, flat face. He greeted each of us cordially as we entered his expansive office. A young male assistant served cold drinks as we found places at the large table and along the back wall of the room.

Mr Tam welcomed us to the country. French-educated, he spoke English with just the slightest accent. He wanted to know what state each of us was from and about the major farming enterprises, marketing systems, farmer cooperatives and rural credit schemes in the areas. He was disappointed no one was from Virginia because, as he explained, he had fond memories of visiting some outstanding beef cattle farms in the Culpeper area of that beautiful state.

I liked him immediately. He seemed human: solid, real. He carried his burdens well. Mr Tam seemed like an agricultural aficionado, the kind of man I could enjoy having a chat and a quiet drink with. Perhaps in a roadside beer garden festooned with orange and purple bougainvillaea… I was musing when he started speaking again.

'Well,' he said, getting down to business, 'my minister, myself, all of us in the Ministry of Agriculture welcome you and hope you will have a pleasant, productive stay here with us. For various reasons we are short of trained, experienced agriculturalists like yourselves, particularly at the province level where the important work has to be done. Your contributions toward improving the productivity and the living standards of the farmers will be extremely valuable.'

Mr Tam described the different regions of the country and the natural advantages and capabilities each had to produce certain crops or livestock. He mentioned some of the most serious problems preventing the full use of the nation's agricultural resources, then listed several projects he hoped we would be able to help with once we got to our province stations.

He shifted to the rice situation and spoke of the potential in Vietnam to produce large amounts of high-quality rice. He said the professional staff deeply regretted the country had to continue to import rice but explained they were now ready to address the rice production problem. I felt sorry for him, sitting there in his big office having to explain to us the difficulties he faced, knowing we knew, or soon would know, how screwed up everything was. I bet he'd rather be farming, I thought as I studied this muscular man with the sad eyes.

'This country, like most Asian countries, lives or dies because of rice,' Mr Tam said seriously. 'You men must understand that rice is more than a food; it is a deeply felt necessity of life. It is a religion. The Vietnamese people must have rice every day – usually two or three times a day, topped with a bit of fish sauce or meat or a few sprigs of greens. It is especially important to the peasants who have never learned to eat anything else. Never forget that life is sustained in this country by rice. You will see this is so when you get to the field.'

No one spoke. A paddle fan suspended from the ceiling swished slowly. I listened intently for his next words. This is what I wanted to hear: his thoughts about the country, the people. 'Rice is life itself to the peasants, as important as water or even air,' Mr Tam continued. 'Our language and literature are full of references to rice and its importance in our culture. Harvesting rice is a semi-religious rite, done mostly by women and girls who, with a quiet, worshipful attitude, gently gather the seeds so as not to offend the gods of the field.'

Mr Tam paused for a moment. His eyes scanned our faces. He's good, I thought. He'll be one of the first shot when the communists take over... He spoke again, his voice vibrant, hinting of meanings I could only guess at. 'There is an old Vietnamese saying that sums up our feelings: "Don't break my rice bowl." Essentially, it means don't deny me my life; do not deny to me the right to exist.'

Late in the afternoon, Howard, the chief of the Agricultural Division, bounced into the conference room to welcome us. He was a snappy, heads-up sort of man, confident, poised. 'We're very glad to see you,' he said from the head of the table. 'You will be our first provincial advisors, and from you, we expect big things.' Howard seemed in a hurry, like he had other, very important duties to attend to.

'The agricultural programme here is critically important. If this country is to survive, it must produce the food needed to feed its people. At the same time, those who produce it – the many small farmers all over the country – must benefit from their efforts. They must have an important stake in the success of their government. This is not the situation now. The peasants feel no allegiance to either side. Like farmers everywhere, they just want to be left alone to get on with their lives. At the moment they are harassed by both sides in this conflict, and they give nominal support to whoever happens to be in their area on any particular day. The VC kill their leaders: village chiefs, headmen, teachers. The ARVN take their young men for the army, steal from them, and at times, often on the basis of unconfirmed information, accuse the peasants of collaboration with the VC and take revenge.

'Is it any wonder the peasants don't trust anyone? Is it any wonder the amount of food produced is less each year? But you men are here to help reverse that trend. You are here as part of the US's last desperate effort to help the South Vietnamese government win the support of its people. These are the "hearts and minds" President Johnson talks about.

'Put very simply: if this effort to win the support of the peasants throughout the countryside fails, if they cannot come to feel a personal commitment to the success of this government, there will be no South Vietnam. It's all or nothing.' Howard stopped talking and looked around at us. 'Believe me, I'm delighted you're here,' he said warmly and got up to shake everyone's hand.

The Docks

'Another Saigon tea?' the girl whined, stroking Ted's arm as he idly sipped his beer. We were in one of the cheesy joints along Tu Do Street not far from the hotel. Another bargirl, one we'd named 'Slabs' because of the prominent flat moulding of her forehead and cheeks, perched on a stool next to me.

'Huh? No, that's it, Chi, I'm getting out of the tea trade this evening; just leave me alone, OK?' Ted answered distractedly. He'd clearly lost interest in the girl; was bored by the tedious conversation in broken English; the empty questions like, 'Where are you from?' or 'How old are you?' or 'Are you married?' Besides, at a dollar a glass, the tea was just as expensive as the beer, and for what any of us got out of paying for it – a lot of silly drivel – we might as well burn the money.

Chi, like most of the Saigon bargirls, was a tough nut, made so by too many men with extra money, too many propositions. The ground rules were clear: if the fellow a girl latched on to didn't keep her supplied with glasses of tea, she moved on to another customer; there was no shortage. No hard feelings, either; a girl had to make a living while she could. After all, as one girl had said to me earlier, 'The war can't go on forever!'

Chi promptly spun around and started rapidly chatting with a couple of girls entertaining some American soldiers in a booth. When she felt the connection between herself and Ted was broken, she quietly slipped away to seek a more generous customer. Ted seemed relieved to see her go. Already we were both tired of these women, their excessive cuteness, strutting sexuality and incessant yakking. They seemed tougher, shrewder than the Manila bargirls, or at least more than Rosita and Divinia. And I could understand it; the Saigon bargirls had to learn to survive in their own kind of war zone.

'What's wrong, Ted? Feeling out of sorts; not in the mood for your darling "Chi-Chi"?' I teased. 'Is that ravishing, nubile virgin drinking up your pin-money?' Slabs, who understood only a dozen words of English, sat alongside grinning stupidly. I reached over and pinched her padded bra. She shrieked.

I was feeling good. Earlier in the day I'd learned of my assignment to Gia Dinh Province, an intensively farmed area surrounding the city. From the little I knew, it seemed I was in for an exciting tour of duty. Poor Ted, however, his hopes dashed for a Mekong Delta assignment, had to stay in Saigon and work at the AID office. Bad luck, I thought, but it will be great having him around.

'No. Just tired of listening to her. She natters like a chipmunk!' Ted answered as he emptied the last of the beer into his glass.

'Hey, man, a chipmunk; that's crazy!' said a young soldier who sat half slumped over the bar a few seats away.

'Yep, crazy,' Ted said, turning to face him, a skinny kid of about 20. He wore the standard dark green fatigue uniform with some patches and stripes that meant nothing to me. 'How're you doing, fella?'

'Not bad, could be better,' the soldier answered.

'Where you from?' Ted asked.

'Toledo, Ohio. You ever hear of it?'

'Of course, don't they make those Trojan rubbers there… or is that Akron?' Ted said. It was one of those times when I couldn't tell if he was joking or not.

'Beats me, I never use 'em.'

'What's your name?'

'Bob.' He spoke with the flat, nasal accent of the Midwest, pronouncing his name like it was spelled 'Bab'.

'I'm Ted. That's Eddie and Slabs,' he said, pointing over to us. I nodded.

'Slabs?'

'Yeah,' Ted said, without explaining.

'How long you been in Vietnam, Bob?' I asked, emphasising the 'o' in his name. The soldier didn't seem to notice the full, round sound.

'Eight months, one week and, eh… three days, tomorrow,' he answered.

'Why tomorrow?'

'Because when you hate a place like I hate this place, you keep the days remaining as few as possible,' Bob said emphatically.

'Yeah, I see.'

'How long you guys been here?' His speech was a bit slurred. Been drinking a while, I guessed.

'About a week,' I said.

'Damn, fresh stuff. Me, I'm a short-timer now,' Bob said. 'What're you doing here?'

'We are agricultural advisors.'

'Here in Saigon?! You trying to grow things in this sewer?'

'No, we'll be going out to the field soon. At least Eddie will. I'll be here in the AID Mission,' Ted answered.

'Oh,' Bob said, then paused to take a drink of beer. 'Did you get sent here or volunteer or what?'

'Volunteered.'

'You're crazy, man! It's a shitty place. War going on, too damn hot, nothing to do, girls rip you off. Bad news, man.' Bob shook his head slowly and stared into his beer glass.

'What's your job here, Bob?' Ted asked. Slabs had jumped up to hug and joke with a heavy, middle-aged civilian who had just entered the bar. The way she acted it was obvious he was a regular customer, a big Saigon-tea man. His fleshy jowls quivered as he stroked her back and ran his hand down across her tight ass. He'll have ten gallons of tea invested before he gets a look at that, I thought.

'I'm stationed at the docks. Security guard.'

'Well, that's not so bad. At least you aren't out in the bush fighting a war,' Ted pointed out.

'Oh, I don't know, sometimes I think I'd prefer that to the Mickey Mouse at the docks.'

'Hell, you've got it soft,' I said. Bob motioned for the boy behind the bar to bring him another beer.

'Maybe, but it's got drawbacks too. It's spooky as hell at night. There's a lot of valuable stuff coming in down there, and a whole lot of people who want to get their hands on it. I've been offered bribes, big bribes, to keep my eyes closed.' He closed his eyes to show how it was done.

'What do you mean?' I asked, smiling at his facial expression.

'People with big money, man, piastres, dollars. They want to buy an hour of your guard-duty time. You know, only one hour. Just don't be anywhere near warehouse number six between, say, midnight and one o'clock, that's all. No problems, no shooting. Just a regular, everyday sort of break-in at warehouse number six when you happen to be patrolling over at warehouse number ten. You know, no big deal.' Then, almost as an afterthought, he added casually, 'There's a job on tonight.'

Bob poured his beer straight down into the middle of the glass. 'Look at that,' he said, 'no head. How the hell they gonna win a war if they can't even make beer?! The damn slopes have perfected the art of making flat beer!'

'Slopes?' This was a new term for me.

'Yeah. Slopes, VNs. You know, the *Vietamese*,' he said, mispronouncing the word.

'Who offers the bribes?' Ted asked.

'GIs. They take the stuff. You know, stereo equipment, refrigerators, booze or other stuff brought in to sell at the PX on base. These guys sell it to *Vietamese* guys and it ends up on the street. It's the black market, man. There's a lot of money in it.'

'Have you ever taken a bribe?' Ted continued in his questioning mood.

'No, man. Like, I've been tempted, you know. It's so easy. At least I'd get something besides VD out of this damn place. But I haven't done it. Don't have the nerve, I guess. Man, I just want to put my time in and get the hell out of here.'

'What will you do when you get out?' Ted asked.

'If I get out!'

'Ah, you look like a guy who will make it,' I said lightly.

'Yeah, sure.' Bob took a gulp of his flat beer. 'Ohh, I don't know. I thought maybe I'd go to *callege,*' he said, flattening out the 'o'. 'Maybe do a course at Bowling Green State, you know. It's not far from Toledo.'

'Sounds good,' Ted responded.

'Yeah, maybe. I'm not so sure now. After this shit I need some peace and quiet, and that's no place to get it! My sister studied there. I went to see her once. Jesus, talk about a racket! Like 1200-watt stereo units blasting from one end of town to the other. And it wasn't even the weekend! Crazy. Those students are noisy. I mean, you get no peace. I don't know if I could take that shit now.' Bob looked up and grinned. 'This place makes ya kinda fragile, you know.' I laughed. Cute kid. I bet his mom misses him.

The bar emptied out a bit; just a few couples and groups of soldiers and civilians remained talking and laughing in some of the booths. The six or so girls without customers lounged on their elbows at tables in the back of the room. Occasionally a couple of the girls heaved themselves up to shuffle around in a desultory dance to the music hissing from a cheap tape deck.

As Ted and the soldier continued talking, my thoughts drifted to my upcoming assignment in the field. Ted's disappointment lingered after George's meeting but everyone else was pretty excited about their province assignments and anxious to get going.

At a later meeting, George and I had discussed the importance of Gia Dinh Province as a producer of rice, livestock, and fresh fruits and vegetables for the city markets. In terms of the war, too, George explained, the province was strategically important because if the VC hoped to make successful attacks on the city they would have to control the area. To establish a broad belt of secure and productive villages around Saigon was a top goal of the Vietnamese and US policymakers, George explained, and said I'd be able to make an important contribution to that goal. Although I'd been expecting to work mainly on rice, the variety of farm activities in the province would make the job more interesting, I thought, and my experience with vegetable production and marketing would be helpful.

George suggested it would be best for me to live in Saigon since the provincial office was just across the city line and housing of any kind was hard to find out that way. Thinking about it now, I decided it wasn't important where I lived if I could get on with the work and do something that might make a difference. I was just anxious to get started, anyway.

The barboy placed more bottles of beer on the counter and padded off to the other end of the bar, his loose sandals flapping on the wet floor. That's the last one for me, I thought, beginning to feel the effects of the beer. Ted and the soldier were talking about the break-ins at the dockside warehouses again. Ted sounded sceptical.

'Nah, I don't believe it,' he was saying as I tuned in on the conversation again. 'You run into a couple of guys just one week in-country and you give them this fat war story!'

'The hell I do!' Bob said belligerently. 'What I'm telling you is for real. You guys are just innocents.' He rolled his bloodshot eyes at us. 'Some weird things go on here… hell, a couple guys I know make a lot of change selling the same fridge to bargirls over and over!'

'Now what the hell does that mean?' I asked, beginning to wonder about this soldier.

'They make a deal with the bargirl, see – a nice fridge at half the black market price. These queens are country girls and when they get money one of the first things they want is a fridge. And believe me, they got money! Well, these guys I know load a fridge on a truck and take it over to her place. She pays up gladly. "Cheap" she says, a great deal, stupid soldiers, she thinks. Then, wham! She opens the fridge and a dead GI is folded up inside.' Bob made the motions: slumped body, twisted head, dangling arms. I smiled. He should do drama at college, I thought. 'But, of course, he ain't dead, see, he's breathing through a plastic hose in the back. Christ, she panics… happens every time. Know what her first thought is? The money? No. See, as long as she has tits and ass she can make more of that. No, she thinks of the national police – you know, those shitheads in the grey uniform at every corner. Only one thing certain in her life at this point: if she falls into their hands, she's finished; raped, locked up… She's scared stiff, see? Usually just takes off; doesn't want to be anywhere near a dead American soldier. Or she begs the guys to take it away…'

'And the money?' Ted quizzed.

'Well, shit, I mean if the girl bolts away screaming, who can they give it to?' he said, stroking his chin and smiling slyly.

'I don't know, Bob, pretty hard to swallow that one,' I said.

'Well it's true all the same. This place is rotten right through, man, full of things like that. Look at all the junk on the black market up and down the streets. Where do you think that stuff comes from? Jesus!'

'From guys buying it at the PX and passing it to their girlfriends or selling it to Vietnamese dealers on the streets,' I answered, taking a guess.

'Yeah, that happens a lot, I grant you that. But that's chicken feed, man. That's just one bottle of booze or a carton of cigarettes at a time. Sure, that happens. I do it myself with my booze allowance when I'm short of cash for these Saigon-tea hustlers. No big deal. I'm talking about lots of stereo sets, boxes of cigarettes, cases of booze. It's big-time, man!' Bob said firmly. 'Look, I'll show you. I happen to know a guy who sold an hour of his duty tonight, between 11 and midnight. Do you wanna see what happens?'

'Yeah,' said Ted.

'Sure, let's have a look,' I agreed, the beer doing the talking.

'OK, what time is it?'

'10:30.'

'All right, let's finish up here and go on over to the docks. It's not too far,' Bob said as he poured the last of his beer into the glass. 'Then you guys can see what this place is really like, see what you're in for here.'

We teetered out of the bar and stopped a taxi. Bob named the street that ran alongside the river and pointed in the direction the driver should take. After going a number of blocks we paid off the taxi driver and stood on the sidewalk across the street from a series of warehouses. In front of each one, a waist-high loading platform led to a set of large doors. A single, dull light, shaded by a metal hood and fixed to the front of each warehouse, just barely lit up the number painted on the door. We stood across the street from warehouse number three.

'I don't know which one is going to be hit, so let's just walk along this way,' Bob said quietly as he started off towards the higher numbers. 'Just act casual, like we're going this way after a few drinks. Talk out loud, don't whisper.'

We strolled up the dark street, talking and sometimes laughing softly as we pretended to be joking with each other.

Since we were half loaded anyway, it was no trouble at all. We reached warehouse number six and walked on. The area was deserted, completely still except for an occasional car or motorbike that shot up the gloomy street. I noticed a few faint lights bobbing on small boats as they passed on the black river behind the row of warehouses.

Suddenly, from out of the shadows across the street, a harsh voice barked, 'Hey, you guys, what the hell are you doing?! This area is restricted. Get the hell off this street!' A soldier stepped into the circle of pale yellow light in front of warehouse number eight. He held an automatic rifle and pointed it towards us; we heard a metallic click from the gun as the soldier stood with his legs braced; a dark menacing shape, tense and watchful. When I heard the gun click my heart stopped, the beer buzz gone. I was scared sober in an instant. Stupid, bloody stupid, was all I could think, wandering down here in the dark with this damn soldier! Just a twitch of a finger on that gun and we're all shredded to pieces. Stupid! A couple of aggies, half crocked on lousy beer, don't know where the hell we are… my legs trembled as I stared at the guard across the street. I wanted to speak to him, say something reassuring, like 'Hey, buddy, we're all Americans, how you doing? Cool it, pal,' but my mouth wouldn't work.

'OK, man, take it easy,' Bob shouted over to the guard. 'We're just going up to the next corner and turning off. Where the hell are we?'

'The docks. It's restricted. Go on, get up to that corner and move out of here,' he yelled back.

'OK.'

'Relax, pal. We're just looking for a bar,' Ted said, somehow managing to sound casual.

'None around here, you dopes. You'll get your balls blown away if you keep wandering around here. Get moving!' the guard said sharply.

We quickly walked on while the guard stood watching. At the corner we turned off into a small side street leading away from the river. In the darkness, Bob slipped back to the corner and looked down the road towards the area where the guard had stood. He watched for a few minutes, then stepped back and joined Ted and me. I was still shaken up; no one had ever pointed a gun at me before. I wasn't interested in the break-ins at the docks anymore; I wanted out of here.

'OK,' he whispered. 'He's walking off the other way; if it's on tonight, they'll hit one of the warehouses up here. Just sit tight.' He squatted down against the wall of a large, derelict storage shed and motioned for us to do the same. We waited silently, keeping well back into the shadows of the side street.

Huddled in the dust against the flaking wall of the building, we heard a heavy truck and moved to the corner as the noise grew louder. At a warehouse less than half a block away, a darkened truck turned across the street and slowly backed up to the loading ramp. A couple of men dropped from the cab, jumped up onto the ramp, fiddled with the lock a minute and quietly pulled the sliding doors aside.

Soon shadowy figures were working steadily, hauling large boxes from the warehouse and placing them towards the front of the truck. I heard the sound of scraping wood and scuffling feet as a large crate was humped from the warehouse and across the loading platform. So, it does go on like this, I thought. Crazy! Someone grunted and swore in a low, gruff voice as the crate was shifted clumsily onto the bed of the truck.

In less than 30 minutes the men had loaded the truck; a heavy canvas tarpaulin was stretched over the boxes and cinched. The warehouse doors slid shut; a couple of people jumped down from the ramp, the engine started, and the truck turned away from the warehouse in a wide arc to head up the street. We watched as it picked up speed and finally disappeared along the silent row of warehouses.

'See, there goes another load of goodies for the black market; tomorrow you'll find a nice new fridge in one of the fancy shops downtown,' Bob said, keeping his voice low as we hurried away from the docks area towards the main business district.

'I can't believe it,' said Ted. 'Where the hell are the Military Police?'

'Oh, they're too busy breaking up GI fights in the bars or taking drunks to the tank. Besides, this place is guarded by soldiers. Why would the MPs have to worry about security here?' Bob answered. We were approaching a busier, well-lit street.

'Hell, doesn't anybody miss the goods? Don't they keep records of what comes in and what goes out?' I asked.

'Yeah. I guess they keep records all right, but I figure the records get fixed up and somebody else gets paid off too,' Bob answered casually.

'It's wild,' Ted said as we turned onto a main street near the all-night market. The area was bright with gas lanterns and street lights.

'Sure is. This is one crazy place, man. Everything is happening so quickly. There's so much stuff arriving at the docks no one can set up a system to control everything. I've heard of whole barges of goods, just unloaded from a ship in the middle of the river, vanishing completely. The barge just gets towed upriver instead of over to the warehouses. I mean, it's all too fast, too much.' Bob spoke quickly as we dodged around the thickening traffic and groups of shoppers. 'A few guys are going to go home from this war very rich men.'

Bob stopped at a corner. 'I'll see you guys. I go this way,' he said, pointing. 'My girl works at a bar down here. She gets done soon; I've got to check in!'

'OK. Good luck,' Ted said as Bob started walking off.

'Yeah, sure. No sweat.' He turned back, smiling. 'If you guys ever get to Toledo, look me up at Harrison's Building Supply. If I don't go to *callege*, that's where I'll be working. I'll never leave Ohio again!' he said over his shoulder as he settled into a fast pace and vanished among the sidewalk stalls.

The night market was crowded with late shoppers as Ted and I headed back to the hotel. Pressure gas lamps cast intense white light and deep shadows on the faces of the vendors and their customers. We walked past flimsy, canvas-covered stalls loaded with bottles of good liquor, cigarettes and perfume. Displays of electric fans, stereo sets and radios cluttered the sidewalk. Foreigners and Vietnamese picked their way through the goods and haggled over prices.

'Do you think any of this has to do with the old "hearts and minds" thing we keep hearing about?' Ted said sarcastically as we pushed past a smartly dressed woman clutching a carton of American cigarettes.

'Of course, don't be silly!' I answered brightly. But I had been shocked by what we saw. What kind of war is this, I wondered? Why are the Americans bringing in all this stuff in the first place? Is this our idea of fighting a war? Somehow I'd expected to find shortages of things, especially luxury goods, and a country tightening its belt, doing without; people pulling together and sharing hardships. This was madness – a town glutted with American and Japanese goods while war raged around it.

During the next few days, the guys started to leave Saigon to take up their work in the field. Steve was the first to go, managing to talk himself onto a military flight that would put him down in Nha Trang, from where he somehow planned to get a lift to his province. That part of his journey was a bit vague but he didn't seem concerned. Five of the men flew as a group to Can Tho for assignments in the huge, watery Mekong Delta. Julio and Larry left for their posts in the III Corps area north of Saigon. Ted and I went around to wish them all good luck and say goodbye as they packed up.

Shoop was one of the last to leave. We helped him load his gear into a taxi for the trip to the airport, then stood on the sidewalk talking awkwardly for a few minutes. We shook hands before Shoop settled himself down into the back seat of a pokey, blue taxi and hung his head out the window as the car started off.

'Be steady, Eddie. You too, Ted,' he called.

We waved at him one last time and watched as the car got smaller then disappeared at the end of the street.

Colonel Horst

My office was on the second floor of a building behind the Vietnamese provincial chief's headquarters; both were inside a large, well-protected compound at the centre of Gia Dinh town, the provincial capital. My assistant, Mr Phu, and Linh, a young Vietnamese woman who worked with the orphanages and refugee programmes, shared an office down the hall. American health and education advisors had a room next to mine. The translation and typing pool, a typically military caged-in mail room, the communication centre and offices of the police and senior US military advisors were on the ground floor.

As with the other civilian advisors, my job was not clearly defined; it just sort of happened as one thing led to another. Basically, anything having to do with agriculture was part of my responsibility. This meant working closely with the Vietnamese chiefs of the various technical services in the province, such as crops, livestock, fisheries and irrigation, to improve their assistance to the farmers. I attended a lot of slow-moving meetings, which were maddening, but also got out to the villages and worked directly with the people on problems they felt were important. This part of the job put a bounce in my step.

I was learning that Vietnamese bureaucrats were not too different from those in any country, always armed with a dozen reasons why something or other couldn't be done. This came with the job, I figured, and so settled down to plead with, or sometimes even badger the chiefs into trying projects that often broke some of their sacred rules. Knowing the language and applying a little psychology: compromising here, pushing there, and trying to keep a sense of humour made it possible... but not always easy with people like the irrigation service chief, a hard-ass little engineer who went strictly by his damn equations and formulas too complex to understand. I suppose controlling the dollar budget for new agricultural projects didn't hurt either!

Since my province was an important provider of fresh vegetables and animal products for the city markets, I tried to concentrate on these two areas during my first weeks on the job. Later, as I got more familiar with the province and the people in the different agricultural offices, I was able to help with other projects such as rice production and fisheries. These were exciting days for me; I was charged up, enthusiastic and excited as I'd never been before. Even Colonel Horst, the senior American officer in charge of our advisory team, and my immediate boss, couldn't dampen my spirits.

He was a trim, short, stiff man in his late 40s, always dressed in an impeccable uniform, from highly polished boots to the glittering eagles on his shirt lapels. After a relatively tame duty during the Korean conflict, Vietnam was the colonel's last chance to be involved directly in a war.

'This is the only war we've got, so make the most of it!' he said to me once with evident pleasure. He enjoyed this opportunity to be what he called 'a front-line soldier' – something he'd been preparing himself for since he joined the army 20 years ago. For the colonel, Vietnam was the action he'd been seeking, and the one place in the world where his chances for promotion were the greatest. Colonel Horst had volunteered to return for a second tour of duty; he was serious about this war.

He was a good soldier: disciplined, tough and willing to suffer personal hardships or even expose himself to danger.

He often spent nights in the field at the tiny base camps with some of his military advisors and their ARVN counterparts and had been involved in a number of hot skirmishes with the VC. He loved to talk about these encounters. If America had to send anyone to a far-off place to do its dirty work, I couldn't think of a better person for the task than Colonel Horst.

But the colonel had one basic problem: he couldn't for the life of him understand why civilian advisors were involved in Vietnam at this stage. He firmly believed that first you fight the enemy with everything you've got; you wipe him out. Then, and only then, do you have a civilian assistance programme. It was this belief of his that separated us so irrevocably. I probably didn't help the situation, though, by going out of my way, when I was in the mood, to make myself appear the untidy civilian – in the colonel's opinion, a lowly form of life.

I was at my desk finishing up some paperwork when one of the pretty Vietnamese secretaries from downstairs appeared at the door. 'The colonel wants to see you now,' she said as she rolled her expressive eyes down towards the floor, indicating roughly where the feared, white colonel sat waiting.

'Aha,' I said, with a smile for the secretary, 'what now, pray tell?' I jumped up from the chair and opened my arms wide to give a better effect for the lines to follow. She quickly backed out of the room.

'Hmm. No appreciation for the dramatic arts in this place,' I mused. 'The colonel wants to see you.' I started talking to myself. 'Yes sir. Right now! Yes sir. Do you want to see the colonel? Yes sir, no sir! Right now!' I shouted and did a quick step, stopped, snapped my heels together, threw out my right arm in a Nazi salute. '*Heil, Herr Reichsmarschall! Heil, mein Fuehrer!*' Just like in the old war movies…

A loud hammering sounded on the wall of the office. 'For God's sake, knock it off, Eddie!' Henry, the education advisor, shouted from the next room. Maybe he was getting used to these outbursts by now and didn't really mind; probably figured I was just mad enough to be balanced, crazy enough to survive this chaotic place.

'*Jawohl*,' I called out and prepared to go below to see the colonel. I was wearing a brightly coloured Hawaiian shirt printed with giant clusters of red hibiscus blossoms front and back. I lit a cigarette and stepped to the door.

The colonel sat at attention behind his huge desk which was bare except for a pencil and yellow pad of paper. The office was clear of everything but the desk, a filing cabinet, the colonel's chair and two straight-backed, grey, army-issue chairs in front of the desk. The colonel was deep in thought as I casually approached the office and leaned against the doorway, puffing on my cigarette.

'Damn it, man, where did you get that shirt? Put that cigarette out! Stand up straight; what happened to your backbone?' the colonel snapped as he looked up to see me lounging by the door.

'Where's the ashtray,' I asked innocently and came over to the desk waving the cigarette above his paper.

'Outside, man. Get that damn thing outside!' The colonel cupped his hands to prevent ash from hitting the desk and nodded with his head for me to take the cigarette out of his office.

'OK, Colonel,' I said and stepped out of the office to toss the cigarette into the butt can. 'What's up?' I asked as I returned and sat in one of the grey chairs.

The colonel glared. 'Where the hell did you get that shirt? Do you wear that sort of thing to the field?'

'A Christmas present, and of course I wear it to the field. The Vietnamese farmers love it. The women often come up to me to touch it when I'm in a village. This is nothing, you should see...'

'Good God, it looks awful! Sloppy, Eddie, sloppy,' the colonel said in disgust, shaking his head slowly.

'Oh, I don't know. It's colourful and comfortable and makes it pretty obvious to anyone who sees me that I'm a civilian. You never know, the VC might take a shot at someone in uniform but not a guy poking around in a flowery Hawaiian shirt.'

'Don't count on it.'

'I won't, Colonel, but just the same, I'd rather not be confused for a soldier.'

'You're part of a military operation; this is war, man. You should look and act accordingly.'

'Look, Colonel, I'm a civilian. I did three years in the navy some time ago, but that's over now and I'm a civilian through and through. Don't expect me to stand to attention or wait in line. Now, any complaints about my work?'

'No, your work is fine, as far as I can see. It's just your bearing, your posture... and when are you going to get a haircut?'

'Damn it, when I get a haircut is my business. Long hair is the style now, anyway; college guys have hair to their shoulders these days. Hell, they're tying it back in ponytails...'

'Don't talk to me about those fairies, man!' The colonel was getting angry. He had no greater disdain, even hate – except for communists, of course – than for the upper- and middle-class college kids of America. 'Anything to save their asses, they'll do anything: swear to any half-baked philosophy, claim a great moral outrage at the very thought of war to remain just where they are, playing their damn guitars and singing those heart-jerking, self-indulgent songs in a falsetto voice!'

'Some of them may have a legitimate complaint about this war,' I challenged.

'Sure, of course! Some! But what percentage? Huh? Five, ten, even 20? There'll always be conscientious objectors. I respect them. They do at least follow through on the logic of their stand; they'll go to prison, if necessary, for their beliefs. No, Eddie, I'm talking about that bunch of self-centred, over-mothered drips who will save their asses at any cost. The ones who take and take from our system of government but won't give a damn thing back. Shirkers! And even shirkers are OK. I can even stand them, but not when they want the whole nation to think they're the only people with any moral scruples. No. No way. They should be drafted and sent over here for a tour of duty. That would sort them out in a hurry! Make men of them, make them lean and mean!'

'Lean and mean,' I repeated and smiled. It was one of the colonel's favourite phrases.

'The trouble with your college guys, and guys like you, Eddie – the do-gooders of the world – is you think you can love your way through life!'

'I'm not a do-gooder, Colonel, I'm only an agriculturalist,' I said lightly, relishing these little chats with the colonel.

'Yes, exactly. You think your fertiliser and seed are going to bring peace. You think setting up cooperatives and making credit available to peasant farmers is going to mean victory for decency and democracy. This is an armed conflict, Eddie. It's a godless armed conflict; a war pure and simple; a military struggle between forces of good and evil!' The colonel brought his clenched fist down on the desk for emphasis.

'And we are on the good side, right?'

'You're damned right we are!' the colonel said sternly. 'We want nothing for ourselves in this conflict. We are pouring in men and material; our young soldiers are losing their lives every day to ensure this democratic, sovereign nation survives.' The colonel had the words, and he obviously believed them. And probably half the time I agreed with him, but I couldn't help debating a little. He seemed to bring that out in me.

'I guess it can be called sovereign, but it's not democratic and you know it,' I said.

'OK, sure. There are priorities, we both know. First you have to secure the peace, then you can think about elections and all that. Even so, it's a hell of a sight better than a communist dictatorship – even for your precious peasants.'

'I'm not sure they'd notice much difference,' I responded mildly. I didn't feel like arguing these matters with the colonel anymore; it seemed fruitless. 'Whether it's this government or another, they would still go on doing the things they've done for centuries. Besides, the main question is are we doing more harm than good?'

'What do you mean?' he demanded indignantly.

'Well, how many of our soldiers and how many of South Vietnam's young men have to be killed before the price is too high? How much destruction to the country should be suffered before someone says, "Hey, that's enough guys, it's all off"?'

The colonel just stared at me like I was out of my mind. He really couldn't understand someone being in Vietnam voluntarily and not fully supporting the effort. 'You're a self-righteous bastard, you know that Eddie?' he said angrily. 'You don't have to be here, you know? After all, you chose to come here; you're not in the army – as you're always saying. If you don't like it, go home, man!'

I had sounded self-righteous, I knew it. Somehow, if I said what I felt was the truth about Vietnam to a guy like the colonel, that's how it came out. Hell, I didn't have any answers. And he was right about a lot of things. I could get out if I didn't like the way things were done. But that was just it, I didn't want to get out. In some ways I'd never been happier. But that didn't mean I couldn't bitch.

'If the troops are bitching, they're happy, Colonel!' I said with another innocent look.

'Not in this case. But look, Eddie, it can't go on much longer. Our forces are getting stronger every day. We plan major offensives soon...'

'Good luck,' I said sarcastically. 'So what do you want to see me about?'

'Oh, yes. The province chief has asked if you could visit some of the orphanages to see about getting some gardens going. They need the food, I guess. Should be just the job for you.'

'Sure, why not?' I answered. Linh had already spoken to me about this and we'd agreed to visit one of the orphanages here in town soon.

'Good. Major Keene has the details. He's been helping out in one of the orphanages and wants to take you over there with him. OK?'

'What about Linh? She's working with the orphanages too, you know?'

'Oh, sure,' he answered, almost as though he'd forgotten she was on the staff. 'Take her along also. All right? Let me know how it goes.' He dismissed me with a wave of the hand and bent back over his paper. Probably planning those new offensives, I thought. Mustn't disturb the colonel!

The Orphanage

Major Keene was clasping two coffee mugs with one hand and some sheets of paper in the other as he carefully pushed into my office, turned slowly and slid the door shut with his foot.

'What's this, Harry?' I asked, reaching for the papers and accepting the coffee.

'Colonel Horst's report to headquarters about the civilian assistance programmes. Thought you'd like to see it since your projects are featured.'

I flipped through the report, tossed it on the desk and sipped the coffee. 'Well, I'm glad to see our fearless leader has a good word for some of the things we're trying to do. What a stiff arse!' I said with a touch of a cockney accent. 'Tell me, Harry, is it true our beloved colonel gets his underwear starched?!'

'Why sure, of course... if that's what the regulations call for. The colonel's big on regulations, you know,' he replied breezily. 'By the way, you'll notice the colonel is requesting more loan funds for cooperatives. He wants to see more help going that way.'

'Well, whatever next?! Never say you don't get a fair shake from the US Army!'

'You bet, Eddie. We're from the government; we're here to help; your cheque is in the mail...' He laughed and kicked his feet up onto the corner of the desk.

The major was an easy-going career soldier from Kansas. Unlike most of the military men on the ground floor, he didn't take himself too seriously. As supply officer, Harry was able to get things for some of my projects and he offered great practical advice. Also, because he was in close daily contact with Colonel Horst and the other military people in the province, the major knew what was going on and kept me informed.

A trim man in his late 30s, he had a cowlick hairline of wavy blond hair and expressive blue eyes that revealed his continuing amusement at many of the army's ways, despite his years of military service. Harry managed to get a lot done without fuss or paperwork. He kept quietly at his job, neither wanting nor causing waves, just checking off the days until his one-year tour of duty in Vietnam was over and he could get back to his family in the States.

Harry came up for a chat from time to time and seemed to enjoy some of my crazier moments when I was climbing the walls about something or other. Normally, I expected a visit from the major when Colonel Horst had 'gone crackerdog', as Harry called it. 'So, our intrepid leader is at it again, I see! Strange, I didn't hear him from up here this time,' I said, taking another sip of my coffee.

'Just got to worrying about you working so hard up here. Thought you probably could use a coffee break to rest your mind from these heavy and no doubt deucedly important labours,' Harry responded.

'Sure, all of a sudden you got terribly concerned I hadn't had a break this morning, right?'

'Well, yes, something like that, but don't forget my burning interest in corn, rice, chickens and such,' he answered with a smile.

'So, the old man's launched a verbal assault, huh?'

'Yep.'

'What is it this time, the mail clerk caught handing out a perfume-soaked letter before regular mail call?'

'No. No serious breach of military discipline like that, Eddie. Just a bad mood, I guess. Things not going well; one of those days.'

'Well, too bad. How is everything going with you?'

'Pretty good. Keeping busy and maintaining a low profile at all times... standard survival tactics around the colonel.'

'Yes indeed, keep a low profile,' I chuckled.

'The reason I came up to see you this morning – besides bringing the coffee, Horst going apeshit the floor below and, of course, my abiding love for all things agricultural – is because I want to know when you can come with Linh and me to visit one of the orphanages here in town.'

'Oh, yes. The colonel mentioned it, and I talked to Linh about it briefly. What's the story?'

'It's a poor kind of place, damn pathetic really, run by some Catholic nuns. It's badly overcrowded and short on everything... in fact, it's getting pretty desperate over there.'

'So, you think we could get a garden going?'

'Yes. Lots of things need to be done, but for you, I kind of had an idea. See, one of the main problems is getting enough food for all the kids, and there's a small area inside the compound where I figured a garden might be possible. I wondered if you'd have a look, then give us some ideas about what we could do.'

'Sure, Harry, no problem. Name the day.'

We drove down a series of small, crowded back streets where people rested in the shade of the closely packed houses, sitting on back steps or squatting against the walls eating and chatting. Motorcycles and bikes were parked casually beside crumbling back stoops under which mounds of rubbish fermented in the heat. I had to swing the vehicle from one side of the alley to the other to avoid the obstacles as I followed Harry's directions. Linh sat in the back seat.

'Stop in front of those metal gates on the left just up there,' Harry said, motioning with his arm to a spot past some small carts used by soup vendors that were piled up as though they'd been dropped from a truck and left to rot. A pair of large solid doors were set into a high, plain concrete wall along one side of the alley. Harry jumped out of the vehicle, walked up to the gates and pounded on them with his fist. Soon a face appeared at a small opening, some words were exchanged, and the doors were pulled open. I squeezed the vehicle past the broken carts and into the orphanage.

The front courtyard was covered with fine gravel that crunched loudly under the wheels, the sound echoing back from the walls of the low, open buildings. My first impression was of hardness, bare cement walls and floors. Then I noticed the silence. I'd expected a noisy throng of kids whooping it up and raising hell while being chased by some harried nuns. There was none of that. It was silent: a stony, unnaturally quiet place set in the middle of the crowded neighbourhood. Where are the kids? I wondered as I walked gingerly over the crackling stones to join Linh, Harry and another woman who were talking in front of one of the buildings.

The woman wore a dark blue, mid-length dress with a large faded blue apron over the top. Although her face had few lines and a certain freshness, her tired eyes and slackness about her mouth, as well as the wrinkled skin of her thin neck, made her appear older than the 40 or so years I first took her to be. Her hair, a medium-brown colour streaked with grey, was cut short with no attempt at stylishness.

'*Enchanté*,' Sister Claire said warmly as she took my hand after Major Keene made the introductions. 'I'm glad to meet you, Eddie,' she said, emphasising the last syllable of my name. She was French but spoke English well. Her voice had only a hint of an accent, mainly a slight, pleasant buzzing sound on certain letters. 'Please come into the office and have a cup of coffee. Afterwards, we can have a look around.'

Another nun soon entered the office carrying a tray with the coffee, some glass cups and a plate of small cakes. She was younger than Sister Claire and wore the same type of blue dress and apron. She greeted Linh warmly and nodded to me. I was surprised when Major Keene began to speak to her rapidly in French, teasing her a bit and making her smile. 'Sister Monique doesn't get on so well with English,' he said and pulled a chair around for her.

'So, Linh and Major Keene,' Sister Claire said, starting to get the cups set up, 'what brings you two and your friend Eddie to see us today?'

'Harry. Every time I come here I must remind you to call me Harry,' he said in a gently scolding manner.

'Ah, yes. You Americans, always on a first-name basis. Even with your worst enemies, I expect.'

'Especially with them!' Harry said cheerfully.

'OK. Harry, it shall be,' she smiled. 'But what brings you to us today? Surely you have more important duties.' She handed the cups around while Sister Monique passed the cakes.

'Well, Sister, Eddie here is an agricultural advisor and I've brought him along to look at the garden area.'

'Oh, *magnifique*!' She beamed at me. 'The food costs are very high; they get higher every day it seems. And, of course, we keep getting more children all the time.'

'How many children are in your care now?' I asked.

'Well, last night we got another,' she said. 'We heard a loud banging on the gates and when we opened them, there he was.'

'A baby?' Linh asked.

'Yes. Wrapped in some dirty rags and tucked inside a cardboard box on the ground just by the gate.' Sister Claire spoke quickly in French to Linh who nodded and left the room. So, this social and welfare officer knows French as well, I thought.

'And so, one more mouth to feed,' Harry said.

'Yes, of course.' She reached under her apron into a pocket in her dress and fished out a small, red packet of local cigarettes. 'Here, let's have a cigarette. They're not so bad. I have one sometimes when I'm in here alone. It helps me try and figure out how we can get food for all the mouths.' She shrugged her shoulders and handed the cigarettes around.

'So how many children do you have now?' Harry asked.

'As of last night, 147.'

'That's a few more than you had when I was here a couple of weeks ago.'

'Yes. Two brothers might be adopted soon by an American nurse who is going back home in a month or so. That helps. But the government makes it so difficult. They can't care; not really. It takes months and months to process the documents. You can't believe it!' Sister Claire said, not trying to hide her frustration at the government's inaction. She ran her dry hands through her hair, then brightened up quickly as Linh came through the door carrying a tiny baby wrapped in a green, army-type blanket.

'Aha, here's our new man now!' Sister Claire stood up. 'Just look at this one, eh!' She reached a finger into the cloth covering the baby's head and stroked his cheek. The infant, cradled comfortably in Linh's arms, gurgled contentedly. His thin, pale arm poked above the blanket; his tiny fingers clutched at the air. Sister Claire lowered her head to the baby's face and made a gentle cooing noise. The baby crinkled his mouth and eyes; his legs kicked and jerked beneath the blanket.

'This one will make it. Regardless of the war, this one will come through!' Sister Claire declared as she patted him. Harry and I stood watching her gaze at the newborn. 'He acts like he's been on this earth before, no? He knows all about it! God has directly intervened in your life, little man. He brought you to us. You will make it, *mon petit*. You will make it!' It was almost an incantation... Sister Claire pressing her incredible energy and urge for life onto this tiny spark.

She said a few words to Sister Monique, who took the baby from Linh, then turned to me. 'Let's go look at the garden area.'

'Where are all the children?' I asked as we left the office.

'They are resting. Come, we will have a peek.' We crossed the courtyard and entered a large, darkened room where we had to stop just inside the door to avoid stepping on the children. Scattered on the floor, with nothing to soften the hardness of the bare concrete, children lay on their backs or curled up alone or in twos or threes. Many slept while the few who were awake turned to look at the visitors standing in front of the open door. The room was quiet except for the gentle breathing or occasional scraping of a foot or leg as a child shifted position. A strong smell of urine and disinfectant filled the room.

'These children are anywhere in age from three or four to about 12,' Sister Claire said as we stepped outside again. She quietly closed the door and started to walk along a path protected from the sun and rain by the low overhang of the building's main roof. 'They might look a bit tattered and thin to you but they're quite clean and not badly fed, at least not at the moment. We get plenty of clothing as donations from various relief agencies, some of them American.'

Sister Claire led the way to another room, much smaller than the first one. 'Here we have the babies,' she said as we entered the room and greeted another nun who was sitting bottle-feeding an emaciated baby of about six months old.

'Ah, this one is not doing well,' Sister Claire said as she touched the baby's head. 'He was left with us about three weeks ago by a bargirl. This baby is one of your countrymen, I would say. Look at the hair, the eyes. He'll never see California or New York or wherever his father is from.'

The room was full of babies. They were lined up on plastic or canvas cots or whatever could be found to keep them in. One tiny girl lay on her back with her feet in the air inside a wooden packing box. Harry reached down and put a finger under her chin. Her tiny hand clutched at his arm.

A young Vietnamese woman appeared from a back room carrying another little one. She had just bathed the baby and was drying her off with a green towel.

'Did you provide the towels, Harry?' I asked.

'Yeah, a few; and some blankets and other things. But really, it's all because of Linh. She got me out here.'

'Harry has been a wonderful help for many months now,' Sister Claire acknowledged. 'He has been able to give us lots of things we desperately need. These towels and lots of blankets – we cut them up to use as baby blankets – he brought to us. He gave us bags of rice and bulgur wheat and dried milk, as well as the coffee we just had. We have a year's supply of paper towels, thanks to Harry!'

'Well, there are quite a few of us involved,' Harry said. 'Linh, here, of course, for encouraging us, making us see the need. Corporal Howard, Captain Rubinoski and others have not only brought supplies over here but have spent hours of their spare time fixing things, painting the rooms; they even installed a new water storage system and did all the plumbing.'

'Oh yes. Linh and these men have kept us alive!' Sister Claire said brightly as she picked up another baby and held it in her arms. 'I don't know what great plan President Johnson had when he sent you here, Harry, but the Good Lord guided you to our gates.' She paused. 'Or perhaps it was Linh who guided you here, on second thoughts,' she said with a smile and took Linh's hand.

'It isn't much help, really,' Linh said. 'More is needed.' She picked up a baby boy and carefully handed him over to me. 'Here, hug this one.'

'It's critical help,' Sister Claire said in a serious tone.

'Where do you get the items?' I asked Linh.

'Oh, here and there. Some of it is brought in from the refugee programme. Some of it is army surplus. Some of it… well, after all, Harry's a supply officer and I have my contacts,' she said, smiling. 'There are ways.' Linh looked away and started fussing with another baby. It was obvious she took great pleasure in helping the orphanage but was easily embarrassed when talking about it.

'And some of it just gets bought at the army commissary by Harry and the other men and brought out here, I know,' Sister Claire added.

'Really?'

'Yes,' Harry said. 'But look, many of these orphans are fathered by Americans. The Vietnamese society won't take to these mixed-race kids, and their mothers know it. So, often they get dropped off at places like this. It's only right that we help.'

I put the baby I was holding back into the makeshift crib and moved over to pick up another. 'There must be thousands of kids like this all over the country,' I speculated while hitching the baby up to my shoulder, placing one hand behind its head and neck as support.

'Sure, thousands. After all, we've got over 400,000 troops here ourselves, and if you add in civilians like yourself or people from other countries such as Australia, South Korea… why, hell, just think of the number of kids that will result from years and years of that kind of foreign presence,' Harry continued.

'A grim thought,' I said, for the first time becoming aware of the problem.

'Exactly. So what any of us do here is nothing, not compared to the need. Of course, at other orphanages, people are helping out too, but it's nothing really. The way I see it, America is a big part of the problem. The war effort… well, that's something else; I still believe we're doing the right thing there. But this other thing, this tremendous number of orphans that results because we're involved here in the war, that's our problem as well as Vietnam's, and I don't think we're doing enough to help. We don't even admit the problem exists, or if we do, we don't accept any responsibility for it.'

'Anyway, I think it's great, you guys helping out where you can…'

'Sure. If that means getting a load of groceries at the commissary, no big deal; if it means slipping a carton of paper towels or some blankets out of the army's stores, that's OK too. These kids are entitled to American goods; they're here and in this shabby state because of us.'

We left the nursery and walked out to the back of the compound where a crudely built wall marked the property's boundary. The soil had been dug up in places by the kids and was thrown into rough piles.

'What do you think, Eddie?' Sister Claire asked, spreading her arms wide to indicate the area she thought might make a decent garden. 'We have a good all-year supply of water now, thanks to our army friends, so we could irrigate the garden during the dry spells.'

'It doesn't look too bad,' I said, stooping to scoop up a handful of the soil for a better look at its texture. 'The soil is quite light… a lot of sand, and it probably won't provide much nutrition for the plants at first, but it can be built up over time. We could get a pretty good garden going here with a bit of work.'

'The gardening tools in the warehouse – could we use them here?' Linh asked. She doesn't miss much, I thought.

'Yes. They're provided by CARE and other humanitarian organisations like it, so that won't be a problem.'

'That's good, Eddie,' Sister Claire said, obviously pleased by the nearing reality of a garden at the orphanage.

'Maybe I'd better come back and help get the area dug up first; then, when we're ready, I can get seeds from the Taiwanese Agricultural Team. They're developing some good varieties for this kind of situation. We could run a water line out from the tap at the base of the storage tank for watering the plants.'

'I can get some pipe from a pal of mine,' Harry offered.

'Someone will have to look after the garden each day; be responsible for the watering and weeding and so on,' I explained.

'Oh, yes,' Sister Claire answered quickly. 'I'll select one of the nuns to be in charge, and there are two older girls who can look after the plot daily. They're both good girls, willing workers and quite responsible.'

'They should do fine,' I said and took a last look around. 'Well, I think that's about all we can do for now. Perhaps we'd better be going.'

'Yes, of course,' Sister Claire said, walking with us as we headed back to the jeep. 'Thank you for coming today, Eddie. Getting enough food for the children is a constant problem, and I'm sure a garden will be a big help. Perhaps you think I'm a bit forward in asking for help, but when it comes to these little ones, I'm not ashamed to ask, even beg, for assistance from anyone. Isn't that right, Linh?' she said as she put her arm around Linh's waist.

'Yes, and thank goodness you do,' Linh answered. '*C'est très difficile.*'

'I'm starting to get the picture now, and I'm glad to be of help,' I responded.

'It's very kind of you,' Sister Claire said in a serious voice. 'Linh, Harry, thank you once again for everything. Until next time, God bless you.'

An old man held the gates open; Sister Claire stepped to one side and waved as we drove out.

The Cooperative

As we waited by the vehicle, I looked straight up into the tall mango trees arched gracefully over the narrow road, their foliage a thick dark mass against the colourless sky. Back along the road, I could see the early morning mist drifting through leaf-cluttered clumps of banana trees, then curling against the houses and trailing off to thin smoky wisps above the fields. Nearby, a woman worked silently in the tangle of mature plants, cutting the drooping, seed-heavy panicles of rice.

Cool and serene, I thought... like a pale Japanese watercolour. After a few months in the province and many field trips, I still couldn't believe the delicate beauty of the Vietnamese countryside. The peaceful quality of the hushed landscape of soft greys, muted earth colours and greens and yellows constantly amazed me. I hadn't expected this. Perhaps the stark contrast between the ugly, noisy concrete towns and the unspoiled villages made the beauty of the countryside even more striking. I don't know, but I could feel myself responding to the tranquillity of the place.

Mr Phu and Linh and I stood on the dusty road near the centre of Thanh Loc village watching the women at work. Before sunrise we had started out for the small village to meet with a group of farmers interested in forming a cooperative. The leader of the group, Mr Sang, had stopped at the office several weeks earlier to see Linh, his niece, about the possibility of getting help from the Americans. I'd met him briefly at the time and agreed to come out to talk with the farmers if Mr Phu and Linh felt the idea of a cooperative made sense and if there was anything we could do to help.

Because she had some experience with cooperatives, and because it was her uncle who was trying to organise the group of farmers, Linh was involved in the discussions about the cooperative right from the start. I didn't mind a bit. About 30, she was a lovely young woman with clear pale skin and glossy black hair pulled straight back and wrapped into a thick, tight knot at the back of her head. I knew her in the office as a friendly but quiet person who always seemed to be going off somewhere to attend to one problem or another. I had enjoyed visiting the orphanage with Linh and was looking forward to working with her more and getting to know her better.

Mr Phu was a different matter altogether. In his mid-60s, he was an imperturbable, courteous older gentleman from another era. He spoke the very precise English he'd learned many years before during his schooling in North Vietnam, where, after studying agriculture, he worked for the government. Forced to flee to the South to avoid being persecuted as Catholics, Mr Phu and his family had settled near Saigon some years before.

He hated the communist regime with unwavering passion, blaming it for putting his life permanently out of balance by forcing him to leave his homeland. As I got to know him better, another interesting side to Mr Phu's personality surfaced. He harboured a not-so-secret pride in being a Northerner and felt superior to, and even intolerant of, the South Vietnamese with whom he now lived and worked.

Mr Phu was a displaced person who disliked the attitudes and, as he implied, the lazy, undisciplined ways of the people of the South, and was unable to see a day when he could return to his home. Like so many people in Vietnam, he lived with divided loyalties. His heart ached for an earlier, quieter, more rational time, an era he couldn't bear to admit was gone forever.

Mr Phu and I were the agricultural section of the advisory team. He had worked with the Americans for a number of years and when I arrived was filling in for the US Army officer I replaced. I was glad to have him with me. We got on well and I certainly appreciated his extensive tropical agricultural experience.

When we arrived at Thanh Loc, we learned the farmers were in the fields. Linh sent a young boy out to bring Mr Sang and some of the leading farmers back for the meeting. As we stood talking on the road, Mr Phu pointed across the nearest paddies to a group of men walking along the narrow clay dykes separating the fields. They were old men, wearing dark trousers rolled up to the knees, loose-fitting shirts and conical hats. Mr Sang led the group and waved as he stepped onto the final dyke leading to the roadside.

Although not particularly big by American standards, I felt huge as I shook the rough hands of the peasant farmers. Their thin muscular arms and legs were caked with mud, their brown bodies taut from a lifetime of hard labour. They grinned encouragement as I haltingly tried to comment on the hard work needed to grow a crop of rice. One man, with a happy face, nodded and agreed the work was indeed hard but declared it was his life, it was what a farmer did in order to feed his family.

After the greetings, Mr Sang led the way to a nearby house where two naked babies played on a worn wooden porch while a few scrawny chickens scratched around the yard in search of insects and seeds. Linh went ahead to greet her relatives. We stepped into a small room with a few heavy wooden chairs and a low table. Hot black tea in tall glasses and a plate of fried banana chips were brought in by a young pregnant woman. She placed a large teapot, a clay ashtray and some local cigarettes on the table then disappeared quietly from the room.

'My daughter,' said Mr Sang.

'She will have a baby soon,' I said in my stilted Vietnamese as Linh returned to join us.

'Yes. Number three,' he answered proudly. 'Perhaps we will have another boy.'

'There are few young men around. Is her husband in the army?' I asked, accepting one of the strong homemade cigarettes from a tiny, shrivelled farmer seated on the floor.

'He is dead; killed... the war.' Mr Sang sighed and looked pensive for a moment, then, remembering he had guests, quickly smiled and offered the plate of chips to everyone. 'He was killed in an ambush in the mountains... he was 25,' he added somewhat matter-of-factly.

'Oh, I'm sorry,' I mumbled uncomfortably and glanced over at Linh. She sat perfectly straight and still, looking at her uncle.

'There isn't a family in the village that has not lost someone,' one of the farmers spoke up sadly. He shook his head very slowly, his eyes opaque, blank. I struggled to follow the quickly spoken words and turned to Linh and Mr Phu for help with some of the more difficult or local expressions used by the farmers.

'The war bleeds us,' another man said softly as he exhaled a cloud of white smoke and casually brushed it away with a lazy wave of the hand. 'Our young men leave and never return. Often we are not even informed how they were killed. Two in my family are listed as missing, one of them my son.' Smoke still clung to the old man's bristly white beard as he bent forward slightly and looked out the open door and across the fields.

'It is hardest for the women, the mothers and wives,' Mr Sang said. 'My daughter will have three children. At her age, and with children, she will never be able to attract another man. She is only 21, and for the rest of her life she must live without a man. Imagine what that means for a young woman?' He paused, looking at me and then Linh, and added: 'For her this war is already decided; she has lost. It's the same all over the village.'

'And we old men, who had looked forward to our children and grandchildren, now must carry on alone in the fields,' another farmer spoke up. 'In our country, to have a son is everything; it's our joy and security. To have our sons taken is almost unbearable,' he added in a shaky voice as he squatted against the wall staring at his mud-coated feet.

'Young men should work in the fields; they should grow rice for their wives and children and look after their parents. That's how it has always been,' a little man with clipped ash-grey hair and tiny oval eyes said harshly. 'Now, they get dressed up in green uniforms and wear heavy boots and carry guns. They even put metal hats on their heads. They hide from the sun because now it's too hot for them. They lie in the shade of trees in their heavy clothes. They think they are tough in their shirts with many pockets; they chatter like girls! They strut around the army camps and speak bad words to each other and to ordinary people. They learn evil city ways and come to like them!' he said in disgust.

He picked up his glass of tea, gulped it noisily, then spoke again. 'These soldiers are not men. A man works in the sun and feels the heat across his bare shoulders; he has mud between his toes. In the evening, with tired body, a man sits with his friends or family. He knows how to be quiet.'

For the first time since starting work in the province I felt helpless and frustrated; my usual buoyancy gone. I'd been too busy, too excited about everything to notice the sadness, the sense of futility the villagers were experiencing as their traditional ways were displaced by a new, brutal kind of existence. I began to see how this fragile culture, one that evolved over the years into a stable lifestyle with well-established community values, was rapidly changing as the war brought frightening new experiences the villagers couldn't assimilate. It was clear the peasants were victims of new forces beyond their control. The endless, inexplicable loss of their young men in distant places pulled their world apart. I looked around the room. Whatever joy the locals got from their work and customs: the planting and harvesting, the marriages and births and even the deaths of their venerable old-timers, now was made impossible by this war.

The old man who had offered me the cigarette was talking again. I tried to focus on his quickly spoken words. Almost as though reading my mind, the farmer continued, '…and even if they do survive this war, our young men will not be willing to return home to the village. They've seen too much; they are ruined for this kind of life.'

To break the sombre mood, Mr Sang refilled the tea glasses from the teapot, then said, 'We want to form a cooperative. We want to group together and organise ourselves into a legal farmers' cooperative that will be able to buy the things we need like fertiliser and seed and pumps for irrigation. We want to make group purchases at lower costs and offer these goods to our members for less than we must pay now at the dealers. If possible, we want to be able to buy these things on credit and pay for them after the harvest of our crops.'

Mr Sang had given a lot of thought to how the cooperative would be organised and managed. With Linh's help, he had gone to talk to various government officials in the provincial capital about his plan. He had prices of the different fertilisers and tools and equipment the cooperative would stock.

'How many members will the cooperative have?' I asked. I was glad to deal with the details of organising a cooperative and put thoughts of the villagers' lives out of my mind.

'Right now, about 40 to 50 families in this area are ready to join,' Mr Sang answered. 'If it is successful, we could provide help to over 100 families.'

We discussed the idea in detail, including a suggestion from Mr Phu about the type of building needed to store the cooperative's supplies. The farmers said they would provide a piece of land for the building and agreed to build it themselves if a loan could be approved for the materials. This led to a discussion of possible ways to get the money and the need for someone to act as a manager and bookkeeper.

That was the first of many meetings held at Mr Sang's house to organise the cooperative. In the following weeks, we managed to get approval for the initial loan so the group could buy the building supplies for the warehouse. About 20 of the villagers, including a number of women, worked in shifts to put up the simple brick and concrete structure. A small office was constructed on one side, with the rest of the area left open for general storage and for handling crops the cooperative would eventually buy from the members. A large, corrugated metal bin was built for communal grain storage where the villagers could keep their cleaned, sun-dried rice safe from rats and insects.

I was able to get some of the building materials from the army thanks to Harry. An old truck was also located with the major's help to be used for picking up and delivering supplies. After the building was completed, Linh and I prepared a request for a second loan to purchase fertiliser and some simple office furniture as well as money for basic operating expenses. Mr Sang was elected director of the cooperative board and a part-time bookkeeper was hired. The cooperative was ready for business, so we planned the opening ceremony. I was feeling good; we were getting somewhere now.

Chairs, brought from the surrounding houses for the official opening ceremony, were lined up in front of the newly whitewashed warehouse. A cloth banner was tacked to the building with the name the villagers had chosen, in translation: 'The New Life Farmers' Cooperative.' A small, raised platform had been constructed and Mr Sang, Linh, Mr Phu and I, as well as several officials from the provincial capital, sat facing the crowd of farmer members and their families.

Mr Sang thanked everybody for coming and expressed his and the other members' appreciation for the assistance received from the provincial government and particularly from the American advisory team. He introduced the guests and spoke of the time and effort we'd contributed to help establish the cooperative. Then he walked over, took my hand and asked me to say a few words.

I hadn't spoken in public before and was surprised to do so here. I plunged in with vigorous, if less than perfect, Vietnamese about how little we had done compared to the efforts of Mr Sang and the other organisers. I started to say how glad we were to have been able to help get the cooperative going, but the sentence construction and attentive faces got to be too much. Linh rescued me, stepping over quickly and going on to speak about the cooperative, predicting a long life of good service to all the members in the years ahead. Everyone clapped enthusiastically when she was done. It was apparent Linh was well known and liked in the village.

The head of the Provincial Cooperative Office, an old-line bureaucrat who hadn't been of much help to date, spoke briefly about the meaning of such an enterprise, its opportunities and responsibilities. He expressed his hope that the New Life Cooperative would serve as an example to other farmers in the district of the benefits of working together.

Finally, the ribbon was cut by a low-ranking officer on the province chief's staff who seemed a bit confused as to why he'd been sent out this way at all, and the villagers shouted and applauded and pushed their way inside. I went with them and looked around. The warehouse contained a couple of tons of fertiliser, a few small irrigation pumps, some cans of pesticide and two bags of rice seed. Not much, I thought; still, pretty good, considering how recently the group had organised themselves.

Drinks and cakes were served from rough boards braced up to make a table. Linh looked happy and proud as she greeted the farmers and guests moving around inside the warehouse.

'Congratulations, well done, Linh!' I said with a smile as we stood near the table.

'Thank you,' she replied sweetly and handed me a cool drink.

Later, with Mr Phu driving, we headed back to the office. As he carefully steered the vehicle through the deep ruts in the road, past silent, drab houses and the occasional farmer working late in the fields, I sat looking out and thinking about what we had achieved.

'It's good; the cooperative should make it,' I said after a while. Mr Phu turned the vehicle onto the busy main highway leading back to town.

'Yes. Mr Sang will see the project succeeds,' he said. 'After all, he is related to Linh, and we all know how successful she is with her projects!' he added with a rare touch of humour. Linh looked pleased but remained quiet.

I sat back, feeling a sense of satisfaction. Since I'd arrived in the province I had done a lot of talking, had contributed ideas and offered help at many meetings and during the frequent field trips Mr Phu and Linh and I had taken. But the cooperative was different. It was a physical thing that now existed, at least in part, because of our efforts. Linh had told me, and I agreed, this was the best way for the American advisors to help in Vietnam: find a group of people who want to do something – something they feel is important – and help them do it. I was learning, able to see now that the peasants usually know what their problems are and probably how best to solve them. My job was to continue to find and work with people willing to commit their time and energy to solving their own problems.

Traffic was clogged up as we approached the narrow bridge leading into Gia Dinh. Motorbikes darted around the cars and trucks with a sudden blast of noise. A man, a woman and two tiny children, balanced precariously on a motorbike, moved along slowly in front of us. I watched the wriggly toddler perched on the far back edge of the seat, clutching on tightly and burying her face in her mother's back.

'What the…?! That's dangerous on roads like these!'

'Yes, Eddie,' said Linh.

'You wonder why they do it,' I said, thinking aloud.

'Because they have to. To take the family someplace, that is how it has to be done,' Mr Phu said.

'Yes, sure, but…'

'Also, Eddie, you will see, we Vietnamese love our children but always expose them to danger,' Mr Phu said enigmatically.

'What on earth does that mean?!' I asked.

Mr Phu didn't answer. He turned the vehicle across the rushing traffic and, with the help of a guard at the gate, pulled inside the provincial headquarters compound and parked by the office.

I got out, still puzzled and more aware than ever that I had a great deal to learn about the Vietnamese people. Mr Phu went straight into the office. I turned to look at Linh.

'Don't worry, Eddie,' she said softly as we stood by the car. 'We are not that difficult to understand.' I looked at this lovely girl. It seemed as though I was seeing her for the first time. She's beautiful, I thought.

'No?' I asked, not thinking what I was saying, just wanting to study her face.

'No. I can help… if you like,' she said shyly.

'Of course I like!'

'You can help me with English. I will help you with Vietnamese and will explain about Vietnam and our people and customs. OK?' she said, looking quite serious.

'A deal, Linh,' I said, pleased. We stood on the hot pavement. Then, like we were just meeting for the first time, we stepped closer and shook hands as our eyes met.

Ted

'Hello, Ted, is that you? I can hardly tell with this lousy connection,' I said as the phone crackled and hummed. The sergeant on duty in the communications room smiled and nodded; he was evidently familiar with the Saigon phone service. 'Sounds like you're calling from a boiler room! Where are you?' I was a bit surprised to hear Ted's voice; he was busy at headquarters and often on trips to the field with ministry officials. He had come out to the province to help Linh and me plant the garden at the orphanage but, except for that, we hadn't seen each other for weeks.

'At the office. Look, before this thing goes dead, Will wants you to come here to a meeting with the rice programme guys on Friday,' Ted said, his voice fading out then coming back loudly. 'He thinks it will be good to have some of our fieldmen present to keep all of us honest. You'll have a chance to meet him and learn about the programme.'

'Righto. No problem. Who else is coming?'

'I think Shoop and maybe Larry will be in town. Can you make it?'

'Sure,' I answered. 'I'm looking forward to seeing this new chief of the rice programme in action. What time's the meeting?'

'Nine o'clock sharp. Why don't we meet for dinner tonight and catch up on what's happening?' he said flatly. Was I detecting a note of weariness in his voice, dejection? I wasn't sure, probably the field trips or just the terrible phone connection. 'I know a nice French restaurant,' he added.

'OK, I'll meet you for dinner about 8,' I replied, just as Colonel Horst bustled into the room with some papers for the sergeant.

'Phone is for official business only, Eddie,' he said. 'Have to keep the lines open for important...'

'Yes, sure,' I said to him and nodded.

'What?' Ted asked.

'Nothing, Ted, just my *superior* officer telling me to shake a leg!' The colonel scowled, shrugged his shoulders indicating how impossible civilians were, and walked out. 'Go ahead, tell me where the restaurant is.' Ted managed to give me the name and address of the place before his voice was blotted out by rapid clicking noises on the line.

Not sure I'd heard the address, and unable to get through on the phone again, Ted appeared at my apartment early that evening. He seemed tired and a bit withdrawn but brightened up when he saw the new stereo set.

'Hey, what's this?' he asked, looking over the Sansui receiver and amplifier, the turntable and two speakers. 'This is a good set. Doing your bit for the war effort, I see. Black market?'

'Nope, got it at the PX along with some records. I figured if the army is going to all the trouble to get these goodies in here...'

'And losing half of it at the docks!'

'Exactly! The least I could do is go over and buy a set with hard-earned dollars; thought they'd appreciate that. Besides, it really has a full, rich sound. Jean always thought a set like this was an extravagance, so we made do with a clunky portable and a couple of records, old show tunes she liked... *South Pacific* and that kind of thing,' I said. 'You know, now I think about it, we were always just "making do"!'

'But now you're going first class? Come on, then, let's hear it!'

'Would you like to hear the sweet tones of classical guitar... perhaps the amazing jazz piano of Dave Brubeck. Or maybe the ladies: 'Downtown' by Petula Clark, or anything by the sultry voice of Shirley Bassey, an incredible Welsh singer I discovered when I was living in England,' I responded, feeling the confident host, full of myself with my varied record collection.

'Let's start with the Segovia record I see over there and work our way up to your sultry singer!'

I showed him how the set worked and put on the first record. The mellow notes of the classical guitar reverberated through the apartment. We stood listening for a minute, and then I went back to the kitchen for a couple of beers.

'Now ain't war just hell?' Ted said. He sounded oddly bitter, not his usual dry, joking tone. He was sprawled out on the couch, his shoes off, his feet now perched on the wobbly coffee table.

'Sure is,' I agreed. 'I wonder what the other working folks are doing right now?'

'Oh, up to their asses in muddy water trying to get an obstinate carabao to plough a straight line!' he replied, eyes twinkling.

'Or shovelling snow in New Hampshire,' I added. 'I sure don't miss that backbreaking chore!'

'Yep, or that,' he said with a sigh of unconcern, then rolled over onto his elbow and looked at me. 'Speaking of that frigid place, how is your dear wife doing?' The question surprised me; coming, it seemed, from something he had on his mind rather than any great concern for me.

'Just fine. She's been promoted to first assistant to the second vice president for consumer loans... or something like that.'

'Hmm... hard-driving gal, that one; or maybe she's sleeping with the boss. Who knows, maybe even more than sleeping! Strange, she seems to be blossoming in your absence, Eddie,' Ted said, sounding more like himself, a smart-assed smile on his face as he settled himself more comfortably and closed his eyes.

'Yep,' I said, knowing she was getting on well without me and glad of it. The better Jean did the less guilt I felt, and I had to admit that feelings of guilt about leaving didn't enter into my life very much anymore. Lately in her letters – which arrived less frequently and, as always, were very brief – she seemed almost a stranger to me. 'I think we're finished,' I said abruptly, the words surprising me as much as Ted.

'Finished?!' he said, his eyes popping open as he sat up.

'Hold on,' I said quickly, not wanting Ted to run away with this. 'I just have a gut feeling, that's all.'

'A feeling in the gut is worth one in two testicles... or something like that! This calls for a toast!' he said and headed back to the kitchen to get more beers.

I thought about Jean, that cool, self-sufficient woman. She'd do all right. Would she want a divorce or just let things drag on as they are? That was more her style. She had infinite patience; could wait and wait for something, for just the right time before making a decision. Maybe that was why I'd always felt so damn tense around her; we were such opposites. No, it's not fair to her, I realised, she's OK. It's me, I'm just irresponsible!

'Do you think I'm irresponsible, Ted?' I asked as he returned.

'Yes, of course; never any doubt about it,' he said casually then flopped on the couch again. 'That's beautiful,' he said, his head tilted as he listened to the intricately fingered notes tumbling from the speakers. He was silent for a while and I thought he was just listening to the music, but then he spoke again. 'It's not a problem for you, in your situation.'

'What isn't?' I asked, puzzled.

'Being irresponsible. I mean, it's just you and your wife, right? That can be worked out one way or the other. Simple, nothing to it,' he said, snapping his fingers. 'No kids involved. It's the kids, Eddie, they make all the difference; they make everything so much tougher to deal with.'

Ted hadn't spoken much about his family life before. I knew he was married and had two kids, but that's about all. I'd always understood that it was too difficult for him to talk about. 'Yeah, I see,' I said, thinking that was the end of the matter.

'Do you? Do you really understand how it hurts to know you won't be part of your kids' lives; that they won't be part of yours?' he said.

'Must be tough,' I said, wondering what kind of hell that would be.

'Oh, it's all fucked up, Eddie!'

'Hey, what's eating you?' I asked, surprised at his vehemence.

'A snooty, cold-ass letter from her lawyer.'

'Her lawyer? Divorce?! You?' Christ, what a guy for keeping things to himself! 'And here's me just saying I felt I was heading that way! Damn, good news! Divorce, one of the nicest words in the English language!'

'Yeah, sure. But it makes me sick! That woman made my life so miserable there was no choice. For the sake of my sanity I had to get out, leave the kids, break off my career…' Ted went on, apparently unleashing thoughts he'd been holding back for months. 'I planned my escape 20 times but when the day came I would look at the kids and fall apart. Finally, long after I should have, I got out, but I still can't let myself think about it. And now comes this letter – proceedings for divorce; making it sound all my fault, opening it up again…'

'Well, never mind. What the hell, you don't want to be married to her anyway. One day you'll see…'

'This isn't one of those cases where it took two to make a wrong,' Ted cut in, ignoring me. 'I did everything possible to make that marriage work; brought the most important thing needed to make any relationship work: a sense of humour. I know it sounds shitty and self-centred and all that, but it's true anyway.' He attempted a weak smile.

'Yes, people will always figure it takes two to destroy a marriage; probably because it usually does. True in my case, at any rate.'

'But it's not always that way,' Ted said. 'Hell, I wanted us to be happy. I didn't even think there could be anything but happiness. I thought it just happened when you did all the proper things. But it doesn't.' Ted stopped talking and stared at the wall. I didn't know what to say. He pulled himself up off the couch and went to the window. He stood looking out for a minute, then spoke again.

'There's not a damn thing a person can do to make a relationship work if the other person won't try,' Ted said sharply. 'She would talk about happiness constantly, or about not having it, I mean. But when it came to doing something, some little thing to help it along, why, hell, she couldn't do it. My wife, Eddie, I'm talking about my soon-to-be ex-wife,' he said as he turned to face me.

'And the kids?' I said, not really sure what I was asking.

'That's the hard part. Now they're hers. She will influence them in ways I could have prevented by a word or a look or a little encouragement. And they'll grow up OK, I'm sure. But they'll be separated from me, will barely consider me their father. She won't have to say a word against me – although she will, of course. The distance will open between us; already has. Spoken or not, the kids will know I wasn't around when they needed me, and in later years when they need a father less they'll see no reason to keep in touch.

'Oh, shit, it's a lousy system. In order to save my life – yes, save it – I had to make a choice. And now, because I had the guts or was the one who was so damn sensitive that I couldn't carry on, well, now, I'm the one to suffer. She could have gone on forever living in the tension she created; she wins no matter what! Ha! And for the rest of her life she'll play the role of the abandoned wife – the sniffles, the hang-dog look, the poor-me act spread as thickly as peanut butter on a kid's bread! Yuk!' Ted was shaking his head bitterly. He seemed talked out.

I felt sorry for him. I could see he was hurting badly but nothing I could say seemed appropriate so I kept quiet. I stepped over next to him at the window and looked down at the river now shimmering with the reflection of the evening sun. The Vietnamese navy yard, just off to the left beyond the roundabout, was quiet. A river patrol boat rocked and bumped gently against the rubber fenders on the docks as ripples passed beneath its hull. Across the river, on the opposite bank, the bare wooden houses – their supporting poles looking like long slim legs in the glittering water – huddled beneath groups of tufted coconut palms. We watched quietly as the light slowly disappeared.

'Beautiful, hmm?' Ted said, finally.

'Yes, it sure is. Come on, let's go see that French restaurant you're so hot about. After all, important life decisions should never be made on an empty stomach!'

As we walked to the restaurant, Ted told me about Will who recently had been transferred from the Philippines to head up the rice programme. Quite a dynamo, according to Ted. It was good to hear the programme was receiving some attention now and I agreed to show up for the Friday staff meeting to contribute any ideas I had.

We stepped into the restaurant, a little place tucked away on a side street. 'Ted, you are here!' a gorgeous, shapely girl of about 19 called out happily as we entered. She jumped down from a high stool at the bar and hurried to the door.

It was obvious why I hadn't been seeing much of Ted lately; she was a charmer: fresh, animated, with flashing eyes; her long hair brushed straight down to the middle of her back. She looked captivating in her dainty sandals and a long, cream-coloured silky dress that flowed across her smooth curves and hollows like skin. She folded Ted's hand between her slender fingers and looked at him with evident pleasure. Just the ticket for Ted tonight, I thought and wondered what was going on here.

'You look so handsome; where have you been for such a long time?' she said gaily. Then, remembering she was reproving him gently, she dropped her thick eyelashes even though her eyes continued to sparkle.

'Been busy, Tu,' Ted said. 'Here, I want you to meet my friend, Eddie.'

'Your friend? I am glad to know your friend,' Tu said.

'She speaks English without using contractions,' Ted said. 'I tried to teach her to say "I'm" instead of "I am" but she refuses; she says it does not sound good and is not "proper" English,' he explained.

'Your friend, he also is very handsome!'

'It's true,' I said, enjoying her wonderfully expressive face.

Tu flashed a devastating smile at me. 'Are you going to eat?' she asked pleasantly.

'*Oui*,' Ted said. He was loosening up now and smiled. 'A table for two, *mademoiselle*.'

Tu gave a slight bow and led the way past the bar to a table. We sat down while she went back for the drinks.

'Tu is sort of a hostess in the place. For a small fee added to the bill she sits and talks with a lonely customer,' Ted explained after I asked him about her job here. 'She's good; likes people, speaks English and French well and has a lively interest in many subjects,' he added, as Tu returned with the drinks, including one for herself. 'I come here once in a while when I don't feel like cooking or when I want a beautiful, sensitive woman to talk to,' Ted said, touching her hand. Tu beamed at him.

'Oh Ted!' she said, loving the compliments, as she moved a chair close to him and slipped into it.

'And now for a toast,' I said, picking up my glass. 'To your new life, Ted, and, of course, to all the beautiful Vietnamese women!'

'Here, here,' he said as the three of us clinked our glasses together.

'So Tu, what have you been doing?' he asked.

'Studying, of course,' she purred.

'Studying?' I asked.

'Yes. Ted has not told you? I am a student at the university. Ah, ha, you think I am a bargirl, no, Mr Eddie?'

'No, he did not tell me, Tu.' I smiled as I realised I was beginning to drop the contractions from my sentences.

'You Americans. What do you talk about all the time? I am Ted's most beautiful friend and he does not tell you about me?' Her shadowy chestnut eyes flashed merriment, her lips pouted.

'Oh, we talk about many things, Tu,' Ted teased. 'Such as the war…'

'Foo! War! You are silly! Art and music, history and literature are what to talk about. In Vietnam we have always loved music. The sounds of our classical stringed instruments and our flutes will break your heart. Our people have a long tradition as carvers of stone and wood. Our lacquerware is the most lovely in the world, each piece receiving many, many coats of lacquer. We have a noble, ancient literature, beautiful stories about our folk heroes. We have exciting romantic legends and, of course, many stories of love. These are things to talk of…'

'Yes, Tu. You are right.' Ted lifted one hand to touch her fingers resting on his shoulder. 'Let's talk of love.' He moved his other arm to encircle her waist and brought his head close to hers.

'Ted! No! Not here!' Her eyes danced. She squirmed away from his arm then took his hand and held it on top of the table. She giggled at herself for jumping.

'What are you studying, Tu?' I asked from across the table.

'History. We Vietnamese have an ancient culture, we have a long, glorious history,' she said, having a little trouble with the word, pronouncing it more like 'grorious'. It was one of those English words the Vietnamese had difficulty saying.

'Glor-ree-us, Tu, glor…' Ted made the sound for her.

'Glor-re-us,' she said hesitantly. 'In Vietnam we have a glorious history.' She was doing well and smiled her thanks to Ted. 'We achieved our independence from the final period of Chinese rule in AD 1427; that was the birth of our country.' Tu looked like a prim young schoolteacher as she recited her historical facts. 'What was happening in America in 1427?' She waited for an answer.

'Well, not too much that we know about, Tu.' I shifted in my seat. 'There probably were some hot battles between the Indian tribes.'

'Oh, you talk of Indians and battles. We had a culture, a great civilisation. We fought and defeated the barbarians from the north in 1287.' Tu sat straight and proud as though she herself had fought against those brutes. 'Now you must tell me, what was New York or Ok-la-ho-ma like in 1287?'

'Ok-la-ho-ma?' Ted said, surprised she knew the word. He laughed and patted her hand. A beautiful girl's magic, I thought. 'You know as much as we do about that, Tu.'

'Yes. I do. America was not even discovered until 1492. Vietnam was not discovered; it was always here and everybody knew it was here!' Tu smiled sweetly and asked, 'Now, what would you like to eat?'

After the main meal, Tu wheeled out the dessert trolley and brought us some coffee, then went off to check another table. Ted and I started talking about Will and the action he was bringing to AID's Agriculture Department as chief of the new rice programme.

'Would you like crème brûlée, rum baba or the pro-fit-er-roles this evening?' Tu said on her quick return.

'Decisions, decisions! Two rum babas, please, with a large dollop of whipped cream on both,' Ted announced, continuing to gaze at the trolley display. 'It's crazy good, and I know a quality dessert is kinda important to a field officer like you, Eddie!'

'I need no convincing... Shoop is certainly missing out! He cracks me up, especially if he is anywhere near a bottle of low-grade whiskey.'

'Hey, what the hell was all that Baby Sandy stuff? Who is that?' Ted chuckled, thinking back to that night.

'Ha ha! Shoop is certifiably bonkers. You've got to watch those quiet ones. Now then... this new "accelerated rice" business, Ted. Is the new rice programme going ahead now?' I asked, trying to refocus the conversation.

'Yes, definitely,' Ted said, still smiling from my reminiscing. 'Our top guys, Mr Tam and Will, have agreed on the basic target: rice self-sufficiency in Vietnam within three years.'

'Wow! How the hell is that possible?'

'Good planning and organisation and day-to-day management of all the details by both Mr Tam on his side and Will on ours,' Ted said. 'Plus about four million bucks. That helps!' he added with a smile.

'We're going to crack the whip, right?'

'Afraid so,' Ted answered. 'It's going to be non-stop action for all of us, including you guys at the province level. It's going to be exciting as hell, but it will be a heavy-handed American presence.'

'Damn!' I said, seeing, as I knew Ted did, the good and the bad in it. More pushing and cajoling... even threatening. '"The old technological fix" with a vengeance, hey?'

'There's no other way. Over 400,000 metric tons of rice were imported into this country last year. You can't turn that kind of a situation around without a big programme and...'

'And we are the only ones with that kind of money? And you know that means throwing our weight around and banging some heads and...?'

'Yep,' Ted said coolly, and for the first time I thought I detected in him what I disliked in many of the Americans here: a willingness to impose their ideas without much thought about the long-term effects on either the country or the people. I was doing it in the province on a minor scale and I loathed it. There seemed no alternative.

It reminded me of what we had done to try and help Rosita back in the Blue Moon. I wanted to believe she was happy in sewing school now. Was this arrogance on my part or wishful thinking? What was the difference here? Wasn't it just help on a larger scale? Either you jumped in and slammed around and made things happen – hopefully good things – or you backed off and left things alone and the country continued to stumble along, the economy and standard of living getting worse all the time, at least for the majority of the people.

'Well, I'll be at the meeting,' I said, somewhat reluctantly.

'Cheer up,' Ted said, sensing my feelings. 'After all, it's for the good of the country.'

'Sure. Only I guess it's just those things we Americans think are "for the good of the country" that worry me.'

Dynamo Will

I arrived at the AID office early and was introduced to Will. Then Shoop showed up, looking properly bemused by all the scurrying around, as any good fieldman will on a visit to his headquarters. Still the same old Shoop, I thought, always somewhat detached; not quite connected to this hectic bureaucracy. He looked good: tanned and relaxed; the impish glint in his eyes even more pronounced. Ted went after some coffee while Shoop and I swapped stories. Shoop was describing a new professional association he had decided to form – something special, for people like ourselves who work in agricultural development overseas, he was explaining as Ted came back.

'What's this, Shoop?' Ted asked.

'Look, our very own association; here's a letter to prospective members,' Shoop said with extreme seriousness, putting a paper on the desk. It had a heading in bold print: **Foreign Agriculturalists for Research, Training and Extension**.

'Hey, Shoop, what's this all about? It sounds odd, somehow,' I said, studying his deadpan face.

'But why not? Every professional group has its association. Hell, even orthodontists. I know, because they've united to jack up the prices so I can't afford to get the kids' teeth straightened,' he said. I couldn't be sure, but Shoop seemed to be suppressing a smile.

'Come on, Shoop, out with it!' Ted said.

'You guys have no faith! Look, we'll send copies to the people at the Department of Agriculture in Washington; they could be associate members. They'll love it; will see how their boys in Vietnam are really serious professionals in their work. We can design a uniform…'

'A uniform?' Ted said loudly, now starting to grin.

'Yeah, I've already got some ideas: blue polo shirt, green khaki trousers – the sky and the earth, see; a patch on the left shoulder… maybe a corn borer, or a rice midge.'

'What the hell's come over you?' I said and slapped Shoop on the back. 'You've been in the field too long.'

Shoop was clearly enjoying himself. He sipped his coffee, looked at Ted and then over at me. 'You guys know how government-types love acronyms, I suppose?' Shoop said, now unable to keep from smiling.

'Sure, but…' Ted hesitated.

'Ah, Shoop!' I bent over to look at the sheet of paper again and formed the acronym from the first letters of the heading: 'F.A.R.T.E. FARTE!… You old fart, Shoop!' We were all laughing now.

'Yeah. We can say we are forming this association; we leave the 'E' on, see, to show we aren't aware the letters…'

'We could have a competition for the uniform design,' I broke in.

'Sure,' Shoop agreed generously.

'The members can select a "FARTE of the Month"!' Ted added.

'Of course! A profile could be featured in each issue of the FARTE Newsletter!' Shoop sputtered.

'You mean the *Bend With The Wind*?' Ted asked.

We were laughing loudly when Clem stepped to the door.

'What the hell's so funny? We've got a meeting, you know?'

'Hey, one of our future members!' I said.

'Shit, you guys…' Clem was saying.

'Exactly!' Shoop said and we trooped over to Will's office feeling like three incorrigible schoolboys.

Will sat behind a large metal desk with a blackboard at his back. Andy, the senior credit/cooperatives specialist and Will's deputy, perched on the corner of the desk talking to him. The rest of the group sat shoehorned in on folding chairs arranged in a tight semicircle facing the two men.

Although I hadn't seen much evidence of it in the province, it was clear from what Ted had told me and the tension I felt at headquarters that the new Accelerated Rice Production Programme was in full swing. Helping Vietnam reach rice self-sufficiency had now become a top priority and the programme had received quick approval in Washington. Money was allocated outside of the typically slow routine administrative channels with a minimum of paperwork. Will had complete authority to bring together the people he needed as a management team; he was moving swiftly. Ted and other advisors had been shifted from their previous jobs to join the group.

'OK. Come on you guys! Let's get going!' Will announced suddenly. Everyone looked up, surprised at the urgent tone in his voice. I sat calmly, watching the new chief. Ted had told me about Will's method of causing a stir, of motivating people by creating excitement and tension, even concerning the most routine of business. 'I've got to see the director soon so let's quit fooling around!' I smiled. According to Ted, this was another of Will's standard management techniques: he always had someplace to go, someone else to meet. 'Now, let's go around the room quickly. Stan?'

'Two tons of IR-8 seed will arrive at the military air terminal on Tuesday,' Stan said briskly. 'We worked a deal with some air force guys who went to Manila on a joy ride or…'

'OK,' Will broke in, 'that's good. We want the first seed to go to the irrigated areas. Then, for the big push, seed and fertiliser and farmer credit – everything – should be in place well before the rainy season, so let's not shit around. Now, what about the IR-5?'

'Well, that's the taller variety with the longer…'

Will slammed the desk. 'God damn it, Stan, don't tell me about IR-5 or any other variety of rice developed at IRRI. I was in the Philippines for six years working on *their* rice programme! I know every damn rice expert in the country. I've had dinner or gone whoring with everyone in the Philippines who knows anything about the miracle rice! I want to know about the seed.' I had to laugh; this was great! Where the hell was this guy when we were at rice training?

'Well…' Stan faltered, 'I mean, since the IR-5 has a longer growing season, the seed won't be available from IRRI for another month.'

'OK. Keep on top of it. We want both varieties. Maybe IR-8 won't be to the liking of the Vietnamese; IR-5 has better eating qualities… we want to introduce both. And remember, our message is "a new rice… new hope".' Will made a quick note on a yellow pad. He held up his hand as if to command silence as he wrote, then looked up.

'Sally, I want you and your home economics gals to be working on this grain quality thing. Hell, if folks won't eat the new rice we've got a problem. The Filipinos didn't mind it, but who knows. Vietnam has always produced some high-quality rice. Plus we've got the damn VC propaganda to quash – "IR-8 causing leprosy and impotence",' he said with exasperation.

'OK, Will, I'm on it,' she answered enthusiastically.

'Get some of the milled rice we brought in. Cook it up different ways; do some taste tests here and in some of the rural areas. Got it?'

'Yes, we've already started,' Sally confirmed. I knew her slightly. She'd worked for AID in many developing countries for the past 18 years and knew her way around. Sally didn't seem to be knocked over by Will's fast-paced style, either. She appeared to be thoroughly enjoying herself, relishing the sense of urgency and commitment he'd brought to the office.

'Good,' Will said. 'Tom?'

'We're getting set to plant four more research trials, two of them in the Delta. Also, I'll be going up to Nha Trang this week…'

'Adaptive research, Tom. Always call these tests "adaptive research", or better, "adaptive trials". Someone will get the idea we're introducing a crop before the basic research has been done if we're not careful with our terminology. Some damn congressman will hear about it, he'll make a call to AID, Washington and I'll have all sorts of questions to answer. They've got over ten years of research on these new rice varieties in the Philippines so the testing we do here is strictly *adaptive*, not basic. I want everybody to remember that… probably better if we avoid the word "research" altogether. OK, who's going with you?'

'Mr Lan.'

'OK. Remember, nobody from this office goes to the field without a Vietnamese counterpart. This is their country, their programme; they'll have to make it work. We might push a little bit,' Will said, half-smiling, 'but we are *advisors*! Everyone got that?' He didn't wait for an answer. He looked around the room. 'Floyd?'

'We've got the last two IRRI-type grain threshers set up in the ministry workshop. One was damaged slightly in shipping but it's being welded today and should be fine.'

'What about the threshers and grain dryers already in the field?' Will asked, looking down quickly to scrawl another note.

'They're being tested at different locations. So far reports are good about performance.'

'What about local manufacture? Are you having any luck finding people to make these machines in-country?'

'We have a Chinese fellow with a small foundry and machine shop who's interested. He has the drawings and all the specifications. We'll meet with him sometime this week to get a sense of his commitment. One thing's sure, he's going to need some credit to get started.' Floyd looked at Andy. Will nodded for Andy to speak.

'A special loan fund will be established soon in the Agricultural Development Bank,' Andy responded. Not the ADB, I thought. I'd had some frustrating meetings with the people at the branch office in my province. Nothing but an overstuffed bureaucracy… 'I'm meeting with the senior bank officials to work out the details. We're proposing $200,000 for the initial revolving fund for machinery and equipment manufacture. More will be added as needed.'

'OK. You got any thoughts, Clem?'

'Yes, Will. We will be visiting some manufacturer facilities to evaluate their repayment capability. I'll go with Floyd to visit this Chinaman he's dealing with on the threshers.'

'OK,' Will said. 'Floyd, you and Clem work together on the machinery credit issues. What's the status of the farmers' credit programme?' he went on, rapidly changing subjects.

Clem flipped through some papers. He was an easy-going man in his late 30s; before coming to Vietnam he'd been a farm credit manager for a large bank somewhere in Iowa. 'Seems under control,' he said in his relaxed way.

'What the hell does that mean?!' Will shot back, his face tightening and voice rising an octave.

Clem seemed amused by Will's annoyance and answered slowly: 'Well… two-thirds of the provincial ADBs have their first loan funds for farmers growing the IR rice…'

'You got yours, Eddie?' Will asked.

'Nope.'

'How about you, Shoop?'

'Might be at the ADB office but I haven't seen it or heard about it.'

'They'll be there next week,' Clem said. 'Now, loans will be "in kind": seed, fertiliser, pesticides – or in cash.' Will was tapping his fingers on the desk. 'The procedures are set in the major rice-growing areas and we're working on the rest of the provinces as quickly as possible. Andy and I will be meeting with the ADB people next week to keep it moving.' Clem folded his papers and looked across at Will.

'OK, listen up. Everybody should know there are three credit funds being set up as part of this programme.' He held up his hand and put up fingers as he went on. 'First, the production credit for farmers. This is only for farmers who agree to grow the IR rice. Second, the credit to small manufacturers who will make the threshers, dryers and small field equipment like weeders. And third, the credit fund for grain buyers and processors: the grain milling industry. If you need details check with Clem or Andy. And remember, no give-aways. That's the deal. OK?' Will looked around the room, glanced at his watch then continued.

'Now, you should know we're bringing out a three-man team of grain marketing consultants to work with us for about eight weeks. Al, our in-house man, is spearheading this. We want a complete inventory of all grain handling facilities and a clear picture of how grain moves and how it's priced throughout the country. From that we'll know where and how much to invest in long-term grain processing and storage facilities. Once the production problems are licked, you can be sure there will be plenty of problems in the entire grain marketing system. We want to be ready for the future.'

'If there is a future!' somebody joked.

'God damn it!' Will exploded. 'You can't do this work if you don't believe in the future!' His face was hard, his eyes narrowed angrily. He didn't care who had made the remark, or if it was a joke or not – it didn't matter. Will had no appreciation for cynical comments like that. 'If you don't feel there's a future for the country you should be honest with yourself and get the hell out of here!' Will spoke loudly, looking around the room and addressing no one in particular. 'You can't do your job properly if you feel that way. You've got to care. If you want to do anything worthwhile here, or anywhere for that matter, you've got to care,' Will repeated.

'Remember, it's only because we're here… I mean all of us, everybody involved in this process – Vietnamese and foreigners – and each of us doing the best job possible in every area: health, education, agriculture and the military guys fighting the war… that this country will make it.' Will was cooling off and paused. His fingers uncurled from the hard fist he'd slammed on the desk. 'OK, let's move along, I have to see the director in a few minutes. Ted?'

'The 5000 IR-8 demonstration kits are being made up and will start going to the provinces any day now. Some on ministry trucks where security is good, some on military aircraft where we can get space. I'm preparing a letter for our field guys. We'll make up the IR-5 kits as soon as the seed arrives from the Philippines.'

'Good, what about the leaflets?'

'The Information Service is running them off now. I brought some of the first copies.' Ted stood up and handed out the single-page leaflets.

'Terrific!' Will said. He took a stapler off the desk and quickly stapled one of the leaflets to a corkboard on the inside of the door. He was pleased. 'Every farmer growing the new rice will have one of these how-to-do-it leaflets.' Will reached into a desk drawer and pulled out a thick paper-bound book. 'You see this? This is the "Rice Production Manual" from IRRI. Some of you guys are familiar with it. We've boiled this 300-page book down to this one-page leaflet, not bad, eh? The absolutely essential steps for growing the IR rice are here: 20 steps to success, in Vietnamese… I like it. Good work, Ted. What about the training centre?'

'It'll open in about five weeks. The first class of 25 field technicians from the important rice-growing areas are being selected and will be notified when to report to the centre. I'm told the Minister of Agriculture has agreed to attend the opening ceremony. He'll probably talk to you about joining him out there.'

'Did you get the bedding and cooking supplies?'

'Yes. The ministry came up with some money and we bought what we needed on the local market.'

'Super. By the way, Ted, I want you to go over to Cho Lon next week and have dinner with the Taiwan Agricultural Group. It's time for their contract to be renewed and they're oiling us up a bit. We need a couple of people to represent the division. Better if I stay away. How about you and Eddie going over? Don't make any promises, just enjoy a terrific dinner, OK?'

'Sure, sounds good,' Ted said.

'Eddie?'

'OK, Will. Fine with me.'

'All right. Look, I have to run. We'll cut this off now unless anybody has anything else important.' Will stood up and pulled his papers together.

'Ah, Will…'

'Yeah Lou, make it quick.'

'Well, we're having lots of problems with the irrigation pumps. Some were damaged in shipment, there's no fuel in some areas, a system for regular maintenance hasn't been set up, intake screens are missing or not being used, and this is clogging…'

Will cut him off mid-sentence. 'What are you doing about these problems, Lou?'

'Well, Will, I'm just reporting them to you and…'

'Damn it, man!' Will boiled up again. 'Don't you "Well, Will" me. I don't want to hear problems; I want to hear about solutions!' He stood holding the door, ready to leave the room. 'I can get any ten-year-old kid off the street to tell me what the problems are. Hell, I can guess most of them! I don't need you for that! You're a highly paid irrigation technician; your job is to solve problems, not report them. Now I'm going to tell you something: if you can't deal with these things, I'll have you shipped out of here about as quickly as it takes me to write the word "incompetent"! You understand?' He glared at Lou. 'How would you like a tour or two in some godforsaken place in Africa? That's where you're heading, pal!' he said coldly and swept from the room.

Very Big Luck

It was early evening when Ted and I got through the heavy traffic of downtown Saigon and entered Cho Lon (meaning 'big market'), the huge, sprawling Chinese quarter of the city. Bike repair shops, food stalls, tiny tea rooms, medicinal herb sellers and crowded little shops lined the narrow streets. Gaudy, hand-painted signs shouted out the wares and services available. Exhortations on wide cloth panels hung in front of shops or stretched across narrow alleys, the black or blood-red Chinese characters painted on the banners in angular, vigorous strokes.

Crowds of people in drab clothing scuttled through the maze of sidewalk stalls and open fruit displays with incessant, almost instinctual busyness. Oblivious to the stench and din of their surroundings, the Chinese moved reflexively through the daily routine, absorbed in their centuries-old patterns of life.

Tightly knit and family-centred, the hard-working, self-sufficient Chinese were misunderstood, distrusted, even hated by the xenophobic Vietnamese. As a group, their economic power was respected, and at times feared; their willingness to do menial tasks for years – to sacrifice the passing moment in their devotion to work and the future – however, was resented by the Vietnamese; a pleasure-loving, more indolent people.

On a side street near the restaurant a boy waving a flashlight guided us to a parking spot. Without words a deal was made: the boy would 'watch' the car for a small fee while we were in the restaurant. That evening, and probably every evening, he worked this section of the street and collected from everybody who parked here.

'He'll own a couple of shops and two or three taxis one day – and that's if he doesn't do well,' Ted said as we crossed the street, picking up our pace as heavy raindrops began to fall. 'Hey, where's that handy umbrella you say you like to carry around to be "ready". We need it… now!'

We climbed the steps to a large floor where two carved wooden screens separated the foyer from the main public dining room: a steamy, bustling place crowded at this hour with small groups and families noisily taking their evening meal.

Dr Tommy Chang, the director of the Taiwan Agricultural Group, stood waiting for us beside a large brass gong suspended from a red frame. Dr Tommy, as he was called by Vietnamese and Americans alike, was a short man in his 50s who evidently enjoyed his food, having some timber about his middle. He'd served in Vietnam for over four years, first as the economist on the Taiwanese team and now as director. He was dressed in dark trousers and a crisp white shirt, looking cool and relaxed as he greeted us. As we proceeded through the lobby, I paused and pretended I was going to strike the gong with my fist.

'Go ahead,' Dr Tommy said, smiling broadly. 'It will bring good luck.'

'Ah, you Chinese and your good luck,' Ted said. 'You're always going on about luck, but you do everything in your power not to have to rely on it!'

'Yes, very good insight into Chinese people, Ted,' Dr Tommy laughed. 'We believe if you work hard you will have better luck!'

'Well, we aren't here to talk about work. Not tonight, Dr Tommy. Where's the legendary food I've been hearing about?!' I asked and patted myself on the belly.

'That is right. Tonight we just want to enjoy your company and have a pleasant meal together. No talk of work... or perhaps only a little. OK?' Dr Tommy had a playful, sly look on his smooth face. He led the way upstairs to the private dining room. 'The rest of our group and some friends are waiting for us. We are ready to eat. Are you hungry, Ted?'

'Starved. Haven't eaten since breakfast.'

'Very good!'

The dining room, decorated with bright red wall panels and large, tasselled lanterns, was overflowing with the 15 or so men, all Chinese, who sat around the long table or stood chatting. Ted and I circled the room slowly, shaking hands and greeting everyone.

Dr Tommy took his place at the head of the table and invited Ted to sit on his left and me at his right. As if on cue, two girls appeared from a side door with large bottles of beer and started filling the glasses at each place. Another server entered with a brown earthenware jug and filled the tiny wine glasses. Next came large serving bowls of steaming soup placed along the table.

I glanced at the man sitting next to me. He was noticeably thin with sharp, high cheekbones and small, weak eyes behind rimless glasses. He stirred the large soup bowl for quite a while, then was ready to serve.

'Good soup,' he said, looking at me sideways. 'You like some good soup?'

'Yes, thanks,' I said and handed him my bowl.

The thin man smiled crookedly. 'My name is Woo.'

'Ah yes, Mr Woo. Aren't you the plant breeder on the team?'

'Yes.' The man brightened and peered at me. 'Yes, I breed the plants. Vegetables now – cauliflower,' he said.

'Oh, cauliflower?'

'Yes. I make the cauliflower adapted to the hot climates,' he said proudly.

'I see, very interesting. Any success?'

'Yes. Vely success,' he answered, having some difficulty with the words.

'Hmm,' I murmured and reached for the porcelain soup spoon; I was starting to dip into the soup when I caught the eye of the man sitting across the table next to Ted. He smiled.

'I'm Lee,' he said.

'Hello, Mr Lee,' I replied, smiling back at the broad-chested, older man with a round face and head stuck directly on his shoulders with no sign a neck existed beneath. 'Good to see you again.'

'He is growing mushrooms,' said Mr Woo, pointing his soup spoon at Ted's neighbour.

'Ah, yes. Mushrooms.'

'Straw mushrooms. Very big profit for small farmer,' said Mr Lee. He then reached for the tiny glass of brown wine and held it up.

'Cheers,' I said.

The man shook his head from side to side, signalling something was wrong, although he was grinning. Then he said a word that sounded like 'gambay'. Assuming this was some sort of toast, I picked up my glass of wine and held it up. Mr Lee nodded his head vigorously, placed a finger from his free hand on the bottom of the glass and stared at me.

'He toasts you,' said Mr Woo.

'I see that.' I nodded, then looked back at Mr Lee.

'Mr Lee wishes you health,' said Dr Tommy.

'Yes. Fine. I wish him good luck too,' I responded, looking over at Mr Lee who still held the glass up with his finger against the bottom.

'Good health is good luck, Eddie,' Dr Tommy said, apparently feeling he was making Mr Lee's intentions clear.

'I agree. Why don't we just drink to it?'

'Mr Lee is waiting for you to place your finger at the bottom of your glass,' Dr Tommy said.

'It's the little things that count, Eddie,' Ted offered.

'Yes, isn't that so!' I said, smiling.

'The finger indicates how much you will drink from the glass,' Dr Tommy explained. 'If placed at the bottom it means you will drink the whole glass of wine at one swallow. Mr Lee wishes you very big luck.'

'Ah, I see,' I said and placed a finger from my left hand against the bottom of the glass.

Mr Lee nodded vigorously. '*Ganbei*,' he said loudly.

'*Ganbei*, Mr Lee.'

We swigged back the glasses of wine at a gulp. Mr Lee turned his glass over in the air to show nothing remained inside and I did the same. The wine was warm with an aromatic, herbal and slightly bitter taste. I shuddered a little at the strange flavour.

Dr Tommy carefully filled Ted's soup bowl and handed it to him.

'Thanks, Dr Tommy,' Ted said. He reached for the soup spoon. Mr Woo watched Ted intently. I thought he was trying to catch his eye and toast him but Ted kept his head down, filled his spoon with soup and sipped it.

'Good soup,' he said to Dr Tommy. 'What kind is it?'

'Duck soup.'

'Never had duck soup, it's delicious.'

'Yes. A favourite soup of ours,' Dr Tommy replied. He looked at him and smiled warmly. Mr Lee continued to study Ted.

Ted bent forward to take another spoonful of soup. He put the porcelain spoon to the bottom of his bowl to stir it a bit. Suddenly he sat up straight, looking shocked and pale. I glanced over when Mr Lee chuckled lightly. Mr Woo was squinting at Ted and grinning.

'What's wrong?' I asked.

'Look,' Ted said tightly. He pointed to his soup bowl, stirring it again. I leaned over and looked closely. A huge, round eye was bobbing on the greasy surface of the soup.

'What the hell's that?' I gulped.

'That's the duck's eye. It is always included in the soup,' Dr Tommy said. 'It is very nutritious. I got it especially for you, Ted.'

'I don't eat eyes!' Ted said hotly and reached for his beer.

'Oh!' Dr Tommy said, looking disappointed. 'Never mind, perhaps we should have it sent away.'

'Yes, I think so,' Ted said, still refusing to look at the glistening mound in his bowl.

'Come on, Ted, don't be so squeamish!' I teased.

Dr Tommy spoke to one of the girls who quickly removed the soup. Relieved, Ted smiled a bit sheepishly at Mr Lee.

'*Ganbei*,' shouted Mr Lee, holding his glass up to Ted.

'*Ganbei*, old pal,' said Ted gamely, eager to blot out the memory of the staring eyeball. He picked up his glass, touched the bottom, nodded quickly at Mr Lee and drained the glass.

'Don't worry Ted,' said Dr Tommy. 'We understand about you not wanting the duck's eye.'

'You mean I haven't lost face by not eating the eye?!' Ted joked.

'Not at all,' Dr Tommy replied seriously.

'It will make a good story for my future grandchildren, anyway,' Ted said. His face was flushed; he looked hot and embarrassed.

'Yes, it will. And for Eddie's grandchildren as well,' said Dr Tommy, smiling.

'Oh?'

'After all, a duck has two eyes,' Dr Tommy said, his eyes brimming with amusement.

'Indeed,' Ted added, suddenly looking extra wise.

'What?' I said, startled. I dipped the spoon down to the bottom of my bowl and felt the solid rubbery object. 'Oh, no!'

Ted chuckled; Mr Lee and Mr Woo giggled boyishly. Dr Tommy said something in Chinese to the men along the table and the group burst out laughing.

At that moment, the girls entered the room with huge bowls of rice and platters of large, deep-fried prawns. The snapping, twitching chopsticks went after the food all along the table. More toasts were proposed and drunk, then the girls brought in thinly sliced beef cooked with almonds and plates of fried bamboo shoots, seaweed and vegetables.

Dr Tommy toasted Ted, then me. The girl with the brown jug continued to fill the glasses as they were drained. Men down the table started to look towards Ted and me to drink to our health. It seemed to be a point of honour for every man in the room to toast the two special guests. After about six glasses of the bitter wine I was afraid to look up in case another Chinese face would be grinning at me, holding up a glass and shouting '*ganbei*'.

A large grilled fish appeared on the table. Once again conversation stopped and chopsticks flew as the men peeled back the crisp skin and gouged out chunks of the tender, light meat. The men nearest Ted and me reached across the table to place an especially nice morsel of this or that into our bowls.

Dr Tommy's face was quite red, he was speaking louder now, explaining his idea about adding another member to his team. I felt hot, half-drugged and stuffed. The wine glasses continued to be filled as different men along the table saluted Ted or me. My mind was fuzzy from the drink... I couldn't follow Dr Tommy's conversation.

'...and there's always a good market for them,' Dr Tommy was saying as I battled to remain conscious in the stuffy, noisy room.

'For what?' I asked, my lips buzzing out of control.

'Watermelons,' Ted said with a silly look on his face. 'Dr Tommy has been telling us of his plans to produce more watermelons. Fascinating stuff!' Ted was slurring his words, just barely managing to keep from tittering.

'Really, watermelons?'

'Yes. Dr Tommy wants to add a watermelon specialist to his team… wants to know what you think.'

'What I think?' I heard my own words running around in my head like echoes in a canyon… 'think, think…' I grinned, not giving a hoot about watermelons, or cauliflower or mushrooms or much else at that moment.

'Yes, Eddie,' Dr Tommy said, somehow remaining coherent even though he was twitching in his chair.

'Dr T. is drunk,' I leaned forward and whispered to Ted, registering the thought through the fog that was closing in on me. I chuckled to myself.

'I don't see what's funny,' Ted blustered, trying to appear stern.

'Hmm. I really don't know what I think about a watermelon man,' I said thickly. Someone down the table had raised a glass to toast me and now waited for a response.

'Well said, Eddie; you'll make a fine bureaucrat one day!' Ted sniffed as he pulled himself up straight.

'We do need a man for watermelons,' Mr Woo said faintly, almost to himself. Hearing his voice, I looked over at the strange, serious person peeping out from the thick glasses. The man down the table waved his glass.

'He wants to toast your health,' Dr Tommy mumbled, pointing to the man with his chopsticks.

'Ted, would you be so kind as to take that man's toast for me?' I said with excessive formality, trying not to sound dim and babbly.

'Oh, my pleasure!' Ted reached for his glass. '*Ganbei* to you, you yellow devil!' He glanced at the man, hitched his arm and socked the wine back.

'*Ganbei*,' the man shouted and slumped over.

'Ted, watch your language, for God's sake! These gentlemen are our colleagues,' I said blankly, resting my head in my hands and staring at the wall across the room. 'Why always red?' I muttered disconnectedly.

'Good luck,' Dr Tommy said between gulps of food and airy sucking noises as he inhaled the rice from the bottom of his bowl, flailing rapidly with the chopsticks.

'Do you think it makes a bit of difference?' Ted asked absently.

'Yes.'

'Then you think it's a good idea, Eddie?' Dr Tommy said with interest as he looked up for a second. His shirt now hung wet and limp over his shoulders.

The girls cleared away some of the mess and put plates of small pieces of fried chicken and mushrooms along the table.

'How many course dinner is this?' I asked, sinking rapidly.

'Fifteen,' Dr Tommy answered. 'Now Eddie, you agree then?'

'How many have we had?' I heard a thump and looked over at Mr Lee. His head was down on the table among the scraps of food. Won't have to worry about any more toasts from him, I thought dully.

'Eleven, I think. When you see the oranges it will be over. Oranges always come last… cut the grease,' Dr Tommy said. He was holding up well, I thought, even though he was drinking quite a lot of beer and had drunk a glass of wine toasting most of the men in the room.

'Watermelons are good,' I said vaguely, feeling I hadn't answered Dr Tommy adequately.

'Exactly so, Eddie,' Dr Tommy beamed, his round face shining with sweat and oil. He reached over and placed a hand on my shoulder.

Ted was grinning; his head suddenly jerked to one side. 'Quite true. Ever so, Eddie,' he said vacantly. '*Ganbei*, old boy!' Ted picked up his wine glass and bumped it to mine making a distinct clink. The wine slopped over our hands. 'You've gone right to the heart of the matter, as usual.'

Dr Tommy smiled, then patted Ted's shoulder. 'Americans are often very… well, stiff; very difficult to…'

'Reserved?' I asked, tilting my head, trying to follow his words.

'Yes. Reserved,' he replied, looking my way but seeing nothing. 'But you are not. Not you and your friend Ted.'

I couldn't eat another bite. I looked over at Mr Woo who was still deftly picking up bits of food with his chopsticks from the plates in the centre of the table and popping them into his mouth.

'How do you manage to stay so thin, Mr Woo?' I asked with difficulty.

'I watch what I eat. I'm very careful. I don't ever drink milk,' he answered, then added: 'Also, I jog.'

'Don't drink milk?'

'No, that is for baby cows!' he answered as he speared another piece of chicken.

'Mr Woo jogs, Ted. That's how he stays so thin!' I said somehow, as the red walls started moving; red walls, lanterns; a swirling splash of scarlet… I shut my eyes.

'Admirable,' Ted mumbled.

I looked at Mr Woo. He seemed higher, taller and quite pleased with himself as he skilfully lifted more bits of food into his bowl.

'We Chinese try to keep fit,' Dr Tommy said, his tongue getting in his way. 'We aren't fanatics, you know, but we keep ourselves sharp.' He casually hooked his hand beneath my arm just in time to keep me from sliding under the table.

'Admirable!' Ted exclaimed again to no one in particular. 'All *very* admirable!' Something crashed at the other end of the room. One of the men had dropped his head and arms on the table, knocking a few dishes and glasses over as he went down.

'Excellent dinner,' I croaked, trying to hold on until the end. Two girls pushed through the side door carrying trays of fruit. 'Ah, the oranges,' I sighed gratefully.

'Yes, the oranges,' Dr Tommy said, wiping the grease from his face with a large handkerchief. The girls managed to find places at the table among the heads and arms and glasses and chicken bones to put the trays down. 'The dinner is finished,' Dr Tommy said with finality, stood up, affectionately patted his swollen belly, belched violently, then, looking composed and dignified, sauntered unsteadily towards the exit.

Ted fished me out from among the food scraps and chair legs; we righted ourselves, and with a lot more difficulty than Dr Tommy, wobbled from the restaurant into the steamy night.

Zoom

His name was Dung – pronounced almost exactly like 'Zhung' – he said, his eyes staring from deep pockets in a thin face; long prominent teeth; a shock of black hair slashed across his pale forehead as he made a swooping arc, like a dive bomber, with his hand and arm, while he said 'zoom, zoom'. Everyone called him Zoom; it suited him perfectly. He was in his early 20s; an angular, restless man, moving in jerks and starts like a puppet and packed with a small dog's energy.

He was the agricultural fieldman responsible for several villages, including Thanh Loc. Soon after we met, he told me – without a hint of humour in his voice – that one day he wanted to be the Minister of Agriculture. After I got to know him and saw him at work, I believed that, given the slightest chance, he could easily carry it off. Zoom was the organiser and the force behind the introduction of the improved rice varieties in his territory: the area around Thanh Loc and three other villages nearby.

We'd met when Linh and I had driven out to the village to attend one of the regular meetings about the farmers' cooperative. Zoom was there, and before long, the talk had turned to the possibility of reconstructing an ancient irrigation system to provide water for rice-growing during the dry season. The old system, built in colonial times, had gradually stopped functioning due to the disruptions of years of war and because fewer young men remained on the land to maintain the canals and water-control structures. Eventually, the siphon tubes split open, the main canal became choked with weeds, wooden gates rotted, and silt filled the distribution ditches. Then Zoom showed up. Transferred into the area, he replaced a sleepy older man who seldom ventured out to the villages.

Zoom was different; he not only came to visit the villagers frequently, but he dressed as they did, ate with them and worked alongside them in the fields. Zoom was a vital presence, and he had ideas; ideas about everything, but mostly about how the farmers could get more from their land. Growing the two high-yielding rice varieties from the Philippines in the wet season as well as the dry season by using irrigation water from the river was his most insistent message to the villagers.

I never found out what made Zoom zoom, but it was clear when I met him he was a special young man. He'd quickly spotted the potential of the old canals and ditches, called a meeting of all the farmers and in one evening, with the help of senior farmer Mr Sang, convinced the village that the people themselves should recondition and open the irrigation system once again.

There was excitement in the air when Linh and I met Zoom and some of the headmen at the village chief's house. Zoom had done a preliminary survey and, with the help of some old maps he found at the province irrigation office, he'd made projections of 100, 200, even more hectares that eventually could be irrigated. It all depended on how much of the system the villagers would be able to clean and repair and the size pump they could beg or borrow, he explained rapidly, as though there wasn't a minute to lose. 'Think of it, 200 hectares double-cropped with miracle rice, yielding four or more tons per hectare per crop...' he raced on, gesturing frantically as he pointed to the maps, his whole body vibrating in place. I was immediately caught up in the excitement. Here was a project that would involve the entire village, physically and directly. It was unlike anything I could imagine happening in the US, where a community project often meant no more than getting a donation from as many people as possible.

And that was the start of it: months of hard labour by the villagers when they had time and energy left from their other work – the people helped and pushed and pestered by Zoom, and loving it – and the scurrying around by Linh and Mr Phu and me to find a suitable engine and pump and the money to pay for it. Ted helped at his level by arranging for a loan to the cooperative for the pump, plus an engineer to install it. We managed to redirect 200 kilograms of IR-8 seed to the village and got a promise of more. Ted sent some of the demonstration kits to my office so planting could start just as soon as irrigation water was available. And later, when the system was ready for operation, Ted was able to get a promise from Mr Tam, the director-general, that he would come out to Thanh Loc to open the project officially. A date was set.

But Zoom wasn't there for the opening of the system and only appeared later after the visiting officials had gone. Linh and I had been delayed at the office. By the time we arrived at the village, the ministry officials had inspected the pump and diesel engine, located in a low pump house built by Zoom and the farmers about halfway down the riverbank, and had gone back up onto the main irrigation canal leading to the fields. Linh went to find her relatives among the crowd of people standing around below the canal in the rice paddy where the first of the water would appear. I joined the visitors on the earthen dyke that Zoom and his work crews had thrown up when they cleaned the canal. Ted, who had travelled from Saigon with the director-general, saw me and turned back.

'Well, at least they haven't started pumping yet,' I said as he approached.

'Probably forgot the diesel fuel,' he commented dryly.

'No, I dropped some off a couple of days ago,' I answered. The village chief and Mr Sang and some of the other village leaders stood talking to Mr Tam. I looked for Zoom but didn't see him. Mr Tam turned to welcome me. He appeared relaxed and happy as we shook hands. I then greeted the other visitors as well as Mr Sang and the village chief.

'What a wonderful day this is for these villagers,' Mr Tam commented, waving his arm around at all the people. 'We are glad you could join us for the opening of the system. The village chief has told us that without your help this would not have been possible.' Although Mr Sang didn't understand the words spoken by the director-general, he could easily guess their meaning and stood by looking very pleased.

I was feeling good too. The efforts of Zoom and Mr Sang and Linh and everybody else – convincing the farmers to clean out the old system, locating the large pump, getting it installed properly – now seemed well worthwhile. It all came together today with the official opening.

After looking at one of the water-control gates, Mr Tam turned to Ted and me and suggested we walk along a bit further. Just to our right, a secondary canal branched off, leading to a series of smaller ditches that opened into the individual fields. As we talked about the network of canals that would feed the irrigation water to the fields, the engine sputtered, made a slapping clanging noise and slowly settled into a steady, powerful roar. Then I knew where Zoom was.

Farmers in the rice paddy called excitedly in anticipation while we moved to the main canal to catch the first sight of water entering the system from the pump house. Soon, a fast-flowing layer of water surged along the canal bottom, was blocked at the diversion gate, then dropped to a smaller secondary canal and ran down to the field ditches where the people stood. The villagers below cheered as they saw the water begin to seep onto the land. Children were kicking the water at each other and running around wildly, splashing and shouting. The director-general smiled, clapped Ted and me on the back, then suggested we all walk into the field.

'Sure,' Ted answered, and I agreed, anxious to get my feet into the mud and water.

We sat down on the dyke and removed our shoes and socks. Ted and I wore our field clothes, which for Ted included one of his favourite misshapen t-shirts, so we didn't mind sitting on the ground, but Mr Tam looked formal in his tailored black trousers. He was unconcerned, however, and quickly removed his shoes and socks, rolled up his trousers, then, holding hands with the village chief and Mr Sang, stepped across the main canal and half-slid down the side of the dyke. Farmers and children gathered around him, smiling and pointing and chirping happily about the water flowing into the field.

Soon, the other visitors followed Mr Tam into the paddy to stand in the water. He moved about the field stopping to chat with a farmer here and there. 'I am a farm boy in heart,' he told us, holding his hand across his chest and looking around with a huge, boyish grin on his face.

'Yes, me too!' I said. It was obvious he was pleased to be out in the fields with the farmers, well away from the headaches at the Ministry. I walked over to where Linh stood with her aunt and some other relatives while Mr Tam talked to more of the farmers.

Later, Mr Tam called to the people to be quiet so he could say a few words. 'This old irrigation system is once more in operation,' he said, speaking above the chugging of the distant engine. 'More of the system will be opened in the months ahead as the project is expanded. The government can do no more than this; it can only help bring the water to your fields. The rest is up to you.' I looked over at the pump house for Zoom. Where the heck are you, this is your day, I thought. Mr Tam continued, 'Three out of four people in South Vietnam work the land. It is for your benefit and for the greater strength of the nation that you must use this land and this water properly.' 'For the greater strength of the nation'… I ran the words around in my head. Is there a nation here at all, I wondered.

'I have some good news for you. Today we have some new rice seed for you to plant. It has been brought from a foreign country, a place called the Philippines. There they have named this rice "IR- 8", and sometimes "miracle rice" because of the large amount of grain it produces, but we shall call it "Than-Nong": the rice of the agricultural gods. There will be more of this new seed available in the weeks ahead,' he said. I held my breath, hoping nobody would shout, 'We've got it already!' 'By growing the new seed and using this irrigation water, you will be able to plant now, before the rainy season, and so grow more rice that is needed by your families and by your country.' Nice speech, I thought. If only Mr Tam knew that on the other side of the village Zoom already has two large seedbeds planted to IR-8. Just as soon as the visitors have cleared out, the villagers will be ploughing the paddy he's now standing in and transplanting the improved seedlings into it soon afterwards. He would be amazed, I thought, and not upset by this small deception.

Mr Tam thanked everybody for their efforts in getting the irrigation system back into working order. He mentioned the good work done by the government technicians and the excellent cooperation and labour contributed by the farmers and their families. 'I am sorry I will not be able to stay here and help get the soil ready for planting, but I will return whenever I can. I wish all of you peace and good health,' he said finally, and the visitors started walking back towards the dyke.

Ted and I said goodbye to Mr Tam on the road. 'We appreciate your help and the help of all the American civilian advisors in the provinces and at your headquarters,' he said. 'Our task is not so... how do you say it?... so eye-catching as the military's. We get no headlines, but what we do is vital for the survival of our country. Do not get discouraged when you see only a little progress for your efforts; this is a slow process, this nation-building. Good luck,' he added and shook our hands. 'Oh, by the way, if you see Mr Dung, please tell him I am very pleased with his work here,' he said with a tired smile, then stepped into his car and was gone.

Once the Saigon officials drove off, the atmosphere in Thanh Loc changed from friendly but formal to wildly exuberant. Ted and I walked back into the field to share in the excitement as people got ready to start ploughing the field. Then I spotted Zoom across the paddy, dressed for fieldwork, as usual, in the villagers' style of black trousers, holding a heavy mattock, joking and slapping himself as some of the village women explained what had happened and what the director-general had said. Kids were hanging onto his arms, laughing and shouting as he joked with them. I looked over at Mr Sang for an explanation. He smiled.

'You are wondering where Dung has been, no, Eddie?'

'Yes.'

'Keeping out of sight while the bosses are around, that is all. He was in the pump house all the time.'

'Yes, I thought so, but why? He, more than any of us, is responsible for the system being opened again,' I said.

'Yes, he certainly is. Without him it could not have been done; we all know that. But you see, he likes it here, likes our village and the people here and he has met a young girl here also...' Mr Sang said, his words trailing off as he seemed to be speculating about the need for such behaviour, or perhaps how he could possibly explain this to me, a friend, but still really a stranger to the ways of the Vietnamese people. 'The villagers have given him a small plot of land near the cooperative; he is building a house there. He is one of us now,' Mr Sang said, looking proud.

'So, all the more reason to…'

'No, you do not understand, Eddie,' he said, touching my arm. 'At his level in government it is better to be unknown. Then you are left alone. If they get to know you, especially if you are good, they remember your name when they need to transfer someone to fill a vacancy. The government is always short of people, a lot of transferring, better to stay low,' Mr Sang explained, slightly crouching down.

'I see,' I nodded, laughing. A wise old one, this Mr Sang, I thought, and I didn't have the heart to tell him about Mr Tam's kind words about Zoom.

'Yes. Here, now, in our culture and at this time, it is better to be a little man than a giant. All Americans want to be giants, I think, but only a few foolish Vietnamese do.'

'Better to be a small man and stay with people you like near the girl you love than be a transferred giant, yes?' I joked.

'Yes, exactly, or a dead one,' Mr Sang said, then took my arm and pulled me towards the area where Zoom, Ted and some of the villagers were already busy digging up the paddy. 'Come, Eddie, we shall get Linh and the three of us will help the others dig up this field. We are going to have the earliest crop of rice in the village for many years. This is a special day. You may never understand how happy that makes us feel. It makes us feel like we are alive, like we are on the move and not stagnating as the times pass us by. We Vietnamese are a strange people; we love to look back over a very long, exciting and meaningful history, but, at the same time, we feel frustrated if we have nothing to look forward to. Now, with this irrigation project, and the cooperative and other activities we are involved with, we feel good about ourselves, we feel we can carry on until peace comes. The Americans in our country have helped us to maintain this hope in the future; that is what we are thankful for.'

Mr Sang and I found Linh, then we picked out tools from a pile on the ground and got ourselves ready. Linh tied a scarf around her head while Mr Sang and I turned up our trousers and put our shirts aside. Then, with the three of us standing in a row, we dug the hoes into the wet soil and pulled, again and again.

'Ahhh,' said Mr Sang, 'this is heaven.'

I looked over at his niece, smoothly swinging the short-handled hoe then stepping sideways, her face radiant in the light shining back from the flooded field. I was enjoying the moment, feeling life in glorious slow motion as Linh glanced up and smiled.

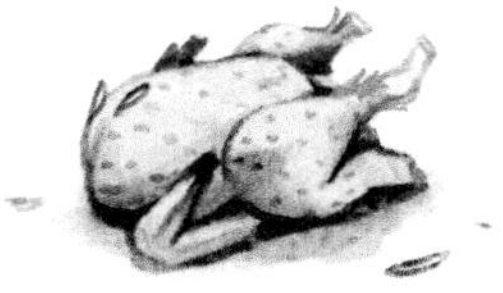

The VIPs

'Look, Eddie, we're doing some very tight scheduling for these VIPs, it's all locked in now; too late to change anything. Just do the best you can; round up some kids, have a cooking demonstration, you know... whatever you can dream up.'

'Why are they coming out, anyway?'

'They're important folks, Eddie, old boy. Community leaders, people with influence. It's our hope to impress them favourably with the assistance programme so when they return home they'll speak in support of our efforts here. That sort of thing gets back to Congress, you know. Helps to keep the bucks coming.' The young officer flashed a witless grin.

'It stinks!' I said, hating this smooth-faced pimp, hating his impeccable white shirt and silly tie and the way he kept saying my name. Had probably read in one of those how-to-get-ahead-in-the-business-world books that it was the way to influence people... win them over.

'Oh come on, don't be so naive, man. It's the way of the world; it's how things get done.'

'*You're* naive, pal,' I said testily, 'if you think some innocent from Nebraska can come out here for a week or so, get briefed by some admin hot shots in Saigon who don't know what's happening in the field anyway, get dragged around to a few staged activities in some secure villages and return home with any idea of what's really going on here!'

'It's out of our hands, Eddie. This schmoozing gets dreamed up by our mighty leaders in Washington. We just respond to their instructions. If you don't like it, write to your congressman!'

'OK... to hell with it,' I sighed, realising this guy was just a two-bit functionary. What difference does it make anyway? Of all the ways money and time are wasted in Vietnam, this is one of the least harmful. 'Got to remember our Zen, right, *Roger*?' I said, emphasising his name. 'Keep things in perspective, balanced; flow with it!'

'That's right, Eddie.' He seemed relieved.

'So who will be coming to my province?'

The officer moved some papers around on his desk. 'Let's see now. Yes, you will have a Miss Cynthia Leggit. She is a journalist, I guess. At least her old man owns a string of newspapers in North Carolina. The other one is Reverend Glen Olsen from Minnesota.' He looked up with a flashy grin. 'You can discuss Zen Buddhism with him!'

'You bet,' I replied lightly. 'OK, send them out. We'll give them a grand tour of the province.'

'Hey, now you're getting the idea, Eddie. Just remember, though, their special thing is rural youth.'

I told Mr Phu and Linh about the upcoming VIP visit. We agreed there wasn't much to see but discussed a few possibilities. Mr Phu said he and Linh would take care of everything; he would visit an old friend of his who worked as an aide to Colonel Long, the province chief, and work something out. Linh knew several people who might be able to help as well and said she would check with them even though she wouldn't be able to accompany the group because of another commitment.

I didn't hear anything about what had been set up until just before the visitors arrived. As I was going over the arrangements for the day with Mr Phu, a group of people appeared at my office door. 'Ah, here you are now!' I said and stepped over to shake hands with Tom, a young AID officer I knew vaguely. He had driven the two visitors to the province and would be accompanying us during the day. Tom introduced Miss Leggit and Reverend Olsen.

'Miss Leggit, Reverend Olsen,' I said, 'pleased to meet you. This is Mr Phu. We work together on the agricultural programme here in Gia Dinh.'

'Please call me Glen,' Reverend Olsen said.

'And I'm Cynthia,' Miss Leggit drawled sweetly as she pressed Mr Phu's hand and studied his inscrutable expression.

Revd Olsen was a tall weedy man of about 40. His pasty white skin, prominent nose and deeply hollowed-out face made him look bloodless, cadaverous. Patchy blue-grey circles showed beneath his tired eyes. He appeared hot and sticky in a white dress shirt opened at the neck. His forehead and lank brown hair were wet with sweat even though the office was still relatively cool.

'Here, sit down, Glen.' I shifted a chair for him.

'Revd Olsen is under the weather this morning, I'm afraid,' Miss Leggit said in a rich Southern accent. She said 'thizmawnin' with a lazy movement of her large, fleshy lips. I found the accent pleasant. Mr Phu, however, who prided himself in his ability with English, looked puzzled as he tried to guess what Miss Leggit had said. He smiled, assuming she was continuing her greetings, pulled a chair forward and asked her to be seated.

'Why, thank you, Mr Phu,' she said, crinkling up her face into a smile. 'Just a little tummy upset, eh Glen? Probably the water.'

'It's not serious,' Revd Olsen replied in a weak voice as he squirmed uncomfortably.

I glanced at Miss Leggit. She was a big woman, quite tall and heavy, in her late 30s. She wore a dark purple dress patterned with white flowers, stockings and shoes with medium-high heels. Her face was perfectly round and pink and surrounded by a mass of strawberry-blonde curls. Miss Leggit looked well fed; meaty and juicy to a hunting lion, I couldn't help but imagine.

I started the briefing by describing the province, the area and approximate population, then reviewed the community development work supported by the US advisory team. I talked about the agricultural programme and mentioned a couple of crop and livestock projects that seemed successful.

'Successful, how?' Miss Leggit asked. She had a stenographer's pad on her knee and was scribbling in shorthand.

'By increasing the amounts of important crops such as rice grown in the wet season and maize or peanuts in the dry season,' I answered.

'Does this really help the farmer?' Revd Olsen wanted to know.

'Well, it can. Many of the peasants are…'

'Peasants!' Miss Leggit interrupted in a loud voice. 'You call these poor dears "peasants"?!' She extended her arm towards Mr Phu and looked at him with sympathy. Mr Phu, not sure why she was pointing at him, nodded and smiled.

'Mr Phu is not a peasant, Miss Leggit.'

'Cynthia, please.'

'Cynthia. Mr Phu is an educated man. He has a degree in agriculture; he is not a poor farmer. A peasant is a person who works on the land – a farmer or a farm labourer,' I explained patiently.

'I don't like it!' Miss Leggit said sharply. 'We come here to help these poor people and what do we do but call them names!' She made some quick notes on her paper.

'It's not a name; it is not derogatory in any way. Peasant just means a poor person who works the land,' I said in a low, even voice.

'All the same, I don't like it one bit, but please go on.' Miss Leggit was bent over her notebook. I was amused as I thought of the articles she would be submitting to her daddy's papers. A lot of good the State Department would get out of paying for her junket!

'Please, Eddie, go on,' she repeated.

'Yes. Well, many of the peasants are subsistence farmers. That is, they normally grow only enough food for their own needs. With increased yields, it is possible to get such farmers to produce food for the market. By selling their surplus…'

'That's very interesting,' Miss Leggit broke in again. She had stopped writing and was looking at me. 'However, I believe you've been told why we are here. Revd Olsen and I have a special interest in the children's programmes.'

'Yes. I was coming to that,' I said irritably. I was getting a bit fed up with the woman and didn't try to hide it.

'I'm sorry,' she said, detecting my annoyance, 'but we only have a limited amount of time. Perhaps we could hear about the youth programmes.'

'Perhaps it would be best if Mr Phu explained what we plan to see today,' I said flatly. 'I'll check to see that the vehicle is ready.'

'Excellent,' Miss Leggit said and beamed intently at Mr Phu as he stood up and moved to get some papers off the desk. I left the room and went downstairs.

When I returned to the office Mr Phu was just finishing. 'That sounds wonderful, Mr Phu. I'm sure you have gone to a lot of trouble to arrange everything,' Miss Leggit said warmly. She stood up and touched his arm. Mr Phu mumbled a few words and slipped out of her grasp. 'Shall we go now?' She turned to me.

'Yes, let's go. Glen, do you want to use the toilet before we leave?'

'Ah, yes, please,' he said, slightly embarrassed. I showed him the door. Miss Leggit stayed in the office talking to Mr Phu, who had a strained, frozen smile on his face.

'Who the hell is this babe?' I asked Tom in the hallway.

'Take it easy, Eddie. She's very influential,' he whispered.

'She's a pain in the ass!'

'I know, but she has powerful connections, or her father does, in Washington.'

'Just a big, fat pain in the ass!' I exhaled loudly.

Revd Olsen returned, and we all went down to the ground floor. Colonel Horst was talking with a young soldier outside his office. He looked up and stepped over to meet the visitors.

As she was being introduced, Miss Leggit grabbed Colonel Horst's arm and moved next to him. A short man, his head reached about to her ample breasts. The colonel looked horrified and tried to step back but Miss Leggit held him tightly. 'Your Mr Phu has just given us a marvellous briefing, Colonel. He's arranged a wonderful field trip for us. We're going out to see the children now,' she said and reached over to pull Mr Phu towards her with her free hand. 'This man is a darling!' she gurgled.

'Well, ah, that's fine,' the colonel said as he tried in vain to disengage himself from Miss Leggit's iron grip. 'Anything we can do to make our guests comfortable and their stay with us enjoyable…' he mumbled. 'Good work, Phu,' he added, nodding his head and coming very close to bouncing his chin off Miss Leggit's chest. 'Have a pleasant trip, ma'am.'

Miss Leggit loosened her grip on the colonel, and he immediately stepped back. 'We certainly will, Colonel,' she said over her shoulder as she marched out of the building still clutching Mr Phu. For a long moment Colonel Horst just stared at me, then his thick eyebrows climbed clear to the top of his forehead.

'Another civilian do-gooder, Colonel,' I said, relishing the moment.

'Good God Almighty!' he growled, shook his head slowly and turned away.

Miss Leggit insisted Mr Phu sit in the back between herself and Revd Olsen. From the driver's seat I could see Mr Phu smiling uncomfortably as she commented about the sights along the road. The minister sat silently on the other side, holding a large camera bag on his knees.

At the first stop, not far from the province capital, we pulled up to an area in the centre of a small village where some children stood in a field. Somebody shouted and, out of nowhere, there was a frenzy of activity. Kids started digging madly in the ground. More boys and girls tumbled over the dyke surrounding the field and slashed at weeds with knives or dug in the soil with hoes and pointed sticks. Wow, what a sight, I thought. Like an ant colony under attack! How did Mr Phu arrange this? I could see we were in for some surprises! Close to 40 kids were hard at work as we walked over to greet the people standing along the edge of the field.

'What's going on here?' Miss Leggit spoke loudly to the first startled Vietnamese she came to. 'Look at those children work; this is fantastic!'

Mr Phu introduced the village chief and some of the other local dignitaries as well as two young women who stood at attention off to one side dressed in faded green skirts and white blouses. Each had a patch on the shoulder bearing the insignia '4-T'. The same patch was sewn onto the centre of each girl's cap – a sort of soft, white baseball cap with a green visor. I noticed some of the kids in the field also wore this type of cap.

Miss Leggit could hardly stand still long enough for the official pleasantries; she was so anxious to get at the kids. She kept craning her neck towards the field until Mr Phu tapped her on the shoulder – staying out of grabbing distance – so he could introduce the two girls to her and Revd Olsen. 'These girls are the leaders of the 4-T club in this area,' he said, looking pleased with himself. The girls shook hands and immediately resumed their stiff pose.

'4-T?' Miss Leggit asked, all her attention now on Mr Phu. 'Like our 4-H clubs at home? Raising prize heifers and huge vegetables and all that?'

Mr Phu didn't understand but nodded and smiled.

'Oh, this is wonderful, Mr Phu!' She gave him a squeeze on the arm. Poor Mr Phu. 'Let's go into the field and talk to the children,' she said and stumbled across the dyke in her heels, half dragging Mr Phu to a boy digging up the soil at high speed. The boy stopped and looked up at this giant blonde woman.

'Mr Phu, please ask this boy what he is doing here.' Mr Phu spoke to the boy.

'Digging the field. I was told to by that man.' The boy pointed to one of the men standing with the village leaders.

'He is preparing the field for a vegetable garden,' Mr Phu said. 'That man over there is teaching the children how to do it.'

'Oh, lovely. What will he do with the vegetables?'

Mr Phu told the boy to tuck in his shirt and then asked him how old he was and if he went to school. The boy answered.

'He will give the vegetables to his mother to help feed the family. He has four younger brothers and sisters,' Mr Phu reported.

'How wonderful, what a good boy! Ask him how long he has been in the 4-T club, please.'

Mr Phu asked the boy if he had ever belonged to a club for kids in the village. 'Never,' he answered quickly.

'He's been in the club for three years,' Mr Phu said to Miss Leggit with a perfectly straight face. I stood nearby, getting the gist of the words spoken, marvelling at this old con artist.

'Good. Now ask him what skills he has learned, please.' She still held onto Mr Phu. She was sweating from the hot sun; large damp patches had formed beneath her soft arms.

Mr Phu told the boy to work more slowly when he dug the soil, then asked him where he lived, how many brothers and sisters he had and how many people lived in his house. The boy gave a lengthy explanation, pointing down the road to where his house was located and described his family.

'He has learned how to grow a garden, how to raise chickens, how to care for fruit trees and how to repair the roof of his father's house. He is working on a project now to build an animal shelter out of bamboo because he wants to keep a goat,' Mr Phu said without the slightest hesitation. I had to turn away to keep from laughing.

'Oh, what an industrious little fellow!' Miss Leggit exclaimed happily. 'You must have a present.' She reached inside her large handbag and after some searching around pulled out a small jar of green liquid, then dove back inside the bag for a piece of wire with a loop on one end. She handed her bag to Mr Phu, unscrewed the lid of the jar, dipped the wire loop into the liquid, held it up to her mouth and blew. Beautiful tiny soap bubbles filled the air… carried on the draft of her steady breath across the wire.

'Well, at least she has some imagination,' I said quietly to Tom as we stood nearby.

The little boy's eyes popped wide open. The other children, who had been watching Miss Leggit as she talked to the boy, saw the bubbles and roared with delight as they ran to see what magic this strange person had let loose. Most of the villagers and the other children standing in the shade along the road rushed over to surround her as she methodically pumped glistening bubbles into the air above their heads. Kids were leaping and popping bubbles all over the place while some of the younger children stood transfixed at the sight of all the lovely bubbles coming from this foreigner's mouth.

'There, this shall be yours because of your industriousness.' Miss Leggit handed the bottle and the wire wand to the boy she had been questioning, then bent over to place an arm around his shoulder. The boy, clutching the bottle and wire loop, danced out of her reach, dipped into the bottle and started to blow bubbles while the mob of children closed in on him. Within a few minutes nothing could be seen but a writhing mass of arms and heads from which, every so often, a cloud of bubbles arose accompanied by a roar of children's voices.

Miss Leggit and Mr Phu returned to the roadway surrounded by many of the villagers and some of the children who were hoping for more goodies from her bag. Revd Olsen, looking quite pale, rested in the shade.

'Well, that was very interesting. Thank you so much, Mr Phu, for translating for me,' Miss Leggit drawled as she pulled a large handkerchief from her bag and mopped her face. 'I think we should push on now. That all right with you, Glen?'

'Yes, quite all right,' he said bravely through a thin smile as he gripped his belly and hoisted himself to his feet. We said goodbye to the villagers, thanked the two girls in the 4-T hats and returned to the vehicle.

Later, at Thanh Loc village, where, thanks to Linh's connections, something had been organised, I pulled the car up next to a group of people standing outside the low school building. I was getting out when suddenly Revd Olsen – his angular features contorted and face blanched – scrambled from the car and raced for a clump of bushes off to one side of the clearing.

'What on earth?!' Miss Leggit looked shocked.

'I think Glen will be feeling better soon,' I said and reached under the front seat for a roll of toilet paper.

'Oh, I see.'

I walked over to the bushes and put the toilet paper in easy reach of Glen. On my way back I chased away a few kids who were curious to see what was going on out that way.

The introductions were made. Revd Olsen soon joined the group looking much healthier, if a bit embarrassed, and we all filed into the school. We were shown to a row of chairs in front of some tables, while behind us the room filled quickly as the villagers squeezed in to get a look at the very important people.

Mr Phu stood with Mr Sang and the village chief who held up his arm to get the crowd's attention. He welcomed us and made some brief remarks. Mr Phu then pointed to a young woman at the front wearing a 4-T cap who stood on one side of the first table. About 18, she was very shy and unable to take her eyes off the floor. Mr Phu explained that the young woman was the leader of the village 4-T Home Economics Club. 'Today the club wants to demonstrate how to prepare a traditional Vietnamese dish: boiled white rice, chicken and local vegetables.' He pointed to four little girls standing next to the tables. They bowed and stepped behind one table to start the demonstration.

'Oh, how marvellous,' Miss Leggit said, shifting her legs and trying to get comfortable on the tiny wooden chair. I shuffled my chair slightly to give us both more room.

A beautiful little girl with glossy, black hair and lovely dark eyes reached into a cage on the floor and pulled out a scrawny chicken that immediately began to squawk and flap its wings wildly as she took hold of its skinny neck. 'Oh dear,' said Miss Leggit anxiously, 'it's still alive!' As she spoke, the girl walked around to the front of the table and stopped in front of Miss Leggit, lifted the little bird up to eye level and with one swift twisting and pulling motion, jerked its head off.

'Oh my God!' Miss Leggit shrieked, aghast at the sight, her round face suddenly twisted in horror. 'How barbaric! I can't stand the sight of blood!'

The girl looked very proud; she smiled and walked around to the other side of the table and placed the headless chicken on a cutting board. She then stepped back as two of the girls started to pluck the feathers from the bird.

'Enough! I can't sit through this,' Miss Leggit whimpered. Feathers were flying in the air as the girls plucked furiously.

Another girl honed a long knife while the first girl waited, holding a meat cleaver.

'Look, Miss Leggit,' I said, 'if you're going to have a chicken and rice dish, someone must kill a chicken!'

'I don't care... I don't want to see it,' she moaned, then added in a hoarse whisper: 'Get me out of here! Explain I've got tummy trouble... anything. I can't watch this!' She grabbed her handbag and stood up. Her chair crashed to the floor as she turned around to see how she could escape. The girls stopped plucking. The villagers started to mumble and laugh. 'I'm leaving!' she gasped, and with that, shoved her way through the muttering crowd and burst out the door.

The crowd grew louder. 'Damn you for getting me into this,' I mentally shouted to that jerk at headquarters. 'You should have chosen your "VIPs" a bit more carefully!' I decided I'd better get this over with as quickly as possible, so asked Mr Phu to explain Miss Leggit was ill and had to go back to town.

'The big one does not like the blood, Eddie,' Mr Sang said with a mischievous grin.

'So it seems.'

'Don't feel bad... we will have chicken and rice later and think of you and your visitors!'

Miss Leggit was in the vehicle and remained quiet when the rest of us climbed in. 'Well, you certainly blew that one!' I said as we drove along the road leading out of the village. 'Super. Really diplomatic, Cyn-thi-a!' I couldn't help adding, exaggerating all the syllables in her name.

'I'm sorry. It was so oppressive in there: so hot and crowded, and that blood...!'

We spent the rest of the day looking at several other projects Mr Phu and Linh had arranged for us to visit. Miss Leggit tried to remain friendly when we stopped at a fruit tree nursery, but on the whole, she was greatly subdued. As she sank deeper into her own thoughts, Revd Olsen brightened up, becoming quite spirited and talkative.

After a late lunch with a group of girls attending a sewing class, we made the last stop of the afternoon at a field on the outskirts of a large village. The kids were having a sports day with sprint and relay races, gymnastic events and volleyball competitions. Here, Miss Leggit cheered up enough to join us in a match with the kids.

She was a game one, I had to admit that. She kicked off her shoes, and her face was soon bright pink, her hair soaked and stringy, her dress wet as the sweat poured from her body. Still, she carried on, slapping the ball as hard as she could with her open palm, shuffling sideways and hoisting her bulky frame to make a difficult play or keep the ball inbounds as her breasts lifted and thrashed around her chest. The kids loved it. They took great pains to hit the ball to Miss Leggit, to keep her in the centre of the action, and howled and squealed at her efforts.

My estimation of her went up considerably. She's not so bad, I thought, as I watched her try to slam a ball and get tangled in the net with the girl from the opposing team. She's a naive, pampered American from another world… not her fault; she's OK, has good instincts…

As we got ready to leave, Revd Olsen retrieved his camera bag from the car, opened it and removed a brown paper bag. Now what's he up to, I wondered. There's been no sign of a camera all day. He reached inside, pulled out a small hard candy and handed it to a little girl who stood close by. The girl didn't know what it was, so he took another, unwrapped the mystery treat and popped it into his mouth. By this time some other children were moving nearer. The girl unwrapped her candy and gingerly put it into her mouth. She said something and smiled. The other kids yelled and began crowding closer to Revd Olsen as he started handing out the candies, one by one, to the waving hands thrust at him.

Cries went up and kids from all over the field headed for this lanky foreigner. They got closer and bolder, putting their hands on the bag. He playfully swatted them away with a laugh. This was the liveliest we'd seen him all day. While he looked one way, a more daring kid on the other side would dive a hand into the bag and quickly grab what he could. Glen tried to give candies to some of the smaller children, particularly the girls who stood back, somewhat afraid of this stranger with the long nose. Finally, the pressure from the kids was too intense; a bigger boy grabbed the bag, ripped it open and sent the goodies tumbling to the ground. It was all over. Revd Olsen retreated looking dishevelled and hot, but pleased. Now that's diplomacy, I thought.

We said our goodbyes and started the return trip to the province office as long, late afternoon shadows slanted across the fields. I was glad this day was over. From the back seat, Revd Olsen chatted on about the attack the kids had made on his bag. 'They are good kids, good people; real people, you know,' he said to nobody in particular. He was silent for a while, then said finally, 'Isn't it sad that I, a Christian minister, never truly understood that real people live in Vietnam until this trip?'

Later, I asked Mr Phu about the arrangements he and Linh had made, about the 4-T caps and the apparently functioning youth clubs we had visited. They had been a big surprise to me.

'It was all smoke,' Mr Phu answered obliquely.

'Smoke?'

'There are no clubs, or only very few; those we visited do not exist. The demonstrations, the sports day… all smoke.' He waved his arm to indicate the insubstantiality of it. 'The 4-T hats came from the province agriculture office. They will be collected and put away again.'

'But why go to all the trouble, Mr Phu?'

'Because we could not disappoint our visitors. It has to do with saving face. They wanted to see youth programmes, so we invented some. That is Vietnam; no problem.'

Carl

Heat waves shimmered over the hazy, undulating strip of tarmac where the silver plane braked to a stop in the distance then slowly wheeled around to head back. I stood in the full, scorching sun until the plane turned off the runway and started taxiing towards the terminal, then clanged down the iron steps and entered the main airport building. Already, a crowd had gathered in the stuffy arrivals lounge where, if all the connecting flights had worked out, I expected my brother Carl to enter from the customs shed. I moved to a relatively uncrowded bit of floor space by a large, rusty air conditioner that wheezed and rattled in a pool of water at the side of the musty-smelling room. A couple of slack overhead fans slapped at the stale air.

Two years older than I, Carl was a perceptive, if sometimes cynical, reporter of the American scene. In his earlier years as a gumshoe journalist, his articles about the local county officials – including a series about the goings-on within the sheriff's department – had been popular reading for the town's people. From clippings he had sent, I saw that Carl's writing was more polished now; he was mellowing, able to balance the acidic tone of the earlier articles with sensitive human-interest pieces about foster children or old people trying to get by on their pensions. He was doing more humorous stories, too, such as the one about recapturing an escaped parakeet called Bixby which had won him some sort of award.

I watched the double doors at the customs area as people from the flight started to emerge. The newcomers being met by friends and relatives created a mob of hugging, laughing people blocking the doorway. I strained on my toes each time the doors swung open to try and catch a glimpse of Carl inside the customs hall. Finally, there he was: medium height, stocky, looking hot and frazzled by it all. He was moving along behind a couple of well-to-do Vietnamese carrying boxes and bags stuffed with goods; a Hong Kong shopping spree, no doubt. Carl spotted me through the crowd, shrugged as the waiting masses enveloped him, then managed to push his way through.

'Just a minute, let me put these bags down,' Carl said as he dropped the shoulder bag next to his suitcase and gave me a hug. 'Good to see you! You look great.'

'You too, Carl.'

'Jesus, I'm sure glad you're here; this place – that place in there – is a madhouse,' he said, pointing back towards the customs area. 'Can you imagine how it feels for someone not connected with all this to fly into Saigon? I mean, damn, there's a war going on; they could shoot the plane out of the air at any time. Who knows what to expect? Hell, the VC could blow up the terminal while you're standing there getting your condoms fingered by the customs inspector!'

'No, it's not like that,' I said, laughing. Same old Carl!

'Sure, you can say what you like. All I have to go by are the reports that keep pouring in from the wire services: body counts, bunkers destroyed, village leaders assassinated. You know, war, man, war!'

'Sells papers, eh?'

'You bet it does. Your everyday, average, peace-loving, won't-screw-his-neighbour's-wife kind of citizen at home loves nothing better than to read about the violence here in Vietnam over his scrambled eggs in the morning. Gets him off to a good start for an aggressive day flogging vacuum cleaners or whatever!'

We crossed to the parking lot and put the luggage in the back of the car as Carl took off his sports jacket and rolled up his shirt sleeves. He looked wiped out from all the travelling as he slid into the front seat.

'We'll go to the apartment now and you can rest up a bit while I take care of some paperwork at the office. Later we can see some of the sights, hit a few bars, whatever appeals, dear brother,' I said and pulled the car into the stream of traffic leaving the airport.

'OK, sounds good. I want to see some of these famous Vietnamese beauties, but right now I'm beat from the endless flying to get to this damn place. Why can't they have a war in the Caribbean? Be a lot more convenient.'

Carl went quiet as he studied the chaos that surrounded us the moment we left the airport. Heavy army trucks with blaring air horns pounded along the road to the city, belching gobs of thick, black smoke. Little blue taxis, an ancient French model of car, moved unpredictably to try for passengers along the route. Motorised rickshaws, a person or two perched out front in the padded seat, belted up the streets with a deafening roar from their open, lawn-mower-like engines. Hundreds of Japanese motorcycles zoomed in and out and around the traffic, their engines a steady scream above the din that boomed back from the concrete buildings. The eye-searing exhaust fumes and smoke thickened as we approached the city centre.

'What a pit!' Carl said suddenly. 'Who the hell could imagine this?! It's not what I've seen on TV.'

'Yeah, it's bad; guess I've sort of gotten used to it.'

'Geez, I thought it was supposed to be a classy city!'

'It used to be.'

'More like a giant compost heap; the shit pot of Asia, now, I'd say! My God, look at the motorbikes! Where do they get the money?'

'With the US pumping money and goods in, there's lots of loose change around.'

'Loose change! Eddie, those bikes must cost a thousand bucks each!'

We stopped at an intersection. The car was surrounded by motorcycles and more kept coming to fill in every possible bit of space. Near the central market, crowds of people were crossing in front of the waiting vehicles. The stalls on either side of the street selling everything from food to clothing and all sorts of electronics equipment were thick with shoppers. Long lines of motorbikes were parked diagonally against the kerb on both sides of the street; boys ran up and down the line selling parking space for one more bike here, one more there.

'Unreal!' Carl exclaimed, shaking his head.

'By the way, you'd better keep your arm inside.'

'Why?'

'One of those hot rods on a motorbike will have your nice watch.'

'You mean rip it off my wrist?'

'Yep.'

'Christ!'

We walked out that evening, past the small bars converted from former shops, now beginning to fill with soldiers and civilians as well as the bargirls, pimps and hangers-on. People making deals in women, drugs, foreign currency and all types of goods were at their posts for the evening business.

On one wide, tiled sidewalk, beggars wrapped in rags were sprawled out on the sidewalk or tucked up against the recessed doors of closed shops, surrounded by their day's pickings from the city's trash heaps. Trees along the street struggled unsuccessfully for life in the poisonous air. In dusty little shops, Chinese herbalists sold mysterious, grey-leafed concoctions or gnarled, dark-red roots and various powders and potions as cures for asthma, worms or a sagging virility.

Carl was fascinated by the sights and smells of the streets. One stretch of the vast night-time outdoor market was devoted to the sale of exotic birds and beautiful handmade woven fibre birdcages. As we looked on, several American women were bargaining for a pair of lovely grey birds in a high narrow cage.

'Now, who would they be?' Carl asked as we stopped to watch the transaction.

'Oh, maybe people from AID or the embassy or some relief agency. Or they could be social welfare types or nurses.'

'And they just stroll along here one evening to buy some dicky birds for their apartment?'

'Sure, what's the problem?'

'I don't know. It just seems incongruous, that's all. Birds of peace or love or whatever, being bought by some American girls to decorate their apartment in this country that's fighting for its life. The war is here and yet it's not here. Up-country the male counterparts to these women are shooting the shit out of villages or dropping napalm around the bush while these dollies buy birds. Crazy!'

'Actually, you don't have to go far up-country to get a war. Right across that river down at the far end of the street is a free-fire zone: anything that moves can be shot.'

'Amazing! There's never been anything quite like this. What do you think goes through the heads of these people: the American girls buying the birds, the Vietnamese women selling them; all of them knowing what they know about what's going on here?'

'It's hard to say. They probably put these things into separate compartments: the war out there somewhere, the birds here.'

'Yes. What an uncanny ability we have to separate things in our minds. It could be the reason for our achievements… and our eventual destruction.'

'Pretty heavy, Carl.'

After a steak and chips and a huge salad plate at one of the army officers' clubs, we walked around the main bar district. Here the cheap bars and nightclubs lined both sides of the street – places with such names as Hollywood Bar or Denver Club. All were small and dark with a low bar and stools, a jukebox blasting out rock or soul music and a line of booths along one wall.

We entered one of the bars where I knew a few of the girls. It was dark and smelled of incense from the smouldering joss sticks in front of a small Buddhist altar at the far end of the smoke-filled room. We found a couple of stools at the bar.

'Do you want a local beer?'

'Sure. What is it?'

'*Ba muoi ba* – 33.'

'33?'

'That's the name of the beer. *Ba muoi ba* means 33. *Ba* is 3; *Ba muoi* means 30; *Ba muoi ba* is 33.'

'I see.'

'Now, *hai* means two. So if you want two beers, you just have to say "*hai, ba muoi ba*".'

'*Hai, ba muoi ba,*' Carl said without any trouble.

'That's it.'

The boy behind the bar came over for our order.

'Go ahead,' I urged.

'*Hai, ba muoi ba,* please,' Carl said to the boy. He nodded and moved off to get the beers.

'Hey, nothing to it!' Carl said proudly, then took a look around the room. A few girls chatted in a booth; a couple more sat up at the bar with some soldiers while another selected music at the jukebox. At the far end of the bar, several girls and their customers shouted as they slammed dominoes on the table.

A slim Vietnamese girl, with the typical schoolgirl's long straight black hair down to her waist, moved over and draped an arm around Carl's shoulder. She wore a white, silky *ao dai,* the traditional dress: close fitting at the neck with long tight sleeves and split at the waist into two floor-length pieces front and back. Beneath the dress she wore silky black trousers.

'You want to dance, Joe?' she asked.

'I'm Carl,' he said, spinning the stool around to get a better look at her. She was in her late 30s and quite plain.

'Everybody's Joe,' she said as she snuggled her head along Carl's face. 'You want to dance?'

'Not now, sweetheart, I'm resting up from my vasectomy,' Carl answered casually.

'You want to play music?' she asked, swivelling on the stool next to Carl and taking his hand in hers. I gave her some coins and she went over to the jukebox.

'She's pretty,' Carl said, looking at her shape as she walked away.

'She's OK.'

'What do you mean? She's beautiful. You've been here too long!' Carl said with a smile.

'Maybe. Or you haven't been here long enough.'

Carl danced a couple of times with the girl and, after she insisted, bought her a Saigon tea. Once she got the drink, and the slip of paper to prove it, she grew less interested in Carl and finally left to greet a tall US airman as he and some pals entered the bar.

'Beautiful but unfaithful,' Carl muttered as she led her new man to a dark booth in the back.

'Just another butterfly, right, buddy?' I said to a soldier sitting a couple of seats away from Carl who had been watching what was going on.

'Yeah, man, that's right,' he grumbled and looked down into his glass.

'Well, how do you deal with that?' Carl had turned to face the soldier.

'I don't, man. I leave these pushy queens alone. They're bad news!'

'How long you been here?'

'Seven months; five to go until I'm out of this shit.'

Carl was about to order a couple more beers but seeing the soldier's glass was nearly empty asked him if he wanted another.

'No, I don't want no goddamn beer from you!' He pulled himself up a bit and glared at Carl through bleary eyes.

'Hey, man, what's your problem? A guy asks if you want a beer, and you turn on him.'

'Damn right! You lousy civilians piss me off just on principle.'

'Why?' Carl probed, getting interested.

'Why? Shit. You bastards come over here to earn huge salaries, you live in fancy houses, buy all the ass you need and drive up the price for the rest of us. You've got safe, soft jobs, all of you. What's worse is you think you're saving everybody's ass; that you're stopping the VC from taking over this swamp!' The soldier was working himself up. 'God damn you bunch of overpaid, under-disciplined farts! It's the troops who are keeping this country alive. Without the American fighting man this whole cockeyed, slimy place would be overrun by the commies in a week!'

'You know, I think you're probably right,' Carl said.

'Damn right, I'm right!'

Carl pointed with his thumb at me. 'You see this guy? He's one of your soft, overpaid civilians and I'm pretty sure he's driving up the price of ass around here.'

'Yeah, and what about you, sport?'

'Me? I'm just a tourist.'

'Tourist?! Jesus, that beats all!' A smirk started across his face; disbelief showed in his eyes as he faced Carl.

Carl picked up his glass and moved to the stool next to the soldier. 'I'm a newspaper man having a little holiday in

Vietnam. I want to talk to you,' he said, then spoke to the barboy, '*Hai, ba muoi ba.*'

'Where'd you pick up that gook talk, man?'

'I just learned it.'

'Damn!'

The boy put two beers down and Carl filled the soldier's glass. 'Now, what's your name?'

I sipped my beer, amused by Carl and his new friend as they began talking. Carl's little notebook came out. I heard the soldier mention Pleiku, a mountain area where there was always some fighting going on, and various references to night manoeuvres, mortar attacks and so on. I figured Carl was in for an education so I settled down to my beer and some quiet reflection, while doodling in my notebook.

Village Piglets

'Looks like our pigs are here,' I said when I saw the truck by the rear entrance of the livestock office. Some of the clerks and other office staff stood in the yard peeking through the slatted sides of the truck as I parked in a shady spot nearby.

'Hey, that's great! Let's get those piggies out to their proud new owners, right, Mr Phu?' Carl had turned to face him in the back seat and spoke in the breezy, friendly manner Mr Phu – always somewhat formal – was getting used to, even beginning to enjoy.

'Yes, it is good,' he replied with a nod that showed his pleasure in these practical results of the pig project he and I and Mr Ngoc, Head of Livestock, had worked on for the past few months. Now, finally, the first 20 pairs of young pigs were ready for distribution to village families.

'They look healthy and frisky,' I said to Mr Ngoc as we stood together looking at the skittish, pink-skinned little pigs snorting and rooting around in the back of the truck. He looked up, smiled and nodded his head. Mr Phu stepped over and vigorously shook Mr Ngoc's hand, smiling as though marking the end of some successful joint venture. They joked and patted each other affectionately.

'You look like a couple of proud fathers,' I kidded.

'We are that!' Mr Ngoc said with a smile on his creased face. He had retired from government service, but because of the shortage of young men due to the war, he'd been asked to return. He and Mr Phu went back a long way together: to the early days in Hanoi, where they attended the agricultural college and later, as young men, when they took their first jobs with the government. After the partitioning of Vietnam, both men and their families moved to the South to start new lives.

'We would like a photograph of ourselves, Eddie,' Mr Phu said, still holding his old friend's hand. 'If you don't mind. It will be an interesting contrast to a picture Mr Ngoc has of our class in the agriculture school taken many years ago. It will show at least that we survived.'

'And certainly aged!' Mr Ngoc added with a laugh.

'And grew even better looking and more dignified,' I pointed out.

'More dignified, perhaps; better looking, no,' Mr Ngoc responded as he turned, and with feigned seriousness, scrutinised Mr Phu over the rim of his glasses.

'Oh, I am not so sure about that!' Mr Phu put in quickly, his eyes brimming with emotion.

I felt a twinge of sadness as I looked at these friends, two gnarled old men, often struggling successfully with today's problems but being, in some fundamental way, anachronisms: remnants from another time of manners and grace. They stood side by side in their dark dress-trousers and long-sleeved white shirts with French cuffs and flashing cufflinks, already appearing like figures in an old sepia photograph. I asked Carl to bring the camera over from the car.

'And just how many years ago was that college picture taken?' I asked as they positioned themselves by the truck for the photograph.

'Ah, that we shall never tell; we shall become perfectly inscrutable!' Mr Ngoc smiled and looked to his old friend for agreement.

'Vanity!' Carl said, getting the camera ready for the shot. Mr Ngoc asked his assistant to get a couple of young pigs from the truck and each man settled a squirming pink bundle into the bend of one arm. With their free arms, they circled each other's waists and faced Carl. They stood stiffly and unsmiling before the lens; a tableau of calm and dignity, of self-esteem and Asian tenacity – made even more poignant by the bright-eyed piglets wiggling in their arms. Carl took the picture.

'Thank you, Carl. This photograph will be a pleasant memory for us and our families,' Mr Phu said as he and Mr Ngoc returned the piglets to the truck.

Some chairs and stools were set out on the coarse grass in front of the village meeting hall. A low, intricately carved table held glasses of pale-coloured tea and plates of fruit and rice cakes. The village chief stepped forward with a few of the elders to greet us as we arrived. Children skipped through the gathering crowd of people, enjoying the festive mood in their village that came with the arrival of the strangers and the truckload of grunting pigs.

Many of the villagers, sceptical of any government pronouncements, believed, only now the animals were here, that the distribution of the promised pigs would occur. Too many promises had been made and then broken in the past; it was a continuing part of the villagers' life. Mr Phu, particularly, had been adamant about not getting the farmers' hopes up until it was certain the project would be approved and that, indeed, pigs would be brought to any village where he and Mr Ngoc had discussions. But on this day, broken promises were forgotten. Here were the chubby piglets, as well as the head of the province livestock department to hand them out to the families selected by the village chief and his council of elders.

Carl was trying to get some photographs of the kids as they quickly darted around the truck or hid shyly behind the men and women in the crowd when they saw him coming with his camera. He focused on a couple of women as they reached over the tailgate to touch the animals. The women giggled, then became serious and stood stiffly facing Carl.

'No posing, please, ladies; make it look natural!' he said in English. Mr Phu called across to the women and they started to laugh and nudge at each other in fun. A young girl peeked around from behind the women who by now had settled themselves into a line as though to be shot by a firing squad.

'Now, now, that won't do!' Carl frowned as he fiddled with the camera settings. *'Mot, hai, ba…'* He started counting the few numbers he knew in Vietnamese while he waited for the right moment to press the button.

One of the women laughed at Carl's mangling of the language and said something to the other women. A couple of men on the side shouted at Carl and the women, obviously teasing them.

'Never mind the hecklers, ladies,' Carl said calmly. 'Just look natural. *Ba muoi ba,*' he added, remembering the name of the local beer, and with that, using up his entire Vietnamese vocabulary. The women doubled over, delighted at this funny person with the terrible accent and strange sense of humour. Carl took a picture of the group relaxed and grinning.

Mr Phu came over to see what all the fuss was about. An old man stepped up with Mr Phu, then clasped Carl's arm and muttered something. 'He wants to have his picture taken with you,' Mr Phu translated.

'Well, fine. Will you take it?' Carl handed the camera to Mr Phu, helped him set the adjustments and showed him which button to press. Carl then stepped over next to the man, but just as Mr Phu was about to take the picture, the man held up his hand indicating he wasn't ready. He took hold of Carl's arm and draped it across his shoulder, then put his own arm around Carl's waist. Now, everything to his satisfaction, he displayed a gaping toothless smile and faced the camera.

'Cheeeeese,' Carl said.

'Cheeese,' the old man sputtered in an attempt to approximate the sound. Mr Phu snapped the shutter. Carl thanked the man, then asked Mr Phu to explain he would send a copy of the picture to Eddie after he got home to America, and Eddie would see the photograph got out to the village. As Mr Phu translated, the old man took Carl's hand and held it for a while, smiling up at him.

'He thanks you,' said Mr Phu.

'Yes, I see that,' Carl replied, moved by the man's friendliness. He looked at the grizzled old farmer in his tattered, mud-spotted shirt, then enfolded him in a hug.

The village chief stepped up onto the open porch of the meeting hall to speak. He was a tiny, shrivelled man of about 70 with wispy, white hair and a puckered face. He was clean-shaven except for one long grey hair that grew from a large dark mole on his chin – cultivated assiduously as a mark of his age and wisdom. He was dressed in black loosely fitting trousers and his best ceremonial long-sleeved black tunic that reached to his knees. His feet were bare. The old man looked over the crowd with a benign, paternal expression and waited patiently for all the people to gather, the children to be hushed. Then he spoke.

'Today, the government is fulfilling a promise to us,' he said in a thin, raspy voice. 'Today the government, our government, has come to our village to help us. We are honoured to have with us today these people from the province capital who care about our welfare.' He pointed to Mr Ngoc. 'This man is head of livestock, a senior official in our government, and thanks to him and our other guests, some of our farmers will receive a pair of piglets. There are 20 pairs of animals, and although this is very few, these can be the start of a better life for us. On your behalf I accept the pigs from the government. These animals seem like a gift, and yet they are not,' the old man said then stopped, appearing for a minute to lose the thread of his message. Then he continued: 'These animals are a small, but to us important, measure of help from our government.'

The chief was silent a minute and looked at the crowd while some children, restless from sitting on the ground in front of the porch, started to fidget. The old man waited, seemingly listening to the faint hum of a distant aircraft as it faded and finally was lost among the sounds of the fluttering leaves on the bushes near the building. The chief dropped his thin arms down by his side, heaved a deep sigh and spoke again.

'We are farmers. We are people of the earth. These are the things we know: the crops and the soil. There are many things we don't know, and many things we do not want to know. What we do want is to be left alone to farm our land in peace. If government experts feel bringing some pigs to our village will somehow help to bring peace, then we accept this. For our part, we will do everything possible to see these animals receive proper care. We will distribute the offspring of these animals in a fair manner to other families in the village. We will keep our side of this agreement.'

The village chief stopped abruptly. He seemed tired of his own voice, sick of words which somehow never were right, never communicated the underlying meaning of village life. I thought he appeared slightly flustered, perhaps unsure now if he had said too little, or too much. He motioned to Mr Ngoc to join him on the porch and invited him to speak.

Mr Ngoc thanked the chief for his wise comments and made some brief remarks about the project. He explained the pigs could help to improve the quality of the other pigs in the village by selective breeding. He outlined how the loan the village was receiving in the form of the pigs could be paid off over the months ahead by returning to the livestock department an equal number of pigs which would be given to other families in this or nearby villages. Mr Ngoc then looked around and smiled. 'But that's enough talk for now; let's hand out the piglets!'

A sigh of relief went through the crowd; people stood up quickly and stretched themselves while children shouted and dogs barked as everybody moved towards the truck where one of Mr Ngoc's assistants was ready to hand down the animals. The chief walked to the rear of the truck with Mr Ngoc, while Mr Phu and I stood to one side. Carl positioned himself to get more pictures.

A young woman had a list of the farmers chosen to receive the pigs and shouted out the first name. A middle-aged woman stepped forward and the chief greeted her. The man in the truck handed a pig to Mr Ngoc; he passed it to the chief, who in turn handed it to the woman. The tiny pig squealed and jostled in her arm as she passed it over to another, older woman. The second pig came along, shrieking as though its life were in jeopardy. The woman smiled and clasped the squalling pig to her chest, then she and the older woman turned away and headed down the road. Quickly, another name was called and the pigs were handed out to more waiting hands.

When all the animals had been distributed, the villagers left for their homes or the fields and the chief invited the guests to join him for some refreshments. Tea was passed around. Carl tried the rice cakes and then, with the help of Mr Phu, thanked the chief for his hospitality.

'The chief says it is an honour to have you visit his village,' Mr Phu translated.

'Perhaps you could ask him why so many of the people receiving the pigs are women,' Carl said.

After a lengthy discussion with the chief, Mr Phu turned to Carl and explained: 'The chief says it's because the young men have gone to the army and now it is mostly old men and the women who remain.'

'How did the chief select which families would receive the pigs?' Carl asked, always on the lookout for information to be used in articles he was writing. Mr Phu once more translated Carl's question.

'The chief says that was easy. He did not make the selections. He asked each of the village council elders to nominate five of the poorest people and then he wrote the names on pieces of paper. These were put into a bowl and his daughter took them out one at a time in front of the elders. The names were entered on a list in the order they were selected. There were more names than could receive pigs today, but the list will be used as the offspring of these pigs are available for distribution within the village.'

'That sounds fair,' Carl said.

'Yes, the villages of Vietnam have been run on the principles of fairness and justice for centuries, Carl,' Mr Phu said quickly, confidently, as he noticed Carl once more scribbling in his notebook.

'And outside the villages, Mr Phu, have the districts and provinces, the nation as a whole, been run on such principles?'

Mr Phu thought for a moment. 'No,' he said reflectively, looking out across the road; past a couple of sun-bleached, wooden houses surrounded by tangled clumps of fruit trees; across the patches of soft, pale green rice plants in the glittering paddies. 'No,' he repeated softly, 'that has been the cause of much of our suffering.'

As I looked at old Mr Phu and listened, a lump came to my throat; the pathetic look in the old man's eyes, his words indicating an acceptance of a lifetime of broken dreams and injustice wrenched at my heart. I saw clearly, perhaps for the first time, the uselessness of these little projects: handing out a few pigs, planting gardens at orphanages, distributing improved rice seed… What earthly good could they do, even if repeated thousands of times up and down the country? It was all too late; too little and too late, I thought sadly as I stepped over to say goodbye to the village chief and the other elders.

Marshmallow and Cricket

Despite his light-heartedness, it was obvious Carl was serious about bringing a couple of girls back to the apartment that evening. But not just any girls. His thoughts were on a twitchy-tailed Marshmallow who this week was going by the name Lena. And for me, he generously suggested that Lena's friend, 'the slim one with the patrician features,' would be a delightful treat!

'A match made in heaven,' he continued, posturing in the middle of the room with his hands together, his head tilted towards the ceiling, rocking on the balls of his feet and his face suffused with a sublime expression, as though he'd just received the word from some angelic messenger.

'You mean the skinny one with the sallow face and fishy breath?' I sighed.

'No, of course not! You must be thinking of someone else; one of the common herd. No, I mean that elegant, svelte beauty you sat with the other night. You were the envy of the bar. If looks could kill, you'd…'

'Yep, that's the one. She had her foot up on the seat, snapping her big toenail. You told her to knock it off, remember?'

'All I remember was the look in your eyes when you were talking to her. The peacefulness, and, at the same time, the look of unbridled passion; the excitement of the male animal when finally, after years of loneliness, he has found that one special woman. It cracked me up.'

'Really? That's funny. The one time you looked up from snuggling with Lena, you told her skinny friend to put her goddamn shoe on and leave her toes alone!' I said, trying to hold back a smile.

'As you like,' Carl said grandly and passed his arm before his eyes as though to erase the distasteful scene from his memory. 'Look, just think about it. All right?'

'Sure. But it doesn't seem right that I have to get with that shapeless Cricket so you can bring curvy Marshmallow back here.'

'Only if you want to; for you I'll do it! What are brothers for?' Carl said magnanimously, continuing to keep a straight face.

'We'll have to see how it goes. Friday night, plenty of action and cash to be earned, they might not want to leave,' I said, not really caring. I knew the bargirls for a miserable lot, and now, since Linh and I were beginning to get along so well, my interest in the Saigon bars and their war-hardened women was at an all-time low.

'With your experience, your skill with the language, I'm sure you'll find a way.'

'Maybe, but you seem to forget, I'm a married man. What are you suggesting?' I said with a laugh as I got up from the seat to go back and take a shower.

'Oh, that. Yes, well, it's on the rocks anyway, right?' He was putting one of the records he'd brought for me on the turntable.

'I suppose so,' I said as I left the room.

'Suppose so? From what you've been telling me, and Jean's response when I called her, it's gone beyond that!' he shouted along the hallway.

'Did she say our marriage was on the rocks?'

'No, not quite, but you did the other night,' he called back over the music. I went to the bathroom, stripped and stepped into the shower. He's right, I thought; I had said as much a day or so after he arrived when we were catching up on one another's news. I'd been telling him how I was getting on with the job and answering his questions about my work, the Vietnamese people and the things we were doing to help. He couldn't understand how anything could be done with a war going on, so I had tried to describe some of the village projects.

We'd talked for hours, Carl scribbling notes in his notebook when an idea interested him. It was later, when he was telling me about things at home, that he mentioned the phone call he'd made to Jean just before he left. She'd received his news about coming out here to see me pretty coolly, he said.

He had asked her, 'Is there any message for Eddie?'

'Oh, tell him I gave some of his old clothes away to the church, a special collection to be sent to Southeast Asia. Tell him to keep an eye out for his Russian hat!'

Carl had no idea what that was all about but laughed when I explained. His theory was that by getting rid of my old stuff, Jean was making a gesture which signalled the end of her old life. 'It's all over, man. Don't you see?'

'Yes,' I said, knowing it had been over for some time.

I finished showering and got dressed, then went to the kitchen to fix something to eat before hitting the town. Supplies were low – tinned foods from the army commissary, some eggs and half a loaf of French bread.

'How about some corned beef hash with poached eggs on top?' I called to Carl.

'Huh? Sure, that'll be fine,' he answered as he looked in the kitchen. 'Not the cuisine I'm accustomed to but if that's the best you can do...' He shrugged his shoulders and leaned against the doorway to watch.

'You've had worse,' I said. I opened the can of hash and dumped it into a large frying pan.

'So have you.'

'No. Jean was a good cook; we ate well.'

'Not the time I came to see you. Remember?' Carl joked. 'Remember when she forgot to properly soak the dried kidney beans and we ended up picking them out of our chilli. It's amazing no one broke a tooth!'

'Oh, yes, that culinary mishap. That was ages ago.'

'Yeah, you hadn't been married long when I drove up to visit… a stuffy second-floor apartment, a toilet that dripped all night.'

'Sure, a terrible hole, that. Remember the paper walls and that Armenian – or whatever he was – and his tall, blonde girlfriend and their hi-fi that made the floors rumble night and day?' I remembered it well. We'd just moved back to New Hampshire after an unsuccessful business venture. 'We were down on our luck, just back from Florida after closing up our boat-rental business.'

'Business? What a disaster! You were going to make a fortune, and have so much fun besides, with that scheme of yours to rent sailboats on the beach at… where was it?'

'Sanibel Island, near Fort Myers,' I recalled. 'Well, what the hell; we had fun, anyway.'

'Only when the wind didn't blow; the only time you liked it was when the Gulf was as calm and flat as a farm pond! Then those crazy tourists couldn't wreck the boats. Of course, while the boats weren't being damaged you didn't make any money either! Great business venture, that. You're the only person I ever heard of in the boat-rental business who prayed for calm days!

'Hey, and remember when you worked for that fly-by-night roofing company and went door to door with the thick folder of glossy photos of the distinguished-looking president of the firm and the company's huge manufacturing plant. But the whole damn thing was run out of the back pocket of that greasy little guy – we met him in that filthy bar, the Hampstead Arms… shit…! What was his name? Doyle Dugan?'

'Broyle, Broyle Dugan.'

'Oh, yeah, Broyle. What a con man!'

'I needed a job. Besides, I learned a lot from old Dugan.' I handed Carl a plate of hash with a couple of badly mauled eggs slopping around on top. 'Here, eat up and shut up!'

'Ugh! What the hell is it?' Carl said, eyeing the dish with revulsion.

We crashed through the door into the apartment; stumbling over each other, singing, giggling and puffing from the ass-grabbing run up the three flights of steps. Cricket had one arm draped around my shoulder as she fiddled with my ear. I felt the hot gasps of her tobacco breath across my face as I groped along the wall for the light switch by the door. Something crashed to the floor the other side of the room as Carl and Marshmallow continued to feel each other on their way past the coffee table to the couch in the non-stop grappling match that had started well before we left the bar.

I found the switch and turned on the light, then, seeing how unattractive my date was, quickly turned it off again. Even in the dim redness of the bar I'd realised she was no beauty; after all, what could one expect? But, here, under the harsh overhead light, she was clearly quite ugly! Why destroy the illusion, I mused as I lunged towards the window with the sprightly girl now wrapped around me; her legs tight scissors gripping my waist, her arms twined around my neck in a modified headlock. I managed to pull the curtain aside to allow faint light from the street lamps to filter into the room before we collapsed onto the floor.

Carl didn't seem to care one way or the other about the lighting in the room. He and Marshmallow were a tangle of elbows and legs as he tried to figure out the locations of the tiny snaps well-hidden across the chest and throat of her *ao dai*. Carl's fingers were busy at her neck undoing what he thought must surely be the last snap as she cooed and laughed lightly, a teasing, tittering sound above his low grumbling and grunting breathlessness.

I had mastered the art of un-snapping these dresses and was busy nuzzling Cricket's neck. I slid my free hand over her flat belly, tucked it under the elastic top of her silky, long trousers and continued half-heartedly.

'Music,' she blurted.

'What?!'

'Music. Ret's pray some music,' she said in her cracked English. She pulled my hand away from her, twisted around, sat up and pushed off from my shoulders as she stood up.

'Damn, not now!' I croaked.

'Yes, we rike music, no?' She stepped over me and went to the stereo set on the table against the wall. I groaned but quickly got to my feet, afraid she would start turning the wrong switches on the new set. I placed a record on the delicately balanced turntable, flipped the proper switches and adjusted the volume to a low setting. I reached for her again but she slipped away and said she wanted a drink now. My passion had cooled considerably by this time so I went to the kitchen to fix some drinks. As I was getting the glasses out, the music suddenly stopped and I knew she must be playing with the set. I rushed back to the front room to find her turning the bass and treble knobs and randomly pushing the on/off switch. The player-arm was raised above the spinning record.

I forcefully escorted her to a chair across the room, got the set working again and told her not to touch it. I returned to the kitchen to finish mixing the drinks when suddenly the volume jumped to maximum: a thumping, rumbling sound which quickly returned to the former low level. 'Don't fiddle with the knobs!' I shouted from the kitchen as I hastily gathered up the glasses.

I tried to get her to snuggle with me on the floor but she refused. She was entranced by the stereo set; couldn't leave it alone. 'Come on, girl, get the hell away from there!' I said angrily. 'Leave the damn knobs alone! That's the only thing in here that's not junk!' She looked at me and smiled vacantly, then twisted the volume up again. The large speakers trembled, the sound blasting through the apartment.

'What the hell?' Carl asked, finally coming up for air.

I jumped to my feet. 'OK, baby, out you go!' I grabbed Cricket by the arm and pulled her towards the door. She started to scream and kick at me. 'You little shit!' I barked as I yanked the door open to push her out.

Marshmallow jumped up, her bare breasts bouncing as she quickly pulled up the front of her dress and skipped to the door to join her friend. 'She go?' she squeaked.

'You're damn right, she go!' I shouted.

'Cool down, Eddie,' Carl said, pulling himself up to a sitting position on the couch. 'Com'on now, settle down and let's all have a little loving.'

'She go, I go,' Marshmallow said and closed the last of the snaps across her chest.

'Right, out you go too, toots!'

'No! Oh damn and blast, man, don't throw them out!' Carl pleaded as I gave a final push to the two snarling girls and slammed the door.

'Man, look what you've done now,' Carl said forlornly.

'Hell, those babes are dogs; this country is full of beautiful women, we don't need that sort of...'

'Yeah, sure, easy for you to say.'

'Oh, don't worry. Will is having a party next week and there's sure to be some pleasant, good-looking women around. Come on, let's have a cup of tea.'

'Well, not quite what I had in mind for this evening. But if that's the best you can come up with for your dear brother... pop the kettle on.'

House Party

Will's house was a low, steep-roofed rectangle set comfortably in a large garden of flowering shrubs and shade trees. Built during the French colonial days, it had a broad veranda with a polished, maroon-coloured tile floor and a plain, concrete balustrade wrapped around the two sides; a wide overhang provided protection from the sun and the heavy monsoonal rains. Two large glass doors opened into a cool, spacious living room.

Will was near the doorway handing drinks to a couple of Vietnamese girls when we arrived. 'Here you are! Come on in!' he called out briskly, stepping forward to greet us as we approached through the garden. 'Good to see you, Eddie! Your gorgeous friend, Linh, is here already; inside somewhere,' he said cheerfully. 'Carl, how are you doing?' Will had met Carl briefly at headquarters a few days previously when I took him in to talk with some people there. 'Are you getting any good material for stories?'

'Yes, sure, Will. A lot more than the folks at home will care to read, I suspect,' Carl said as they shook hands.

'Good. I want to talk to you later, but right now I'm needed in the kitchen. Enjoy yourself.' Will touched Carl's arm, turned to go, then thought of something.

'Wait, I'll introduce you to a nice girl.' Will guided Carl over to the two Vietnamese girls he'd been speaking with when we arrived.

'Carl, this is, ah, let's see now…' Will hesitated a moment as he tried to drag up a name that could possibly go with this petite, attractive girl. 'Hung?' he asked tentatively.

'Hung is a boy's name,' the girl said sweetly. 'I'm Hang.'

'Ah, yes, of course, Hang; I was close.'

'We don't consider that very close!' she said with a lovely smile.

'Hang,' Will said distinctly, as though trying to help Carl get the name correct. 'This is Carl. He's a famous writer and wants to talk to you. But look, honey, he needs a drink first. Can you take him along to the bar and see about that?'

'OK, Mr Will,' she answered, then turned to Carl and shook his hand. 'Hello Carl, I am Hang.' She took his arm and guided him through the crowded living room, past the dancers and other people milling around, and over to the bar. Will flashed a look of amusement at me and pursed his lips slightly as we followed Carl and Hang inside.

'Make a nice couple,' he said, then hurried off towards the back of the house.

I stopped just inside the door to look around. Most of the furniture had been removed and the remaining pieces pushed back against the walls to make room for dancing. Guests were helping themselves to food at a large table near the kitchen. Another table, presided over by a grinning young man dressed in a stiff white coat buttoned to the throat, served as the bar. Loud, big-band-era music from a tape deck filled the room. Will's houseman, Mr Tran, a sober, formal Vietnamese man in his 50s, circulated smoothly through the crowd with trays of drinks.

I walked over to see what foods Will had laid on for the evening. As I was sampling some of the hors d'oeuvres, Fred – a land-use planning expert, who often spoke fondly of his wife and five kids in Austin, Texas – arrived with a flourish, escorting a couple of bargirls he'd picked up on the street on his way to the party. He marched them straight over to the food table. One of the girls was giggling nervously as Fred dished up a mountain of food for her.

It was obvious he'd already had a few drinks. Usually a tight-lipped guy, who, when he did speak, sort of massaged you with his quiet, gravelly voice, Fred now was talking loudly and rapidly above the music to anybody near him. He turned to me and started declaring vigorously how useless he considered 'flat maps' – maps without contour markings, he explained – at the same time absent-mindedly squeezing the other girl's tight ass as he loaded up her plate. She seemed totally uninterested in any kind of maps as she picked up a brown, deep-fried sort of thing about the size of a golf ball from a large platter. As we watched her, she sniffed at the crusty piece of food then bit into it. Fred was intrigued.

'What're those?' he asked, not missing a stroke as he continued to smooth her ass while he pointed to the round brown balls on the plate.

'Fish balls,' she answered and reached for another.

'What?'

'Fish balls; they are fucking fish balls! OK?' she snarled coarsely, clearly irritated and just wanting to be left alone at the food table.

'Oh, fish balls... best part of the fish,' Fred said knowingly. He looked at me. 'This is one crazy war, eh?' he announced over the sound of a loud, jumping Artie Shaw number as he waved a big serving spoon at the food and the dancers and, for all I knew, everything: the whole Vietnam mess from north to south. I was agreeing with Fred when I was surprised and saw Ted. He was joking with the other bargirl in his smooth Vietnamese and leading her off across the room to the dance floor.

'Hey, Ted, when did you get back?' I called after him. I hadn't expected to see him here this evening; for the past few weeks he'd been on field trips to some of the provinces in the Delta.

'Just off the plane, catch you later; feel like a dance right now,' he called back, then looped his arm around the bargirl and moved her in among the other dancers.

Since Linh was talking happily with a friend in one corner of the room, I decided to get myself a drink before joining her. At the bar table, I introduced myself to a stranger who looked a bit lost and uncomfortable at finding himself with all these people he didn't know.

'My name is Jeremy,' he said, and in answer to my questions, explained he was a first-time visitor to Vietnam from the Washington AID office and had been in-country only about a week looking at some of the rural development programmes. He seemed glad to have someone notice him. When he learned I was one of the division's fieldmen he suggested we stroll outside for a chat. We stepped to the far side of the veranda looking for some seats and stumbled across Clem, the credit advisor, and Lucia, one of the Filipina secretaries, as they pressed against each other in the shadows. Although everyone knew they were spending a lot of time together, including frequent weekends at the beach hotels in the resort town of Vung Tau, Clem and Lucia persisted in pretending they were just friends. Jeremy seemed embarrassed.

'Hello Clem, Lucia, enjoying the party?' I asked.

'Oh, I'm sorry,' Jeremy mumbled, seeing how startled the two lovers were as they disengaged quickly.

'No problem,' Clem said, looking down at nothing in particular.

'Did you know that's the Gerald Wilson rendition of "Perdido", played by the Duke Ellington Orchestra?' Jeremy said with a forced casualness. 'Notice the sax!'

'No kidding,' Clem responded vacantly.

'How interesting,' Lucia said in a thin voice as she pulled her skirt back across her knees.

'Yes, indeed,' I said. 'I'm surprised you two didn't recognise it!'

'Hey, are you guys OK out here; need any drinks?' Will said, appearing behind us abruptly.

'Jesus! Sure is a lot of traffic out here all of a sudden! Yes, just fine,' Clem said peevishly.

'Jeremy, come with me. I want you to meet someone.' Will guided him across the room and left him with Andy and his vivacious friend, the office manager for Air Vietnam.

Ted had given up on the bargirl who now was curling herself around Lou, the irrigation engineer, as they did everything but dance to a few slower melodies. So, not off to some awful place in Africa yet, I thought. Maybe Will is all bark. Lou might one day even become a Shoop 'FARTE of the month', I thought, laughing quietly to myself.

'Hey, Eddie, my boy!' Ted said, coming up behind me with two drinks. 'Here.'

I took a glass. 'How was your trip?' I asked as we moved to a couple of seats along the wall near the doorway.

'Good, and bad,' he said. 'The Delta's a hell of a big rice bowl, but it's damn hot, flat, watery and plain boring. Just as glad I didn't get assigned there after all. Say, I've got something to show you.' He reached into his back pocket and pulled out a folded letter. 'It's a complaint about you!'

'Complaint?'

'Yup.'

'Colonel Horst?'

'Nope, an even closer friend of yours, your bosom buddy… Miss Cynthia Leggit!'

'Oh, really? Cyn-thi-a?! Well, she has a bosom all right, as the colonel was made aware!' I took the letter and held it towards the lamp. It was in proper memorandum form, very formal-looking with the 'To' and 'From' and 'Subject' listed at the top. I started smiling as I read her slick sentences about my being the wrong kind of person to work overseas… 'where a fine sensitivity to the aspirations of the local people is so important…' and some other, similar sentiments with appropriate words underlined so the reader couldn't miss the point.

'Hey, this is good shit!' I said. 'She makes some telling points here. Be sure a copy goes into my service file, OK?'

'Sure,' he said lightly, taking the letter, crumpled it into a ball and flipped it into the wastebasket near the floor lamp with a nice hook shot.

'You're not going to get far with AID if you behave like that,' I chided.

'Neither will you!'

'Where did you get it?'

'Will gave it to me this evening. Said to do anything I wanted with it.'

'I don't think that included throwing it away,' I said.

'He did say "anything", after all,' Ted laughed, then took a sip of his drink and looked around the room. 'That must be Carl,' he said, pointing. 'How's he doing?' Carl and Will were by the bar talking. I glanced over at the corner where Linh and Hang and another Vietnamese girl had their heads together smiling and talking animatedly as though plotting some conspiracy. What's up there, I wondered?

'He's fine, having a great time; picking up lots of ideas for articles… he'll want to talk to you about some of his latest findings.'

'Good, I haven't had a chance to talk with him. I'd like to find out if he's got some insights into this place. Never know, perhaps your big brother has this crazy country all figured out!'

'I doubt that. Who has? Certainly not me, anyway. And Carl's never changed the opinion he had of Vietnam from when he arrived – that it's one big shit pot! Not worth the powder to blow it to hell, which he's convinced is just what's happening.'

'Well, that's easy to…'

'Yeah, of course,' I broke in. 'I told him, once you make a commitment here, work with the people to get something going, then it's another matter. It's not so cut and dry, not so easy to take a firm stand on this war. He agrees, especially after we've been to the field, but still, he's just passing through, an observer.'

'There were lots of days during this last field trip when I could have agreed with him; when none of it seemed worthwhile,' Ted said thoughtfully. 'But, hey, how's it going with you? What's been happening here?'

'Not much. Carl and I have been hitting the bars once in a while, we've been out to the field. And, as you might have guessed, I'm seeing a lot more of Linh, ever since we worked on the cooperative and planted the garden at the orphanage. I mean, I see her at the office all the time, but lately we've started meeting after work sometimes. She's teaching me about Vietnam: history and cultural stuff and sharpening up my Vietnamese, while I help her with English.'

'Oh?' Ted said, raising his eyebrows. 'I talked to her earlier tonight. She said something about having a surprise for you.'

'I don't know anything about that.'

'Of course not, you nit, it's a surprise!'

'Fun!'

'What is, having a surprise to look forward to?' Ted asked. He carefully watched the people dancing as though seeking someone.

'Teaching English,' I said, wondering who he was hoping to see. 'Everybody wants to learn English in this country.'

'Sure, just like French some years ago!' Ted said sarcastically. 'Besides, Eddie, meeting some beautiful girl after work is not exactly "teaching English", you know!'

'Of course it is! Hell, Ted, in times of war a man has to find his pleasures where he can!'

'Sure!'

'Linh is special. She's a very competent professional taking care of some important programmes in the province: orphanages, refugees, cooperatives.'

'Hey, you don't have to convince me! So, now the cooperatives are a big part of your work; field trips with Linh to help get the new organisations set up and...'

'Of course, Ted. One has to do these things correctly, you know!'

'Is this a war-time romance... or maybe something else?' Ted asked.

'It could be the "something else". After all, *there is nothing like a dame...*' I sang cheerfully.

'What about your dear wife; how do you think she will adjust to your happy news?'

'Ahh, I don't know. I guess I really don't care, either.'

'I suppose not. Poor woman, married to a rake like you!' Ted said, his eyes open wide, a silly grin spreading across his face.

'You smart ass!' I said as we both started laughing. 'Why didn't you invite Tu,' I asked after settling down again.

Ted got more serious in a hurry. 'Finished with Tu,' he said simply.

'Why? What happened?'

'Well, her main interest is in finding an American to marry and then going to live in France. Somehow it all seemed so mechanical; I didn't want to be tailored to fit that particular slot.'

'Why an American; why France?' I asked, confused.

'Hey, look at Carmelita! Doesn't she look great?! I'm going to ask her to dance,' Ted said, getting up from his seat quickly. 'But briefly, before I go: according to Tu, American men are kind and considerate and all that, but France is the only civilised place to live.'

'So why not marry a Frenchman?'

'Once again, according to Tu – who has studied these things thoroughly – Frenchmen are pompous,' he said and was gone.

As I walked across the room to find Linh, I noticed Will's latest girlfriend – a pushy, over-painted tart who'd latched onto him in some bar a few weeks earlier – was acting the part of the demanding hostess. She snipped at the young Vietnamese bartender, urging him to be more attentive and stop spending so much time yakking with Miss Hardy, one of the AID personnel officers. Mr Tran, obviously put off by the presence in the house of this low-class woman, barely tolerated her and sniffed audibly whenever they ran into each other. This new girlfriend ignored the disapproving houseman. Will stood back watching her as he hovered close to the food table to be sure everything was just so.

'Christ, I can't get rid of her!' he said to me and Al, the grain marketing specialist.

'Why not?'

'I brought her back here one night from a bar thinking it was a one-night affair. Next day while I'm at work she moves herself in… clothes, dozens of shoes, perfumes, an electric fan, everything! She even brings that stupid kid, her brother, to do the gardening.' Will pointed to the young bartender now getting hell from his sister. 'I don't know what to do!'

'Just throw her ass out, that's all,' Al said, surprised by Will's apparent helplessness. Where's the snappy, man-in-charge 'Office Will' who laid into Lou, I wondered.

'Hell, I can't do that; who knows what revenge such a girl can take; she could poison my food… put scorpions in my shoes!' He rolled his eyes in horror.

By this time, Ted was giving all his attention to Carmelita, a luscious Filipina and one of Will's secretaries, who wore a white sweater stretched under great pressure. Her head was thrown back, her eyes sparkling with encouragement as he bent forward, kneading her back with his hand and snuggling beneath her long hair to whisper in her ear. She stepped lightly around his clumsy feet as they moved about the floor in approximate time to the music.

Not far away, Carl and Hang were together again, doing some fancy steps. I was glad to see he was being looked after by Hang on his last evening. It will be a pleasant memory for him back home in his editorial office, I was thinking, when I saw Linh heading my way.

She looked stunning as she wove her way around the dancers. Linh wore a rich, shimmering *ao dai* of dark blue decorated with delicate, pale orange blossoms and the traditional long black silky trousers beneath the flowing, split dress. Her soft black hair, parted in the middle, curled across her shoulder. I'd never seen her looking so lovely.

'Linh, let me look at you,' I said and held her at arm's length for a second. 'It's a good thing you don't dress up like this at the office; I'd never get anything done!'

'It is just because my hair is down,' she said. 'But look at you in your white shirt and dark trousers. You are beautiful too… very Vietnamese.' Linh's eyes were deep and expressive, but something else – something about their softness – gave her an air of dignified vulnerability. Her eyelashes fluttered with pleasure and sparkled in the light as I studied her.

'Eddie, are you going to stand here staring at me, or are we going to dance?' she asked sweetly.

'Dance,' I said and took her hand, slipped my arm around her waist and we glided off. She put her head against my chest as I breathed in the frangipani-scented perfume she wore. Her soft, supple body pressed lightly into mine. I felt the movement of her warm thighs against my legs as we danced quietly to the slow, stirring sound of Elvis serenading us with 'If I Can Dream'.

'Eddie?'

'Yes.'

'This is lovely.'

'So are you.'

'And you.'

'Linh?'

'Yes.'

'This is lovely.'

She pinched me on my side. 'You like to tease,' she said, looking up at me.

'No. I like to dance with Linh.' I pulled her in closer.

'Uh, Eddie, that's so tight!'

'Oops, sorry.' I eased off a bit.

'You and Carl like to joke.'

'Uh-huh.'

'But you are happy. Carl is not.'

'Oh?'

'Yes.'

'Why is Carl not happy?'

'Because he has no woman to love.'

'How do you know? He has lots of girls to love at home.'

'That may be, but he has not just one. It is different.'

'And me, do I?' I asked, trying to look into her eyes but she kept them down.

'Yes.'

'You?'

'Yes,' she whispered and leaned towards me.

'This is something new, no?' I could feel my heart thumping in my throat.

'Yes... new and special.' She tilted her head slightly and placed her warm lips against my cheek.

'Linh?'

'Yes.'

'What if I fall in love with you?'

'Oh, that will be all right,' she whispered, not raising her eyes to look at me when I kissed her forehead softly.

We found a quiet spot on a bench in the garden and talked in the sultry night air, the music and voices from the party in the background somehow reassuring; a reminder that people can come together, even here, and enjoy themselves for a few hours; can take something from each other, some small cheer that makes it easier to carry on the next day. I reached for Linh's hand.

'Ted tells me you have a surprise,' I said.

'Yes.'

'Well?'

'Well, what?' she said. I put my hand on her knee and squeezed lightly. She flinched and quickly put her hand over mine.

'Now look who's teasing? What is it, Linh?' I threatened to squeeze her knee again.

'I'm going home with you,' she blurted.

I was silent for a moment, thinking of what this meant to Linh, to me. 'What about Carl?' is all I could come up with.

'He is with Hang.'

'I know.'

'She is my friend.'

'And?' I asked, not seeing how it mattered.

'She is going home with him,' Linh said in a muffled voice. She was bent forward with her head buried in her arms on her lap.

'Really?'

'Yes, we have talked about it, Hang and I. He does not know yet, but it is all arranged,' Linh whispered. I bent over to see her face but it was hidden again behind her arms. She was silent. I put my hand across her shoulder; a shiver ran up my arm and along the back of my head at the feel of the cool silk of her dress. Linh trembled slightly at my touch.

'Linh?'

'Yes.'

'This is a wonderful surprise.'

'You really think so?'

'Of course.'

'Then I am very happy.'

'So why the tears?' I asked gently.

'Because I have been worried all evening you would not like this surprise.' She twisted her head around and looked up at me. I bent down and kissed her wet eyes. 'I wanted to ask Ted if he thought it would please you, but I was afraid,' she said.

'Did you talk to Will about your surprise?'

'Yes.'

'Did Hang come to the party with you?'

'Yes.'

'Ah, Linh, you are a schemer, a lovely schemer,' I said, putting my arm around her and looking into her eyes.

'I don't know what a schemer is, but you are lovely,' she said, her face beaming as she curled her hair back across her shoulder, then reached over for my hand.

PART THREE

Lunar New Year, 1968

Linh had left the apartment earlier to be at home with her family on this most important night of the year. Now, alone, with midnight nearing and the clamour of the people on the streets becoming more insistent, I pulled a chair to the open window and settled down to watch the celebrations.

Below, crowds of people jammed in near a small wooden platform as twisted strands of firecrackers were lit and began to crackle and explode violently. The thick grey-blue smoke shrouded the heads and shoulders of the onlookers, flattening into pale sheets then drifting up the walls of the building on currents of warm air. The dense smoke and flashing firecrackers created strange surrealistic images: a sharply etched, swiftly changing chiaroscuro of distorted faces and bodies as people laughed and jerked with excitement.

Across the street, a shadowy figure resembling some fantastic, frenzied, storybook creature with a long sparkling tail darted through the crowd, lighting firecrackers from a strip of smouldering rubber that trailed along the ground. Children shrieked and held their ears, anticipating the popping explosions as the costumed creature tossed hissing fuses above their heads.

By the river, long strings of firecrackers snapped angrily in a steady, unbroken celebratory cacophony – a sure good luck omen for the superstitious Vietnamese. Over the black water, tiny sparks of light winked like hundreds of dazzling fireflies as more firecrackers were hurled into the air. People were on the river in all types of boats: little rowboats carrying couples who laughed and shouted greetings and wished everyone well in the coming year; larger craft – like giant water beetles with oars for legs – starting and turning abruptly, going no direction for long; and other boats with long sleek hulls, normally used as ferries, crammed with noisy family groups and shy lovers taking advantage of the holiday celebrations to hold hands and bump knees.

It was the eve of the Lunar New Year, 30 January 1968, Tet! Everyone was slightly crazy! It was expected, the way to be at Tet… this end of the old, start of the new. I felt just as daft as the people celebrating below, caught up in the mounting excitement. Anything seemed possible in Vietnam on this night… maybe even peace.

Inside the navy base, just beyond the roundabout where a large statue of an ancient Vietnamese hero looked pensively towards the river, a searchlight flashed on and bounced wildly across the rippling water. Bells began tolling from churches all over the city, followed by the muffled, vibrating booms of temple gongs. Car and motorbike horns and whistles and sirens on river craft, combined with the roar of hundreds of people in the streets and the explosions of firecrackers, swelled to a crescendo of piercing, dissonant sound. 'Midnight!' I yelled madly into the ringing and screaming and hooting, adding my voice to the wave of emotion that swept across the city.

A shiver ran down my back, my eyes filled with tears as I was swept up in the spirit and uninhibited joy of the people on the streets. I laughed with them and shared in their hopes for the coming year. These struggling people in this filthy city expressed in this passionate outburst their urge to live, to survive. Despite the years, the centuries of their suffering, the Vietnamese people were able to look ahead; with this ear-shattering racket and heart-stopping display of exuberance, they shouted their belief in the future.

The noise and excitement continued. I looked over at a patrol boat tied up at the navy base when someone fired a handgun into the air. Dark figures ran along the dock towards the boat while the sharp crack of a semi-automatic rifle sounded. 'Live ammo?!' I yelled.

I spotted two little girls holding hands and staring at the sky, then glanced up quickly at a place directly across the river as a short, intense light flashed. I felt, or imagined, a charge in the air, a sudden change of air pressure in my head and ears; half-heard a lightning-fast swishing sound overhead followed instantaneously by a tremendous, deafening, earth-cracking blast.

The building heaved sharply and shuddered to its roots as though rocked by a powerful earthquake. Window frames and glass rattled furiously; doors banged against their latches. Bits of tile broke free and clattered across the roof; crusty lumps of muck rained down from the rafters and beams onto the ceiling overhead; dust filled the air.

I was flat on the floor beneath the window, shielding my head and pressing myself hard against the wall as I waited for the next explosion. My God! This building, or damn close. My mind was numb. Fire, I thought; what then? A rocket attack on this night at midnight! Christ! Why? Linh! Is she safe…? I tried to pull myself together, looked around the room, slid along the floor and turned off the lights, then sat braced against the wall staring at the open window. A rocket could come crashing through there, I thought dully; what a large target this building must make from across the river… I was in shock; heart pounding, my legs shook as I slid back across the room and kneeled by the window to peer out again.

The previously happy, celebrating groups of people had disappeared from the street and open area along the river, quickly vanishing into streets and alleys radiating away from the docks area. Except for some strings of firecrackers that continued exploding, only a few sputtering flames and red embers remained where crowds of people had been laughing and dancing only minutes before. On the river, boats moved towards shore or slipped away into the darkness by the warehouses. How quickly gloom and despair replace joy in this country, I thought. Always on the verge of a tragedy, the Vietnamese denied their one night of unrestrained happiness…

The engines of a patrol boat coughed to life; someone barked orders. From the forward deck of the boat, a heavy gun began to pump shell after shell across the river into the opposite bank, the tracers slashing long, luminescent arcs across the black water. 'What good can that possibly do?!' I said quietly from the window, feeling resigned now to the madness outside. The boat pulled away from the dock and headed across the river, its pale searchlight flashing abruptly across the surface of the water ahead.

Suddenly another violent explosion – this time inside the base: a sharp ripping sound, followed by a blunt, powerful detonation. Someone screamed, flames shot into the sky, then slowly subsided. A searchlight came on, flashed quickly across the area and was immediately shot out by a short burst of gunfire. Men shouted from a sandbagged bunker near the entrance gate.

I stared at the scene below, unable to believe what was happening: shooting inside the base, the explosion; those thick-walled buildings I'd seen every day for months blown to bits in an instant. The action felt like pages of fiction unfolding in front of me, a shapeless dark dream. I realised it wasn't just a rocket attack from across the river. This was more serious. VC were in the city openly attacking important, well-protected targets; on the streets around the apartment building, well-armed VC were on the attack with their own brand of fireworks. I knew nothing prevented them from shooting their way into this or any other building and killing every person they found.

As fleeting thoughts crowded my mind, I watched the flickering flames nearby and heard the shouts and sporadic, nervous gunfire from different parts of the base. 'Well, surely you boys have better things to do tonight than rub out an agriculturalist!' I said, sounding more chipper than I felt. Outside, everything was suddenly quiet – an eerie, ominous silence.

I heard the engine of a fast-approaching vehicle grow louder on the street alongside the river. A jeep raced out of the shadows; the white star of the US Army was clearly painted on the hood as it passed beneath the street lamps. The engine roared, tyres screeched as it careened into the roundabout. Sudden rapid gunfire – stuttering, short bursts of bullets from the deep shadows below the building – slammed into the jeep. Glass shattered; bullets rattled against the vehicle. A tyre blew out, the jeep pitched forward, lifted wildly on two wheels, flipped on its side, and with a piercing noise of scraping metal, slammed into the rows of sandbags in front of the base. Everything went silent.

'Jesus Christ!' someone shouted from behind the vehicle. I saw bright muzzle flashes and heard the sharp crack of a heavy machine gun as it opened fire from the sandbagged bunker just beyond the upturned jeep. The shots were aimed at the pedestal and statue in the centre of the roundabout and into the dark shadows beyond.

A soldier crouching behind the wrecked vehicle squeezed off a few rounds from his weapon then pulled his partner free and helped him over the sandbags. 'Hang on, Wayne,' he shouted, his twangy American voice sounding strange against the stillness. The machine gun stuttered again, slapping a few short bursts into the wall of the apartment building, then smacking the huge lead statue with soft thuds. 'Goddamn you idiot!' shouted the soldier. 'There ain't nobody there!' His voice was full of disgust at the Vietnamese gunner. 'Shit, what a mess. Fucking gook navy!'

Inside the base, behind the high fence that ran down to the edge of the river, everything was still. Smoke drifted above the smouldering wreckage left from the explosion. I was surprised not to see more lights and activity on the base; surely they would be on full alert by now. But then I realised that most of the sailors probably had been given leave because of Tet. 'You chose the right night,' I whispered.

About a mile upriver, bright white spots of light started shimmering in the blackness as the first flares were dropped from a helicopter. The warehouses and naval buildings were soon glowing in a flickering pale white glow as the phosphorescent flares drifted down slowly on small parachutes. Another helicopter followed the first along the river as the unnaturally bright starbursts fluttered down, lighting up the docks and storage sheds and the mud-choked water of the river, now appearing flat and greasy in the harsh top light.

I walked back through the darkened apartment to the kitchen and switched on the light. It seemed excessively bright after hours of peering into the darkness. I looked at my watch – just after 3 am. Only three hours, I thought, for the VC to set this city on its ass! Somehow it seemed so easy: rockets, sapper squads and, above all, timing and daring. 'Fierce little shits! You deserve to win; you seem to believe in what you're doing more than our side!' I stuck the kettle on the stove. 'Ay, lad, a nice cup o' tea will make it right!' I said playfully, glad to hear the sound of my own hollow words.

I returned to have a last look out the window. The area by the river was quiet. As I sat brooding, another jeep carrying two soldiers pulled quickly into the roundabout and stopped by the wrecked vehicle. The soldiers conferred briefly, then cautiously searched the area by the statue and the far side of the intersection, now lit slightly by the flares. Finding nothing, they loaded the wounded soldier into the back seat, stuffed themselves and their guns into the jeep and raced off.

From time to time the building shuddered as explosions, sounding like distant thunder, went off in some far part of the city. My head throbbed painfully from the smoke and noise and tension. I flopped on the couch feeling tired and shaken. What a mess... how the hell can this continue? Now that I've found Linh, is it all coming apart? I started to drift into a fitful sleep as pale shafts of light from the occasional flare stole silently across my face and along the wall behind my head. Modern weapons, imported... snatches of thought, disconnected words skittered in my mind as light flickered across my twitching eyelids. I turned from the window and drifted off... a desert, wind-whipped reddish dust against an old wooden door; everything dry, gritty; a skeleton with a thick knot of hairy rope around its bony neck – dancing, jiggling, rattling, grinning.

Deadly Believers

I was amazed at the extent of the damage in the city when I drove across town to Linh's house. She and her family were safe but frightened by the attacks. Like so many people, this was their first real encounter with the war; destruction and violence – up to this point occurring 'out there' in the remote areas of the country – now, suddenly, had been brought to the city. Clearly, the apparent ease with which the VC had infiltrated Saigon and blasted their way into places considered secure had shocked all of us.

For days Saigon was almost completely paralysed. Business and normal government functions stopped and the usually thick, snarling traffic was reduced to military vehicles that raced wildly up and down empty streets. The few people who ventured out moved about cautiously. Shops and even the many bars, normally swinging all through the day and most of the night, were shuttered and locked. The visible damage and blocked-off streets, as well as increased security measures – including earlier, more strictly enforced curfews – and continued shooting as isolated pockets of VC were rooted out of hiding places throughout Saigon, all added to the tense atmosphere in the city.

Reports were coming in. We soon learned simultaneous attacks had been launched by VC and North Vietnamese units against a large number of targets all over South Vietnam. This country-wide action, quickly labelled the 'Tet

Offensive', was to many people a clear demonstration of the VC's determination and daring, marking the start of a new strategy to push the war to a conclusion. To others, it was the communists' last desperate effort.

Stories circulated about how, weeks before the offensive, arms and explosives were smuggled into Saigon and cached in hiding places all over the city, including caskets buried during phoney funeral ceremonies and dug up at the last minute.

In addition to the navy base, the VC had attacked many American and Vietnamese military compounds as well as some of the officers' quarters located in converted, former downtown hotels. On the first night of the Tet celebrations, communist troops broke through the perimeter defences of the airfield just outside the city and blew up parked aircraft and set off explosives in the repair shops. Days later, sporadic fighting was still going on as groups of VC were found in remote parts of the huge airbase.

Colonel Horst released a brief, carefully worded announcement claiming the attacks had been expected all along and no serious damage had been suffered. Despite his morale-boosting statement that the communists had been dealt a stunning defeat, it was clear to me from the destruction in Saigon – and what I was learning about attacks in the rest of the country – that the VC could not be considered a ragtag band of insurgents, as the colonel sometimes characterised them. They were a disciplined and well-led group of believers with a deadly serious purpose and the will to carry it out. While none of the army advisors considered the attacks decisive, they did seem worried about possible psychological effects.

For Henry, the civilian education specialist on the team, the Tet Offensive had a decisive effect: he was packing up, getting out as quickly as he could. One of the rockets fired from across the river had smashed into some cars parked near his apartment early in the morning of the first attacks.

This, as well as the success of the VC in breaking into the heavily guarded US Embassy, the general destruction throughout the city, and his sudden awareness of how exposed he was as a civilian living in an unguarded apartment house, had unnerved him completely. He was packing his books and papers for shipment home when I stopped at his office to say goodbye. He seemed tense, half embarrassed, even a bit belligerent.

'It's all over, man,' he said quickly with a nervous laugh when he saw me.

'What do you mean, Henry?'

'The VC will win,' he said with conviction. He tied a shoddy knot in the twine looped around a box of books, then hauled the box over to a chair by his desk. He didn't look at me but began to sort through a pile of reports and papers.

'Aw, come on, Henry, you're overreacting.'

'Am I?' he said sharply, turning around and arching his eyebrows as he looked up. Then I saw the fear; realised Henry was finished, needed to go, and quickly. 'Next week, next month, they'll take over this place,' he stammered. 'I just don't want to be here when it happens.'

'It's not that serious. Maybe this whole business will prove a good thing in the long run. Everyone will tighten up; the politicians and the ARVN will take the war more seriously,' I said, knowing this kind of reasoning could have no possible effect on Henry now. Besides, I didn't believe it myself.

'Baloney, Eddie!' he said. 'What's to stop the VC from attacking tonight or tomorrow, huh?' His eyes rolled unpleasantly. 'You guys all talk like this offensive was a one-shot deal… it can happen again anytime!' He looked pale, as though even talking about another attack on the city made him queasy.

'Well, I don't know. I suppose everyone is more alert now, security will be better,' I said with hope in my voice.

'Yeah, just don't count on it,' Henry replied a bit more

calmly. 'I've spent two years of my life here: teachers' training, curriculum development, advanced schooling for administrators, new classroom construction... the whole damn bit! It just doesn't matter. In a country at war it's impossible to develop an educational system; can't be done.' He shook his head, turned away and feverishly sorted papers into rough piles.

'Well, we have to keep trying,' I said lamely.

'Do we? Listen, I'll tell you something.' Henry spoke rapidly as though he wanted to get our conversation over with, pack up and leave this place forever. 'The problem here is we're supporting the wrong side. If we had the North Vietnamese and those damn scrappy VC to work with maybe we could do something!'

'Well, we've got the other bunch,' I said. I'd heard that line before; it was the sort of catchy phrase the wire service spit out.

'Yeah, I know. It doesn't matter,' Henry mumbled distractedly. 'I'm a civilian, I came here to do a civilian's job and it's not possible. Colonel Horst is right, it's war; soldiers are needed, not civilians. Not education advisors. Anyway, this is the beginning of the end for South Vietnam. I'm able to see that now. For the first time in two years I'm not completely bananas! Know what I mean?' He broke off abruptly and started to load another box. I moved towards the door.

'Good luck, Henry.'

'Huh? Oh. So long pal, you need the luck.'

The jeep, crammed to the roof with blankets and sacks of grain, rolled heavily through the deep, mud-softened ruts along the back roads. My thin shirt was soaked with sweat; I felt dirty and tired and irritable from the stifling heat and lack of sleep during the past few days. Linh, obviously just as uncomfortable, sat quietly on the seat next to me, occasionally pointing the direction to take.

All the provincial staff were busy helping the large numbers of people fleeing the war. The important needs were shelter and food for the thousands of people forced from their homes by the VC or by the sweeps made by the South Vietnamese Army to drive the communists out. I was helping to shuttle food and clothing to temporary shelters set up in schools and tent villages near some of the rural military posts. Linh often travelled with me to help organise the distribution of the supplies and assist people who had become separated from their families.

I had just turned onto the road leading to the village school where the supplies were needed when Linh gasped and pointed to a huge cloud of dust and smoke rising from the cluster of buildings a mile further on. I stopped the vehicle and stared at the scene ahead. Over the billowing, reddish-brown smoke I could see the sun glinting off several planes as they circled, then one by one, dove steeply towards the ground and fired their rockets at the village. Linh looked across at me, speechless, her eyes round with horror. Strands of wet hair fell across her cheeks as she stared unbelievingly. 'The village is being bombed! The shelter…' she cried out in a quivering voice.

Individuals, then groups of people started to appear, quickly clogging the road with animal-drawn wagons and small carts hastily piled with belongings and bikes with cloth-tied bundles strapped on the seat and crossbar. Women and old men carried children, sacks of clothing and household goods as they scudded past.

I looked at the frightened, pathetic, bare-footed old women and men flapping along the road; at the children, their heads bent down, trudging through the mud. My stomach was knotted tight; I felt sick. How easy it is for a few pilots to destroy the homes and lives of these villagers… for what? I saw the fear and frustration and fatigue on the faces of the sweating peasants as they hurried by. I couldn't speak. Linh sat next to me – motionless, mute.

Sergeant Beach was usually a light-hearted fellow but today he looked stern as he entered the office. 'You've got to go to the field with an armed escort now, Eddie, Colonel's orders,' he said straight off, without any greeting or preliminaries.

'Now, what will the villagers think if I go out with a jeep full of troops?' I said casually.

'Never mind what they think, you need to worry less about appearances and more about saving your ass. The place is all torn up anyway; don't know what you expect to find out there.'

'I just want to see what happened; see how much damage was done to the warehouse and the supplies; maybe talk to Mr Sang if he's around. See what can be done.'

'Jesus, Eddie, ain't nothing can be done. It's finished out there… no more warehouse, no machinery or fertiliser, no office or truck. The cooperative is done. I saw it. Sang won't be anywhere near that place; crazy if he is. If the VC don't get him, one of our guys or the ARVN will. Nothing's moving out that way.'

'Was it hit that badly?'

'Yeah, it sure was.'

'What about the irrigation system, the pump?' I asked.

'Don't know anything about that,' the sergeant answered and left the office.

We first stopped at Mr Sang's house but it had been abandoned. Clothing was scattered around the silent rooms and a heavy sack of food stood on a table in the back room as though at the last minute someone had decided to leave it. By all the signs, the family had left the house in a hurry, but I guessed Mr Sang would know exactly what to do and where to go until it was safe to return to Thanh Loc.

We drove to the river road, past the fields of irrigated rice and on to the pump house. I walked down to the riverbank while Sergeant Beach and another soldier, a young pimply-faced kid named Turner, waited on the road. I was glad to see the large engine, its green metal covers glistening with oil in the dull light, was undamaged. I glanced at the curled-up bit of paper pinned to one of the posts with a nail. It listed the villagers responsible for the operation and maintenance of the pump during the current month. A checklist of jobs to be done at regular intervals was written out by hand and at the bottom of the sheet the village chief had scrawled his name boldly. I closed the pump house door and returned to the jeep.

Ahead on the road, not far from the cooperative, an armoured troop carrier had skidded into the shallow irrigation ditch that ran alongside the mud track. The vehicle's front end was smashed in by a direct hit from a heavy anti-tank gun. The huge engine, tilted almost onto its side, was visible through the ragged hole in the scorched metal. The inside of the vehicle had been gutted by fire; bits of charred rubber and other junk littered the ground.

I stood by the jeep looking at the wreck, trying to reconstruct how it had been spotted and fired upon from somewhere up ahead in the bush-lined road. The sergeant and Turner poked around in the wreckage. A large clump of tiny, brightly coloured wires lay in a pool of oil beneath the engine; gobs of blackened fibre dangled from a crusted, half-burned seat. This is how it will be at the end, I thought: all the machines and war-junk will rot in the fields, and only the kids who will play on them will be free of the terrible memories.

'They sure nailed this one, Sarge,' Turner said as he kicked at a heavy, twisted bit of metal that looked like an oil pan.

'Yeah, the captain was telling us about it this morning. Six ARVN and a US advisor were inside when it was hit.' The sergeant walked around to the other side of the smashed vehicle. 'Hey, Eddie,' he called.

'Yeah?'

'Must have been a comedian in the crew.'

'Why?'

'You know what's written on the side here?'

'What?'

'Communism sucks!'

Further down the road we stopped again when the sergeant spotted a body in the field just off the track. He was a young man, his head lying against the soft earth. Clay was smeared over his ear and across the side of his shaved head and bony shoulders. He wore a knitted short-sleeved shirt faded to a patchy, blue-black colour. His trousers, made of shiny, stiff dark cloth, were bunched up around his narrow waist and tied with a piece of rope.

'VC.' The sergeant touched the bare foot with the toe of his boot.

'Why don't the ARVN pick him up?'

'They will. They're waiting to see if any of the locals claim the body.'

'Why would they?'

'He might be from around here. Their guys don't come from Hanoi, you know; not this type, anyway.'

'No weapon.'

'Probably his pals took it, or maybe the ARVN got it when they came through here on the mopping up.'

I looked around at the land. Now in the wet season, the fields along the road were a lush green carpet of rice; rice so thick you could imagine walking across the tops of the heavy, grain-bearing heads.

I glanced back at the body. The feet and legs were caked with yellow, dry mud. Flies buzzed around the face and over the outstretched arm. Who is this kid, what's his story?

I wondered morosely, looking at his smooth, unformed face. Not much different from Turner, a little younger, maybe. Somebody is rocking in the night, hurting badly because of this skinny boy at my feet.

'Just a kid,' I mumbled, heading back to the jeep.

'Yeah, maybe, but kids can shoot you just as dead as grown men. You saw that personnel carrier back there; probably just a kid did it,' the sergeant replied as we bounced up the road.

The warehouse had taken a direct hit through the roof of the fertiliser storage room. Large chunks of the brick wall had broken off and these, together with strips of roofing tin, were littered over the torn fertiliser sacks. The metal grain bin was split open at the seams, an ugly gash disgorging the rice the farmers had begun to store.

I went into the small office where I'd sat through many meetings with the farmers, where most of the decisions had been made during the previous months about the operation of the cooperative. I recalled the many visitors from Saigon who had been out to see and support the establishment of the cooperative; the opening ceremony with Mr Sang and Linh, the speeches… the laughter and good feelings. I picked through the smashed furniture. Papers were strewn around the floor; the small, steel file cabinet was jammed against the back door.

Maybe the colonel and Henry are right, I thought. If there must be war – this kind of war, anyway – then the objective should be to win the damn thing and get it over with. In the meantime, civilian programmes are a waste of effort and money. The two can't go together. I wondered if we could learn even that from this mess. 'The VC knocked the hell out of this place,' I said bitterly.

'Yes, or the ARVN.'

'What about the roof?'

'Air force'

'American?'

'No, VN,' the sergeant said. 'Everybody panicked when the VC shot out the personnel carrier. The next day the ARVN troops called in air strikes on any place they thought the VC might be hiding.'

'Christ, Sarge, you mean the government blew the roof off this place, destroyed the farmers' cooperative because they suspected a few VC *might* be hiding here?!'

'Sure.'

'A day after the carrier was shot up; the intelligence was a day old!'

'Yep.'

'Damn it, if the VC are known for anything, it's their mobility. Would they just sit around here for a day?'

'Not likely.'

I stepped outside and leaned against the front of a flat-bed truck parked alongside the building. Bullets had been fired through the radiator; the windshield was smashed and one headlight shattered to pieces. I didn't try to fight off the feeling of hopelessness, of doubt that anything could be accomplished in this tormented country.

'Is this any way to fight a war, Sarge?' I asked wearily, knowing the answer.

'Yeah, man, it sure as hell is; that's something you're gonna have to learn.'

I stepped away. In my chest that tight, breathless feeling again – the lunacy, the utter futility of it all; my mind blank, black, empty. I stumbled across some rough-sawn planks piled among the bushes off to the side of the warehouse near a small, half-finished frame house.

'There's one here, too, Sarge,' Turner shouted from the other side of the bushes. I walked over. Turner stood by the body of another skinny kid in rolled-up black trousers and a loose shirt stained with blood.

'Yep, got the bastard! See, Eddie, the VC were hiding in the warehouse,' the sergeant said.

I looked down at the deeply set eyes, the long teeth sticking out hideously from the face, now frozen in a grimace of horror and fear, the distinctive shock of hair across the pale forehead. 'Zoom,' I said quietly. I slumped on some logs and looked away.

'Huh?' the sergeant said, looking over at me.

'He's not VC,' I continued, not caring if they understood, not giving a damn about explanations. But I heard myself speak again, the words flat, cold, not mine. 'His name is Dung, but everyone called him Zoom. You guys have killed the Minister of Agriculture.'

Flies buzzed and darted over the body. Energised, purposeful little bastards; just like the enemy, seizing opportunity when death came…

'What the hell are you talking about, Eddie? Zoom, Minister of Agriculture? You've flipped, man.'

Zoom was a fallen man; the maggots were alive and wriggling. His future children would have learned about miracle rice. They would have cherished their rice, grown it in neat rows, for Christ's sake. I retched as I turned and walked a few paces away, only to then imagine dozens of headless cockroaches inching closer, still alive – cracking, breaking.

'Just another fucking gook, another dead…' Turner was saying when I lunged at him in a rage of stupid, blind hate and smashed through his upturned arms, grabbed his neck, threw him to the ground and shook him with all my strength. I smelled the heat of his jerking body and saw the shock and fear in his bulging eyes as I squeezed and squeezed…

'Christ! Let go, man! Let go, you fucking idiot!' The sergeant slammed down hard on my arms to break my grip on the kid. I fell away; my arms trembled. I felt sick and disgusted with myself, with the whole steaming, stinking mess that was Vietnam. 'Goddamn it, Eddie, you almost throttled Turner,' the sergeant said as he helped him get to his feet. 'You're crazy, Eddie. You think a guy like Turner is your enemy? Jesus!'

I looked over. Poor kid, he didn't ask for this; he's just trying to get through the days and stay alive like the rest of us. 'I'm sorry, Turner,' I said. 'Blew my head; stupid, not your fault.' I couldn't look at him. I felt ridiculous, a complete ass, adding to the misery of this place. Turner just glared at me as he rubbed his neck.

'Look, Eddie, you better take a break, get away for a while. You don't seem right, man,' Sergeant Beach said as he handed some cigarettes around.

'Yeah, thanks,' I responded dully, accepting a light and wondering if a break was what I needed.

'Come on guys, I've seen enough dead bodies for one day. Let's get back to the office, I have a meeting to attend involving a certain punctual colonel,' the sergeant said as he walked off.

'Aren't they all, Sarge?' Turner called out as the colour pulsed back into his cheeks.

'Give me a minute,' I said as I turned to sit with Zoom next to his unfinished house, pondering his unfinished ambitions and dreams of helping his country… I looked at him one last time, struck by the stillness, wishing and wanting to remember him as a busy fieldman with a small dog's energy. I swallowed the lump in my throat, then rose and joined the soldiers for the drive back to the office.

The Weed Killers

I had flipped at the cooperative, just as Sergeant Beach had said, and I was in a sour mood when the colonel showed up in my office a few days later. Zoom's death staggered me; it had blown a few circuits, more than the sergeant could imagine, but the full meaning of what had happened in Thanh Loc – the senseless wasting of this promising life, the destruction of the farmers' cooperative – hadn't sunk in yet. Something in my mind walled it away, to be dealt with later, when the frantic pace of the work lessened. Then, I convinced myself, there'd be time to deal with it, to determine its importance within the larger picture. Still, subconsciously I think I was expecting some change or event or sign – some damn thing to show clearly that the things going on here were for the good of the nation.

During this time I was unfit to live with, yet Linh stayed with me and worried herself. One thing became clear: her concern was not for some vague democracy-versus-communism ideal, nor even the survival of Vietnam, but for me. Linh's love – her friendship and her unstated but obvious choice of the personal over dogma – was unwavering. While I stupidly bent my mind judging things, trying to see the gains and losses resulting from America's role in Vietnam, Linh watched and waited calmly with an intuitive understanding of the essentials.

I was able to function at the office, but not effectively; my heart wasn't in it. The excitement, the unthinking acceptance in the earlier months of our actions, had been replaced by almost complete disillusionment. Even feeling this way, still I hoped. I forced myself to believe that once the emergency situation was over we could make things right again; could bring back order and development. With true American optimism, I wanted to believe the trend was up, with some setbacks perhaps, but generally towards something good. That belief and Linh's quiet support kept me going. But Colonel Horst was a problem.

About mid-morning a few days after the emotional visit to Thanh Loc with the two soldiers, the colonel appeared at my office. I hadn't seen much of him in the past few days, but I suspected that from the sergeant to the captain to the major to the colonel – in proper army chain of command – he'd learned about my grabbing the soldier at the cooperative. He seemed overly glad to see me. I knew his visit had to be more than a social call – they were not his style. I leaned back to study him. He looks fit, I thought, noticing his tanned, clean-shaven face. My God, he's thriving here. He settled into a seat across from my desk.

'Do you want something, Colonel?' I asked, feeling we better get right to it.

'Well, Eddie, yes.' He seemed to be hedging. Not like him, I thought. Maybe he thinks I'm on the verge of a serious crack-up… handling me gently. 'There's a little something we need you to look into.'

'What's that?'

'Oh, the province chief has asked if you could investigate a report about some crop damage in one of the districts. Captain Wells has the details.'

'What sort of crop damage?'

'We don't know. Perhaps just a few dead plants caused by insects or diseases or something,' the colonel said vaguely, seeming preoccupied.

'It's got to be more than a few plants with insect damage if the province chief has been notified about it.'

'Yes. Well, it could be more serious than that. We'd like you to take a look and determine what the problem is, the extent of the damage and make an estimate of the value of the lost crop. We might pay compensation to the farmers.'

'Compensation?' I was surprised. This was something new. 'Why would the US government pay compensation for crops damaged by insects or disease? Those can be common problems.'

'I only mention compensation as a possibility; only if we are the cause of the damage,' he said, now looking stern. Official. More like himself, I thought.

'*If* we are responsible? What do you mean, how could we be...? Oh shit, Colonel! Herbicides, defoliant? Agent Orange?!' I stared at the colonel who was busy removing bits of imaginary fluff from his jacket.

'It could be, Eddie.'

'How? That stuff isn't sprayed anywhere near here; they use it in the forested areas, miles away.'

'Yes, I know. We aren't sure. It's possible there has been some leakage.' The colonel now looked slightly wilted; not quite so sharp.

'Leakage?!'

'Yes. Look, first you better go out to the airstrip where they load the spray planes. Check the equipment and talk to the people out there about their operation. See if you can find out if it's possible for the defoliant to be accidentally dropped over this area as they make their runs to the drop zones.'

'Goddamn it! You mean our guys have been dropping defoliant over the farming areas of this province? Dropping your lousy Agent Orange over the fields of the farmers I'm supposed to be helping grow better crops?'

'There's a good chance that's happened, Eddie. We want your assessment,' he said in his best military voice, trying hard to show who was in charge here.

'You want my assessment?! An assessment by one American of damage done by other Americans to the fields of Vietnamese farmers we were all sent here to save from communism! Hey, fantastic, Colonel. That's just fantastic!' I laughed bitterly. The colonel shot me a worried glance.

'Accidents happen, Eddie,' he said as he walked away.

'Sure, Colonel. Right on!' I snapped flippantly. I was at the point where I thought nothing could surprise me. 'A new counter-offensive, huh?'

The air base was securely guarded by a high fence with double rolls of barbed wire rusted to a dull brown and heavy concrete posts at the gates. Tattered paper and other bits of trash were caught in the endless coils of spiky metal leading away from both sides of the gate. A sandbag bunker, with flat slit openings giving a clear line of fire across the approaches to the base, stood off to the side of the entrance where a sentry scrutinised all vehicles weaving their way around the obstacles leading to the gate. I pulled up to the entrance, stopped and showed my ID card to the American on duty.

'I'm looking for the group doing the defoliant spraying,' I said as the sentry got down on one knee and looked beneath the vehicle to check for explosives. He stood up, glanced quickly around the interior of the vehicle and then answered.

'You want the Weed Killers? Right, just follow the main base road that way past those hangars and buildings off to the left.' He pointed the way. 'There's a large engine maintenance shop about half a mile down the road; your guys are located just beyond it. You'll see their storage sheds and the spray-rigged equipment; you can't miss it.'

'OK, thanks,' I said and pulled away from the gate, turned in the direction the guard had indicated and slowly drove along the main base road. Off to the right, some sleek fighter jets were hidden inside low, heavy concrete shelters; a few planes were out in the open being fuelled or armed with long, thin rockets slung under the wings. Further on, a couple of Forward Air Control planes were parked by a small hangar – these were the tiny, single-engine spotter planes so feared and hated by the VC.

I'd heard of situations where over-zealous FAC pilots had ordered air strikes on farmers who looked suspiciously like enemy troops. From 500 feet up I could understand how difficult it might be to distinguish a group of raggedly dressed farmers, attempting to avoid being detected, from a similar-looking band of VC huddled beneath some trees. As Colonel Horst said, mistakes were made.

I drove past a long row of armoured helicopters used throughout the countryside for quickly landing assault parties. Just beyond the engine maintenance shop I stopped the vehicle in front of a large grey Quonset hut. A sign over the door pictured a soldier in full gear carrying a sprayer on his back and holding the spray nozzle over some scraggly plants. A light stream of painted dots indicated the spray hitting the plants, many of them shown wilted and apparently dying. Above the picture, painted in crude three-inch letters, were the words: THE WEED KILLERS.

I stepped inside where a sergeant worked on some papers at a metal desk in one corner. He looked up. 'Hey, man. You're a civilian, what are you doing here?'

'I'm the agricultural advisor in Gia Dinh,' I said and showed my ID to the sergeant. 'There's some concern in my province about possible damage being done by the defoliant spraying…'

'Yeah, I see. Reports of our good work getting back to the brass, eh?' the sergeant said brightly.

'I suppose you could say that.'

'Well, Captain Rodina is in charge here, at least sometimes; whenever we see him, that is. He's new in-country and just getting himself all squared away, you know what I mean?'

'Can you show me around and explain your operation?'

'Sure, why not? Always glad to entertain one of you important civilian specialists,' he said with a sneer. 'Come on outside and see what we've got.'

We walked over to where some men were working on one of the spray planes. The aircraft was a lot larger than I'd expected. Obviously, these planes can carry quite a load, I thought. Under each wing a long boom was mounted with short drop pipes about a foot apart along its length. Each drop pipe ended in a small, brass nozzle. 'We use a ULV technique,' the sergeant said, glancing sideways at me. 'Know what I mean?'

'Yes,' I answered and took a close look at the tiny numbers stamped on one of the nozzles indicating its size. 'Ultra-Low Volume, a high concentration mix of chemicals with a small amount of water so you can carry more defoliant and don't have to make as many trips.'

'Yeah, you've got it, man, you seem to know your shit,' the sergeant said matter-of-factly, as though I'd just aced an aggie pop quiz.

The men were pumping the herbicide into the plane from drums sitting on a low wagon. I stopped to read the markings on a drum, including the Department of Defence contract number and percentage breakdown of the chemical ingredients. 'Why is it called "Agent Orange", Sergeant?'

'Hell if I know. It's a nice bright name, though, ain't it?'

'You know this stuff, or something just like it, is used in the States under electric power lines and along roadways; it's a powerful broad-leafed plant killer.'

'Oh?'

'Yep. It's a synthetic hormone, really,' I said, figuring he might be interested. 'It stimulates excessive growth and disorganises the plant's cells. It interferes with the plant's ability to produce food and finally kills it,' I added as we watched the men load the plane.

'No kidding! Look, buddy, our guys just spray the stuff where they're told to. That's all; no big deal, you see?'

'How often do you clean and adjust the nozzles?' I asked.

'Hell, I don't know. I'm new here. Hey, Mike, how often do you guys clean the nozzles?' he shouted over to one of the men.

'Not since I've been here.'

'How long is that?' I asked.

'About six months.'

As the men continued to fill the tank in the aircraft, the pressure in the system built up and soon a few drops of liquid started to ooze from some of the nozzles and drip to the ground. 'Look here,' I said firmly and pointed to a slowly dripping nozzle on the end of the boom. 'The shut-off valve isn't closing properly. The defoliant is being dropped all the way from here to the target area!'

'Hell, man, that's just a few drops; what are you talking about?'

'The amount of defoliant leaking out from here to the drop zone can cause a lot of damage.' I knew the sergeant had no intention of doing anything about the leaks. I could feel myself getting worked up and tried to stay calm. 'This is a highly concentrated chemical; in the air it volatilises – it breaks up into tiny droplets that mix with the moisture in the air, gets carried for miles and finally comes down in the rain. This damn herbicide drops out of the sky onto the people and crops all along your travel route.'

'You damn experts!' the sergeant snorted. 'You come along here and bitch about a few drops of chemical coming down in some rain. Hell, we got us a war on our hands, man! We're dumping gallons and gallons of this junk on the jungles; we're killing off the trees and knocking the piss out of those damn commies who used to hide under the trees.' The sergeant was getting steamed up too.

'Look, you don't understand the…'

'I understand plenty, buddy! I don't know about your fancy-assed chemical names and all this plant hormone shit. But I do understand something about this war, something you highly paid civilian jerks don't know nothing about. I understand one thing: we got to knock hell out of them slopes every chance we got… the spraying helps!'

'OK, look. I'm telling you what you're doing is not safe.'

'Safe?! What the hell is safe in this poor excuse for a country?' he said with a half-smile, pleased with himself.

'I'm telling you to stop this operation now until all the equipment is cleaned, adjusted and checked over.' I knew it was hopeless but couldn't stop myself. I looked straight at the sergeant. The other men had stopped working and were watching us. 'Don't let this flight take off. I'll report back to the province military people and an order will come down somehow. Until then, don't make any more runs.'

'Hey, man, you don't give the orders around here. Who the hell you think you are? I got my orders. This plane goes today.'

I was fed up with it. Why isn't the damn colonel out here? This is army bullshit; I want no part of it! That feeling came over me again: what the hell am I doing out here on this hot tarmac talking to these guys; is this how I want to spend my life? How did I get here? I wanted away from the men and their half-assed grins and the damn planes. I walked back to the vehicle. The sergeant stood with his hands on his hips, posing, being a tough guy. He laughed loudly when one of his men spoke up: 'Atta boy, Sarge!'

'Give that civilian hell, Sarge!' another one shouted.

'OK, you guys,' the sergeant said loudly so I could hear him. 'Let's get these crates loaded. We got us some goddamn weeds to kill!'

Evil Machine

We drove out of town on the crumbling, pot-holed road behind a convoy of army trucks belching black smoke into the already filthy air. I eased the vehicle into position behind the last truck in the column. Sweat rolled down my neck; my shirt and trousers stuck to me and the plastic seat as waves of heat boiled up from the fast-running engine. I was thinking of an earlier time in a cool, sane, orderly world; Mr Phu then spoke.

'Turn off there,' he said, pointing. We left the busy highway and started down a much narrower, badly rutted road, carefully avoiding the piles of river rock dumped at intervals along the ditch. At the edge of a small village, we asked directions from some women sitting in front of a cluster of weathered houses, then Mr Phu directed me to drive onto a muddy track leading to a small wooden house set behind a tiny square of clean-swept red earth. A tattered yellow and red Vietnamese flag slapped fitfully atop a wobbly pole in the middle of the clearing; the little public square and the flag meant this was the village chief's house and the village office.

A sun-wrinkled, weary man emerged from the house wearing a faded grey shirt with a large hole just beneath one arm; his trousers were tied with a belt that went almost twice around his thin waist. He moved slowly as he came over to greet Mr Phu and me, welcoming us on behalf of the villagers in the traditional way, then led us to the house with a dignified wave of his arm.

The village meeting hall was a dark, poorly ventilated room with a dirt floor to the side of the building. Before long, tea was brought out by a young girl in a stained, pale pink dress – a party dress an American girl might wear. Probably from one of the many voluntary relief organisations active in Vietnam, I thought. Perhaps she has my Russian hat!

Mr Phu, formal as always in his long-sleeved white shirt and French cufflinks, engaged the old man in the usual casual talk about the chief's wife, sons, daughters, about his grandchildren and all his other relatives. I was anxious to discuss the crop damage but held back knowing this roundabout approach was the best way to deal with the farmers. The villagers couldn't be rushed; they felt themselves part of a larger, slower cycle from birth to maturity, and finally to an accepted, honourable death. And they didn't respond to pushing by strangers.

I was accustomed to this leisurely view of things now and as Mr Phu and the chief chatted, I sipped my tea and enjoyed the deep-set eyes, the leathery look of a man who had survived many seasons and hardships. He was perfectly calm; not intimidated by the smooth-talking Mr Phu or me, a pale-faced foreigner.

Mr Phu moved on to the weather. 'Has it been too wet?'

'No,' the chief answered thoughtfully, 'it has been good so far.'

Slowly Mr Phu got around to mentioning the crops. 'Is it a good year for the rice, the maize, the tobacco?'

The village chief pursed his lips. 'The rice and maize seem all right,' he said, nodding his head. 'But the tobacco died.' He looked at me, a long, unfocused look as though seeing right through me and the walls of the house to the fields beyond.

'Did the chief say the tobacco died, Mr Phu?' I asked quickly.

'Yes.'

'I can't follow him very well; please ask if all the plants in the area died or just a few in one or two fields.'

'All the fields around here.'

'Ask him if it happened suddenly or over a period of weeks or months.'

'All died within two weeks.'

'And the cassava?'

'All dead. At the same time.'

'And the papaya trees?'

'All dead,' Mr Phu said unemotionally, translating the chief's words.

'Well, I guess the reports are correct. It sounds like the plants have been killed by defoliant. Papaya and cassava are highly sensitive; the tobacco too, while the defoliant wouldn't bother rice or maize, not in small amounts anyway.'

Mr Phu translated my words for the chief. The old-timer looked puzzled and remained silent for a long time; finally he spoke.

'He wants to know how the poison got here on the fields,' Mr Phu translated.

'You'd better tell the chief the chemical came from aeroplanes – from American aeroplanes – by accident. Tell him it fell over his village by mistake,' I said, avoiding the old man's eyes. I knew the US was targeting some cropland deliberately to cut off a food source for the VC troops, but I kept that thought glumly to myself. What I had witnessed was a consequence of shoddy maintenance procedures.

The village chief spoke in a low voice, all the while staring at his bare feet placed firmly on the hard mud floor.

'What did he say, Mr Phu?'

'He… he cannot understand. He does not understand how this could happen; how the Americans could kill the villagers' crops…'

'I can't either. Oh, hell, tell him it was because… No, let's just go out and have a look.'

We walked out to one of the fields not far from the chief's house. I inspected the cassava, papaya, tobacco and other broad-leafed plants, now shrivelled and dead. I tried to estimate the extent of the damage and approximate market value of the destroyed crops but found it impossible to place values on the lost fruit and other trees in the gardens around the farmers' houses.

A few villagers joined us as we walked along the narrow track leading to some distant fields. On either side, bushes and trees most sensitive to the herbicide were parched and limp. I could see that some of the plants, particularly the larger fruit trees, probably would set new leaves and recover in time, but it was clear the broad-leafed annuals – the vegetables and tobacco plants – were wiped out.

An elderly woman stood in her garden, like a thickened, gnarled tree with many rings; she was no stranger to this land. She complained loudly to the village chief and pointed to a couple of papaya trees in front of her house where the once lacy, graceful leaves hung as a shrivelled, grey mass of decaying foliage. The chief answered the woman's complaints in a soothing voice and stretched out his arms and upturned hands in a gesture indicating that all of this – the death of the villagers' crops and trees by this strange poison – was incomprehensible.

I studied the woman in her layers of jumbled clothing; felt the contempt such a peasant woman had for these mysterious forces that destroyed life, and her instinctive hate of all military people and their equipment and foul chemicals. 'A war-scarred mess inhabited by humanity,' I once read in Carl's notebook. If there was a neutral in this war, I thought, there she stood, unable even to conceive of the differences that separated the two sides of the conflict, yet knowing in her bones what was happening around her was beyond explanation.

About a half-mile from the centre of the village, the chief and I entered a field of tobacco and walked along between the ragged rows of plants, now twisted and brittle in the hot sun. I stooped down and checked the bottom leaves to see if there was a chance they still might be harvested. The chief stood by quietly.

We were approaching the end of the field when I heard a shout and some scuffling in the nearby bushes. I froze. 'Jesus, Viet Cong! Oh, shit!' The sound of trampling feet and snapping brush grew louder. My heart thumped wildly; I strained my ears for more sounds from the trees ahead and stared intently to detect any movement of branch or leaf. I considered dropping between the rows of plants. How stupid to get caught out in the middle of a damn tobacco field with no protection, no way to escape, totally exposed to any jackass with a gun.

Fear and anger boiled in my chest. 'You idiot!' I searched the bushes for movement; listened for further sounds; my legs twitching, jerking for action. We should run, I thought. They haven't spotted us yet; they might not come out of the bushes for another minute or two... We could be running away, out of danger! I stood frozen in place next to the village chief.

With a rush of clattering equipment and pounding feet, soldiers burst from the bushes. My eyes were glazed; I dimly saw soldiers racing towards us. My worst fear! The men kept coming; more scrambled out of the bushes, dropped to one knee and then, stooping over, ran towards me and the chief. I reeled. It's not possible! They're American troops! Good God! My breath returned in great gasps. 'Americans!' I shouted. I felt weak, drained. 'They're Americans!' I rasped with a nervous laugh to the old chief by my side, who stood with his hands behind his back nervously watching the soldiers trot towards us.

They were in full battledress with automatic weapons held ready as they scrambled down between the rows of tobacco on both sides of where the village chief and I stood. Bits of grass and brush were poked into the netting of their helmets. One soldier had a radio satchel strapped to his back with a long antenna sticking into the air. Their serious faces turned to looks of puzzlement, then amazement, as they approached.

The lead soldier pulled up quickly in front of me. He was in his mid-20s, a lieutenant with a little white bar painted on the front of his helmet. The grass and twigs framed his surprised face. 'What the hell are you doing here?!' he blurted out, still huffing from the running.

'Where the hell did you guys come from?' I asked shakily, slowly recovering from my shock.

'Damn, man, who are you, anyway?!' The lieutenant was confused and irritated. The soldiers crouched along the rows behind the officer.

'An agricultural advisor,' I said, starting to smile at the thought of this bizarre situation. 'Am I glad to see you guys! I thought you were VC; I figured we were done for!'

'Are you some kind of missionary or something?' the lieutenant asked while he screwed his head around and surveyed the surrounding fields and the raggedly dressed villagers strung out along the rows of tobacco.

'No. Just a civilian advisor. I was having a look at…'

'What the hell are you doing out here, man? Are you nuts?!' the young officer demanded savagely.

'Well, I'm just looking at this damaged tobacco.' I waved my hand around and pointed to the fields. 'Oh, by the way, this is the village chief.' I took the old man by the arm to introduce him to the officer. The chief, who had stood by stiffly to this point, cracked a worried smile.

'Get out of here! You are both crazier than hell! There's an operation going on – a sweep. There's VC all over this area!'

'A sweep?!'

'Yes. Look, I don't know who you are, and I don't care. If you and your old buddy there don't want to get your asses all shot up, I suggest you get out of this area now.' The lieutenant waved his arm like someone leading a charge in an old war movie and stepped forward. The men in the squad fell in behind, hunched low and trotted on down the rows. I felt ludicrous standing there with the old chief as the American troops slipped past us without saying a word. Somehow I thought we should talk, say hello, anything. Instead, they rushed on past and were gone, disappearing into some trees on the far side of the field.

We hurried back to the village, then Mr Phu and I said our goodbyes to the chief and other farmers, got back to the vehicle and left. As I drove towards the main highway as fast as the rutted road would permit, I still couldn't believe what had just happened. Damn, I thought; a sweep, a big operation going on and we don't even know about it.

'Didn't you say the security officer told you it was safe, that we didn't need an armed escort out this way today, Mr Phu?' I asked after we were well away from the village. I felt the anger rising and tried to control it.

'He did,' Mr Phu said, then paused. 'He's a new man, though. It would seem he doesn't know the province very well yet.'

'Lovely, just lovely!' I started to laugh nervously, feeling the tension coil around my arms and shoulders as I drove on. Damn it, nobody knows what's going on; it's out of control, a ponderous, evil machine. Simple mistakes aren't forgiven here… no front, no back. Just being in the wrong place in this quagmire can be the end of everything… 'No place for civilians; stupid!'

'Pardon?' Mr Phu said, sounding concerned.

'Nothing, Mr Phu, nothing at all,' I answered distractedly, but knew I was close to my limit; knew I could snap at any time. My hands shook uncontrollably on the steering wheel. Mr Phu reached over and placed his hand on my arm.

'Take some leave, Eddie. Take some leave.'

Broken Rice Bowls

She wore the traditional baggy trousers beneath a dingy white blouse, a lumpy, pinkish bra showing clearly through the thin cotton material. A network of fine lines crisscrossed her sun-darkened face, merging into deep wrinkles around her mouth and swollen eyes. She stood amid the ruins of the house, gently rubbing a bandaged arm and crying her anguish in choppy, disconnected phrases.

Her mother, a tiny dried-out husk of a woman with thin hair tied back, her lips and teeth stained dark purple from years of chewing the astringent betelnut and lime used as a mild narcotic by all the older villagers, sat on a stool staring at the wall. Her eyes were cold, dead; her face a mask of indifference. Occasionally she bent forward and sighed as she smothered a framed photograph in the folds of her dress.

The house was destroyed: the roof burned away, only a shell of cracked mud walls remained. Bits of pottery, cooking pots and broken pieces of the wooden framing that had supported the roof were scattered on the dirt floor. Tufts of charred thatch covered the bed and the battered table, now harshly lit by the bright sunlight pouring into the house. The pungent smell of recently burned grass and wood rose from soot and ashes by the door where Linh and I stood talking with the younger woman.

I looked across the garden to where some children were sobbing and keening in their inconsolable grief. They squatted on the freshly dug chunks of mottled clay next to a shallow hole in the ground. Wrapped in thin, white muslin cloths of mourning – the two girls hooded, the boy with a white sash around his forehead – they moaned and wept openly.

The woman walked to a shed at the back of the burned-out house and returned with a small box cradled in her arms; the children wailed louder when they saw their mother with the box. She brushed away her tears, lifted the lid and looked down at the body of her baby; the child was wrapped in layers of white cloth reaching to her chin; she looked serene and peaceful, as though she'd drifted away in a peaceful sleep.

Linh spoke quietly to the mother, touched her hand and carefully lifted the box from her arms, gently placing a freshly picked pink orchid on top. She then returned the dead baby to the shed. Distraught and unable to remain still, the woman stepped away quickly, clasping and unclasping her arms around her thin body as she paced back and forth. She stopped by some trees at the far end of the small garden and stared. 'That's our rice,' she uttered pathetically. Her voice, thickened with emotion, was barely audible over the noise of the children hovering by the recently dug grave.

I walked over to where she stood. There, scattered in the mud over a large part of the roughly dug garden, was the rice she and her family had recently harvested and put aside carefully as seed for the next planting season, and for food they would need to live on during the coming year. I was deeply saddened by the sight of grain thrown carelessly on the ground. I'd come to appreciate the Vietnamese peasants' feelings about rice; knew how important it was; how it was lovingly nurtured, harvested and saved by every family. Looking at the bloated, ruined grain, I recalled the director-general's words about rice and the old Vietnamese saying he'd mentioned during the meeting at the ministry. Here, certainly, I thought, was a family with broken rice bowls... how could they ever be pieced back together? I turned away.

'Damn it, but why?' I asked Linh.

'The soldiers thought this family was hiding VC,' she said hesitantly, as though afraid to say more, afraid of her feelings… or mine.

Once more, the gripping tightness in my chest I'd often felt during the past few weeks came over me. I had to move. I went to the vehicle and got the water bottle and a bag of the milled rice I always carried in the car these days and brought them back for the mother.

She nodded her thanks silently, gulped some water and sat down with her back against a tree. Linh spoke to her soothingly. The woman remained silent, looking out across the nearby fields. While I stepped over to give the children a drink, she started talking.

'It all started yesterday around noon,' she said, looking at Linh intently, like she needed to tell someone what had happened. Her husband and son, a boy of 15, were continuing to harvest the rice in the fields near the house while she and her mother threshed the grain. Later, she had walked out with her baby daughter to bring the men their midday meal while her mother and children remained at the house to spread the grain on mats to dry in the sun.

'I sat with my man and son on the little roofed-over platform we'd built at the corner of one of the fields; a shaded place where we rested when working the land or where our eldest boy usually slept when the rice was nearly ripe, guarding it from animals and thieves,' she said, speaking deliberately, remembering every detail and choosing her words carefully. 'The baby crawled on the floor as I untied the bundle containing fried rice wrapped in banana leaves. I passed the food to the men, picked up the baby and settled her to feed.

'That was when we heard the sound and looked up: a rapid clicking and swishing noise above the roar of engines. Over the far line of trees at the edge of the field, two large, grey-green machines came to the earth.' Her voice changed pitch, then cracked, as she needed time to compose herself. 'My husband jumped up, grabbed the boy and pulled him off the platform. Holding the baby close, I slipped to the ground and kneeled behind the back edge of the raised floor. Soldiers dropped from the machines then quickly spread out, running towards us. My husband shouted *"Di di!"*, warning me to get back to the house quickly as he ran off the other way, pulling our son with him. Holding the baby, I bent over and ran as fast as I could towards the edge of the field and crashed into the bushes.

'Then I heard shots; at first far away from where I ran through vines and small trees, then nearer; the sharp, crackling sounds coming closer to me. I stopped, very afraid, at the edge of the open field just behind our house. In the distance more shots were fired. I waited, then heard snapping twigs and people moving. I knew I had to reach our house, had to protect the children and my mother. Holding the baby under my arm, I jumped ahead into the open land and raced for the house.

'I heard more shots from the bushes, huddled low, covering the baby and continued running. There was a stinging pain in my arm. I fell sideways, cushioning the baby as I hit the ground. I dragged myself along on my knees and wounded arm, cradling the baby beneath me. I pulled myself to the low dyke by the garden and rolled over it, stopping on my back with the baby beside me.

'It was then I noticed a drop of blood coming from a wound on her neck. I knew then. My hand behind her head became warm and sticky. My baby. I jumped up and ran through the back of the garden. I fell against the door and pushed it open. Dead. My mother screamed. The children under the table began to shriek. We all knew the baby was dead…'

Her lips and chin quivered; with the memory of the fresh tragedy so raw, she threw herself on the ground, nervously twisting her hair, body shuddering, her feet jerking and scraping in the mud as she sobbed uncontrollably. Linh reached down, touched her shoulder and tried to be a comfort. I looked away. I had understood enough. I got up quickly and walked past the burnt-out house and vehicle and carried on along the village road.

I felt dizzy. Hot. Sweat soaked my hair and neck. Fever? Malaria? Half-thoughts, images, unconnected ramblings crowded my brain. My mind zigzagged from the heartbreaking vision before me to my troubles back home. My brain shifted uncontrollably to thoughts of jogging. Should I take it up again, clear my mind? Did I now need it? Jean, jogging… jumbled thoughts, ideas, goals, the tragedy before me. Then words collided in my head.

'Live free or die, Tootsie,' I muttered. Or just die, your rice bowl punched from your muddy hands. The peasants – don't call them names, you insensitive brute! The farmers, then, or the villagers; the only decent people in the whole damn… Not so, come on, be fair. There are good people on both sides: government types, the honest workers, those poor damn kids who graduate from high school and find themselves a month or so later being shot at in some tangled jungle… Sister Claire, Harry, Linh. And Ted, and Will, Zoom, Mr Tam, all well-meaning, all trying. Then why…? Rot! Something stinks in Saigon! Ha! 'The imponderables, old boy!' Such claptrap, bullshit, swollen words… rice and bodies. 'Saving the world from communism… Kee-rist!'

How, buddy? Hey, how you plan to do that there, amigo? Yea? Shoot de villagers, no? Ya, velly good, one more Saigon tea. I'm cracking… cool it. We shoot dose damn varmints, no more trouble! You fucking idiot! Sir? Yes, sir, the Super-Slope-Slapper Mach Two is proving to be extremely accurate, further testing should… We could stack the weapons on top of the Louisiana rice, save a bundle. Ah, you cagey Cajun. Crushing defeat, a crushing defeat! Hmm, like the frogs at that Poo place? Sir? Den Ben Poo, you know, where the frogs took it in the old…

Lean and mean as hell; red ones, screaming eagles, they should do the trick… promotions in it. Ahem, hardly the proper attitude for a professional soldier. Yes indeed, you name 'em, we got 'em. Huh? Oh, standard government contract, you know, 200 per cent markup over existing retail. Motorbikes? The Japanese, mister; got it all sewed up. Where you been? Seeing the need to develop nobility of character to go with our power, sir, that will be the lesson we must learn… must learn from this 'dirty war'. Will it justify the deaths? And the hardware? Yes. What about the hardware? Doesn't matter a damn, after a certain point; morale, discipline, fighting for one's own land, these count. Then, sir, we are in deep shit!

'Don't tell me the rest,' I said as Linh climbed into the vehicle. 'Let me guess. The ARVN took the man and the boy for "interrogation", pulled down the bags of rice stored in the rafters, gathered up the grain drying on the mats in the garden and scattered it around, then burned the house. It's easy when you know the modus operandi, dear girl. An absolute cinch! Never a surprise. Did I miss anything?'

'Eddie, are you all right?'

'Never better. Did I miss anything?'

'Only that there was an American officer with the ARVN soldiers.'

'Really? Just great. That wraps it up.'

'Eddie, what's wrong…'

'Did you get the names of the two missing?'

'Yes. I think we should go straight home.'

'Can you do anything?'

'I will try. I have some friends in counter-insurgency. I'll ask around.'

'Right.' I started up the vehicle and drove off. For the next hour, as we travelled back to the apartment, neither of us could speak.

Face-Off

My head was still throbbing painfully, a bad night. Gloomy thoughts flitted through my mind as I sat in the office waiting to be summoned by the colonel. I'd had to say no to Linh about a trip to some villages – because of Horst; because, really, underneath everything, I'd lost interest; no longer got pleasure from trips to the field. She looked worried, poor girl. 'I'll be all right,' I assured her. But her eyes gave her away… she didn't believe it.

It's not me at my desk; I'm outside it all, looking down at the man sitting there; restless, silent, without power to act. A soldier at the door says the colonel wants me. I pull myself together. 'OK, coming down.'

Colonel Horst is at his papers again; what the hell does he write all the time? He waves me to a chair as he continues writing; yellow sheets with roughly torn edges. I stare at him like a cat nervously watching a contented dog, in his own world, gnawing a flavoursome bone with the marrow yet to suck out.

'Hang on a second, Eddie, I want to ask you something.'

'Yep.' I have a question for him. 'Did you find out about the man and his son?'

'Huh? Wait.' He keeps writing. 'Oh, yes. They're home now; tell Linh, will you?'

So, they did nothing; innocent. Baby shot, house burned, rice trampled into the ground… sorry, a terrible mistake, abusive use of our power, we're taking corrective actions to see it can never happen again...

'To the same family, you mean?'

'What?' A voice from beneath the perfect oval of a fresh buzz cut.

'Compensation?'

'Wait up, man, just have to finish this.' Some men are joking in the hallway; the pencil scratches across the pad. 'ARVN's business. Not like the Agent Orange thing, where we take some responsibility.'

Ha! Now, we know about the ARVN's business, looting... take *some* responsibility! 'How much can it take?'

'What?' He looks up. Cold eyes; fish eyes.

'The society. How much can it take?'

The pencil goes down. 'Before what?'

'When do you quit operating to save the patient? When all the limbs are gone? Do you stop then? Do you want the ears, the eyes? Do you want the cock and balls?'

'Hey, take it easy. You OK?'

'Yes.' But not in the way the colonel is hoping.

'Someone always gets hurt in wartime, Eddie. There's always destruction of life and property.' Words were tripping off the colonel's tongue. War college phrases? War college? War scholars?

'More than that.'

'Huh? You don't seem yourself.' No? Who is this 'yourself'?

'I mean looting, bribery, deals at the docks, whores, dope-pushers...'

'Well, of course, that's...'

'And your guys; their free-fire zones, bombs, rockets, napalm, Agent Orange causing God knows what harm...'

'Well...'

'Your counter-insurgency guys dropping suspected VC out of aeroplanes to make others talk.'

'Sure, those sorts of things are to be expected. It's regrettable but...'

'And the filth; cities and towns like garbage dumps; it used to be a lovely gentle place. When does it end? Do you quit after the thing worth having is destroyed?' I said, tired of hearing myself… oh, hell, Eddie, shut up! You're part of it, you know, you holy bastard!

'When the war is won, when this government has complete control of its territory and its people. When the Hanoi bosses and their local flunkies are bled to death in combat.'

'Years, then.'

'All wars come to an end.'

'Where do we get the right?'

'What right? You're not making sense, man.'

'Can't we insist the Vietnamese agree it's better to be dead than red? Especially as they'll be dead if the communists move in! When we fail here, do we just pack up and go to another hot spot on the map? Is that what Vietnam is for you, a red patch on a map? Are there others?'

'You talk like those college freaks.'

'Maybe… No, they come up with answers. I just mouth the questions.'

'Look, go home. Go home and rest up; there's nothing that can't wait. I just wanted to tell you your report on the Agent Orange problem is very thorough – except for a few snide remarks which some people might not appreciate. I'll be talking to headquarters about the problem. We should get the flights stopped and all the equipment checked and operating properly.'

The 'problem'? It's not the equipment but the… concept, the contempt, the arrogance… He'll never allow himself to see that. Why?

'When?'

'You know the army…'

'Move quickly enough when they want to.'

'Yes, true.' A weak smile spread across the colonel's face. 'We'll see. Maybe a couple, three weeks.'

'Jesus!'

'Come on, Eddie, let up, will you? Look, you're doing a good job on this. After you've rested up a bit, the province chief and I want you to continue with the estimates of crop damage by the defoliant so compensation can be…'

'I won't do it!' It was over.

'What?'

'I'm sick of doing your dirty work; you guys spray Agent Orange around, you face the farmers.'

'You're refusing my order?' He's looking stern now, this is serious business, this refusing an order. Dropping chemicals on people, well, that's in the nature of things, something worth doing, for the war effort, of course. But refusing an order, well now… serious shit!

'Yes.' I'm smiling now, unwinding.

'You can't!'

I'm going to laugh in his face; I mustn't. 'I can't?! Really, Colonel?' Damn, the look on his face tickles me.

'Not and stay here. As long as you work in this province you are under my orders…'

'Fuck your orders!' I was free. I felt it all the way down to the tiny knobbly bones in my toes. I was free, and he knew it.

'No need for obscenities!'

'Obscenities?! You dare talk about obscenities? You and your lousy chemicals; your five-million-dollar aircraft blowing the hell out of anything that moves…' I was laughing through tears. I couldn't help it. I was free of all the Horsts, free of the starchy, self-righteous bastards and bumbling idiots prancing around in their pressed khakis planning some new offensive. Agent Orange! Christ! They changed every real word – every kind of expression that might help to remind people it was human lives they were talking about – to mushy euphemisms. It was this habit, not calling a thing by its real name, that was responsible for so much of the trouble…

'Do you know what you're saying?'

'Do I know what I am saying?! Yes, I finally know what I am saying. I can't stop any of this tragedy you're inflicting on these people – and yourselves – but I don't have to be part of it. I'm not one of your teenage soldiers, those poor kids who do the killing and get themselves killed while you guys write and write on your yellow pads. Spare a thought for their mothers nine thousand miles away who see the body bags on TV. You've lost, man. I chose to come here and do what I could. I had reasons, good or bad, to do that. Now I have good reasons to un-volunteer. Simple!'

'I can have you transferred to the Saigon office; you can get away from the fieldwork. You're too uptight for this kind of…'

'You don't understand. I'm finished, done.' My pulpy ID card tore easily into a handful of pieces; they floated onto the desk. 'I don't work here anymore; I no longer work for the government. I'm a tourist!' The vehicle keys. They dropped on the desk with a jangle. The colonel's huge eyes watched me; he'd never seen a man take back his life…

I raised my arm in a perfect salute. 'I'll be off now,' I said simply and walked out of the office, past the mailroom and water-cooler, through the door and into the hot, beautiful, cleansing sun. Past the vehicles, across the compound with the white flagpole and the fluttering flag on top. Past the sentries at the gate – a nod, a word, a smile… a little blue taxi at the kerb.

'To the roundabout by the navy base. You know?'

'Sure.'

I braced myself on the greasy seat as fumes boiled up through the rusted body, the old engine rocking and clunking and rattling furiously, finally edging the taxi away from the kerb. 'Christ, I'll be dead from the exhaust before I get out of sight of the place!' I laughed. Dead on arrival… DOA? The driver squints at me through the cracked mirror. A formal letter to my wife: *killed in the line of duty… Edward was responsible for some particularly innovative initiatives that served as models for others involved in our government's critically important civilian assistance efforts to revitalise the rural areas of...* 'Such bullshit!'

'Huh?' the driver grunts.

'Nothing. Go there, OK?' Pointing, almost touching his head. Oops, no good, too close. 'Never touch their head,' Dr Leitz once told us. Something to do with the essential self – the spirit. Why didn't we just buy them a new fleet of taxis, re-engineer the city, put in some storm drains? Half the price of a B-52. Hell, it's a mess. 'Stop!'

'Here?'

'Yep.' I put a big tip in his hands and see his eyes goggle; thinks I'm another crazy Yank. I am. Dog shit sizzling on the sidewalk; I step over and around the ice block by the door and go into the dark bar. Empty. 'Yes, early, not working today. *Mot, ba muoi ba.*' What a laugh. The kid switches on the tape deck, sees my look and turns it off again.

'You've let the side down, Eddie.' No, I haven't, they've let me down. They lied to me, said we were to do something worthwhile here... 'and it just ain't so.' The kid ignores me. Good. Not a damn thing you said is true. Since Truman's day we've lied to ourselves, fooled ourselves. An error of judgement compounded over the years by more lies, deception, ignorance. Yes, ignorance of ourselves, of the so-called enemy, of our so-called allies. We haven't even learned the first thing about these people; what they think, what motivates them. We jumped in clumsily and, in the eyes of most Vietnamese people, simply became the next in a long line of foreigners wanting control of their country. From their point of view we followed the Chinese, the French, Japanese, British and again the French as intruders and exploiters. What's to be won? Now, I'm exercising my right to sign off; don't want to play anymore; taking my ball home.

I bent my head low and massaged the tight muscles along my neck. Can't go back, no need to, nothing to be gained by it. I'm finished... yet, somehow, beginning. Funny. Like the rest, I've been beguiled by noble words, snared by the rhetoric of thick-waisted politicians and snazzily dressed officers. Excessive power and super gadgetry unleashed against kids in black trousers, the violence spilling over, twisting the minds and bodies of soldiers on both sides, and civilians caught between. Two nations destroying each other so this small chunk of earth will or will not be ruled for a particular period of time in this or that fashion.

'Another?' the kid asks with a tentative smile.

'Sure.' He puts the wet bottle on the table. 'Ah,' a sigh pushes up from my chest. Finally, a hint of contentment. Mellow... the word passes through my mind like a soft breeze; you're mellowing out, Eddie! Ha! A long time coming, too, you elusive... a clear sense of now, awareness of the immediate moments at the edge of my life as my being; alive in the present; no past, no anxiety about the future. Vietnam is a place to live now, no longer a difficult 'problem' to be solved.

I prop my back against the wall and flip my legs onto the booth's long seat. Horst is right about one thing: all wars come to an end. The hating and fighting will be over here one day too. Imagine that? Maybe we'll even learn something from it; about our strengths and limitations; that we can't bulldog our way around the Third World anymore; that our weapons are useless in these struggles...

Who knows? I laugh. The kid at the bar glances over. A cockroach scurries across the table, daring me to flick it away. Those damn critters are survivors for sure! I'm grinning madly now and the kid looks nervous. Halfway around the world to find a life, to find a special woman! Linh will hear what happened when she gets back to the office and will be looking for me, worried; but I'm all right now, healing. I decide to drain the last of the beer and go to the apartment.

'Madness, no?' I say to the kid in Vietnamese as I get up from the booth and walk over to where he's chipping at the ice block with his rusty screwdriver. He smiles and nods, glad to see me leaving, I guess. I put the money on the counter and step out into the sunlight.

Love Song

Extra ending written in 2021

Dodging the onslaught of fume-spewing cabs and motorised rickshaws, I expertly dance, side-stepping two to the right, one to the left, from the bar to apartment. Carl's newspaper headline flashes before me: 'Saigon: The Garbage Heap of the Orient.' It's the same outrageous Saigon, busting at the seams from overcrowding with a continuous lion-like roar, but I'm acclimatised to the city grit now. I spot one of the familiar sidewalk hustlers, nod and stride off with purpose. Ambitious dreams of 'hearts and minds' – which once had a catchy ring to it – have fizzled and faded, like wispy clouds burned off by an unstoppable rising sun.

My next big move is unknown. For now, it's simple steps: off to the apartment, wait for Linh. A cold tea is poured and in my hand. I'm in the mood for my music, this time a Shirley Bassey number. I pull a chair to the window, gaze outwards, squinting as my eyes adjust to the brightness. I'm refreshed by the drink, stirred by the 'If You Go Away' lyrics Carl and I had once enthusiastically, dumb-drunkenly sung to the stars. The apartment is hot but it doesn't bother me. Nothing bothers me in my moment of Zen.

Miss Bassey's commanding voice continues as the notes drift into the corners. She sings of a fragile love to hold in her hand…

A cracking sound and an impressive round of rifle pops cut through the gutsy ballad. Shards of glass shatter across the floor. I'm thrown from my chair, dazed; looking up at the ceiling now and the walls seem to be closing in like I'm being squeezed in my own shit sandwich.

Viet Cong infiltration in my building? My God, they're a cunning, focused bunch, driven to win. All that's needed is the mere rumour of VC infiltration to trigger ARVN firepower aimed at me!

The music continues… Miss Bassey sings in the hope of holding on to love, whispering to the trees and worshipping the wind.

Fuck! What was that?! Is there a kid with a grown-up AK-47 trying to rub out this agricultural advisor?! No, no! I've got my Hawaiian shirt on, the one with the hibiscus blossoms. The little shit! 'I'm a civilian!' I yell hopelessly into the dusty, charged air.

I'm struggling to move, feeling lightheaded and sweating as memories circle back, stirring, slapping, reminding me of cooling monsoonal rain.

A child pedals by wearing my Russian hat – it's too big, too thick to be useful in this climate, but I smile at her image, close my eyes to thoughts of juniper berries and Jean.

'Is that a rubbery, round eye in my soup?'

'Yes, Eddie. It is very nutritious. *Ganbei*!'

I hear the swoosh and rustle in the flooded rice paddies; I can even hear those otherworldly, almost silent rice harvesters in their act of worship.

'Never forget that life is sustained in this country by rice.'

'Eddie old boy, thank you for your service to this country,' from the crisply dressed colonel. There's no time in the colonel's day for pocket watch presentations. No blind spot, man. I get it. Colonel Horst continues, 'It's war, and what's needed is resolution and defiance.' He holds up his yellow pad with one big word clear to see. '*WAR*, and what's that spelled backwards, Eddie?'

'Yes, Colonel, lean and mean, but what else did the British Bulldog say…? "In victory: magnanimity" and "In peace: good will".'

As the words fade in 'If You Go Away', there's a quiet voice. '*Em yeu anh…*'

I think about my life. The ups and downs. The decisions. The consequences. If Linh could see me now, crumpled and vulnerable, how different compared to that energised man who stood tall in the watery fields of irrigated rice.

I say to Linh, as I sense she's near, 'Hold my hand. Sing me a love song.'

★

Robert 'Bob' Dodd, 1968

Robert (right) with his journalist brother Noel Dodd, Saigon, 1968

Noel, Saigon, 1968

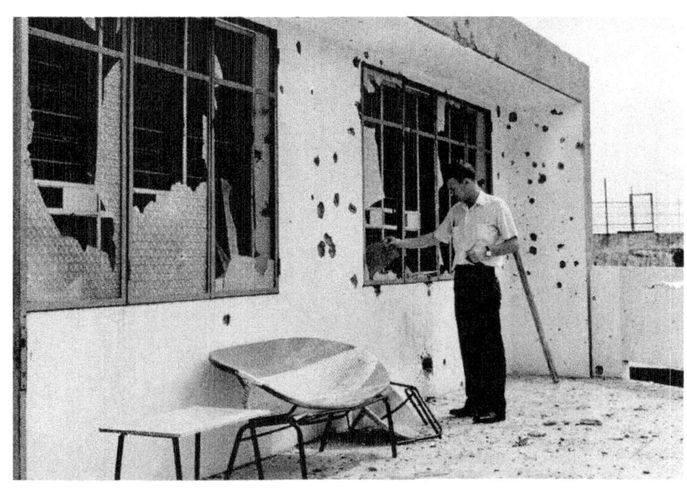

Robert at a bullet-riddled apartment house, Saigon, 1968 'Following Viet Cong'

Photo by brother Noel
He submitted an article with this photo
to his paper in Pennsylvania, USA

Afterword

'If you want a happy ending, that depends,
of course, on where you stop your story.'
— Orson Welles, *The Big Brass Ring* screenplay, 1987

Patricia came across this quote as we were working on Bob's manuscript and it got her wondering (and WhatsApping!): 'Don't you think an extra ending would work? Let's get Eddie back home. I'm imagining an apartment scene at the end.' So, while we wanted to be loyal to the original writing as much as possible, we decided the story could benefit by continuing a few hours more. She was inspired to write the 'Love Song' chapter, where Eddie's life takes a dramatic turn, mirroring the uncertainty in life. Her ending puts forward the contrast between the love song and an emotional Eddie, directly against the cruelties of war. It serves as a stark reminder of the immense loss of life and sustained injuries – military and civilian, Vietnamese and US – during this war; and agriculturalists were indeed among the casualties.

If you search 'If You Go Away' by Shirley Bassey on YouTube, you can follow the 'red thread' of music along with the text to the end. As Bob was stirred by a range of music, played on a quality stereo set of course, we think this idea would be Bob-approved. Does Eddie survive? She paints a deliberately ambiguous picture so the reader may play the stage director in the final scene.

★★★

'Who Lives, Who Dies, Who Tells Your Story' – the song Patricia heard in *Hamilton* that lockdown night was the unexpected impetus to giving Bob's story new life. How fitting that his daughter should be the one to help tell his story, and in so doing, rekindle her own 'kiddo' and beyond connections and affections for her father. As she reminds us, 'Timing is everything', in this project and in life.

When she proposed the idea of helping her get Bob's manuscript into print, there was no hesitation from me. I had previously helped on several smaller projects with Patricia in the UK and me in the USA, so we had a trans-Atlantic collaborative system that worked. Her extensive tech skills and relevant degrees dovetailed nicely with my editing experience, and I was thrilled to help get this story one big step closer to its readers. Her 'get on with it' approach, much like her dad's, has taken this project far beyond anything I could have imagined. When Bob's granddaughter Justine joined in with her enchanting illustrations and book cover design, well, the Dream Team was secure.

We knew finishing the manuscript would involve inputting his words into a word processor as well as some light editing. A surprise, however, was the extent to which we came to feel like team players with each other, and also with Bob. We used WhatsApp chats and Word document comments to consider and debate options, with authenticity always our guide. What were his intentions? Does this make sense? Would this be better? We always tried to imagine what he would have wanted, but knew he had started the editing process himself, trying out the Prologue in the third person rather than the first. We decided to keep the original first-person voice, feeling it brought the reader closer to Eddie, and worked nicely with the writing being a historical novel, from one man's perspective. I knew a metamorphosis was taking place when our WhatsApp chats started talking about 'the reader', and even how the novel sounded when listening to it, thanks to Patricia's broadcast and podcasting background.

We debated the splattering of profanity (at the urging of our grammar checker!) and decided it should remain – the backdrop was war, after all. We considered updating some language to fit current usage and sensibilities, but wanted the writing to reflect the late-1960s setting (e.g. the 'home economics gals', 'Chinaman' and 'Third World'). It would have been disingenuous to sprinkle in 'young women' and 'servers' when the late author chose 'girls'; likewise, we resisted swapping 'congressman' to 'politician'. We settled on using UK-style conventions, given Patricia's UK location, but were mindful that Eddie was American. To both of our amusement, one big discussion point was whether to stay with multiple instances of 'ass' or go with the British 'arse'!

As we became more confident in our decisions, we created chapter names to give the novel a helpful structure and added (and cut) a bit of text here and there. 'Downtown' was one such indulgence – a song that, when it played on the car radio during our Great Lakes camping trip, was enthusiastically sung out the sunroof while on the hunt for pizza in the city. Suggesting that IRRI would be better named RICE was also our creation – an idea from Bob's grandson, Cameron. The flashing an ace of spades comment was included after researching card games played by US soldiers. A newspaper article written by Bob's brother Noel, who visited him in Vietnam, prompted the addition of Bixby the parakeet in the 'Carl' chapter; another provided the newspaper headline in 'Love Song'.

While the book's storyline is from another era and in a war-torn land, there are parts and conversations we can all relate to. Finding love, navigating office politics, enjoying a joke with a friend are timeless themes. Suppressing the VC's high-yield rice propaganda – rumoured at the time to cause leprosy and impotence – is evidence of 'fake news'/ pseudoscience circulating at that time. And there are parallels between the war in Vietnam and recent military conflicts, where we can observe the unintended consequences of war and their repeating patterns.

Don't Break My Rice Bowl is an evolution of a story and of life on many levels. It started as a way for Bob to capture on paper his experiences in a complex time and place, to explore some long-buried thoughts and emotions, and to stretch his creative literary muscles. The project has been one of peeling back the layers (like an onion) as well as putting the pieces together (like working on a jigsaw puzzle) in order to see the whole picture – or as much of the picture as we could uncover. As Patricia and I became immersed in the text, it expanded our understanding of Vietnamese history and culture, as well as Bob's story, his life and how it fits within our own. And we learned that, just like a movie watched twice, this book gives up more details and connections on the second or even third read.

Photos and artefacts show a keen, young professional who was committed to his job and the project goals, and also interested in the local culture and people. Vietnam was Bob's first professional overseas experience. It was an exciting time, trying to make a difference in the lives of the farmers in a war zone, but was also fraught with the knowledge he was separated from his young daughters. You can see some of these emotions play out in the dialogue between Eddie and Ted – a raw and heartfelt section we left untouched. And Bob struggled with the realities of the war as he tried to carry out his assignment. He was deeply affected by the bombing of a real cooperative in the Gia Dinh Province as well as the overall effects of the war. To compound the stress of the assignment, while he was nearing the end of his 'tour' in Vietnam, he got the devastating news his brother Noel had died in a car accident.

When I met Bob in 1979, he was often on overseas consulting assignments but was increasingly drawn to the idea of Thoreau's cabin in the woods, where he could 'live deliberately' and make a difference in his own corner of the world. He gradually persuaded me (via letters through *my* letterbox from Indonesia and Tanzania) to look in that direction as well. In those letters, he also shared his development philosophy, which had evolved since his days in Vietnam: 'The challenge is to help local people develop an efficient yet human-scale technology that solves more problems than it creates.'

Our path to the woods led us to Maine, where Bob wrote the manuscript for *Don't Break My Rice Bowl*. He embraced life in the woods with a positive, always-moving-forward attitude, and seemed driven to create things he could share or leave behind, as if he knew his time here was short. He worked on our house and garden, got involved with the community, and continued with his writing, painting, and creating many pieces of pottery – including quite a stack of 'rice' bowls. Life was good until that fateful spring day when his easy-going 'Love you! Be back soon!' became his final farewell. 'Don't break my rice bowl', you'll recall, can be interpreted as 'Don't deny me my life' – eerily fitting for a man whose life was partially denied.

This book is more than just a story Bob wrote; it is *his* story, demonstrating you can't take the writer out of the writing. Patricia and I have learned that the writing process changes the writer – I'm sure it changed him, just as it has changed us. The message is shaped like working with a piece of clay, where it is hard to predict the exact outcome. It's no wonder he was drawn to working with words, paint and clay, shaping his creations for lasting effect.

The way we have presented his novel, sandwiching it between our thoughts as the 'bookends' and wrapped in a family-designed cover, offers a layered story within a story – about history, relationships and family over a few years in Eddie's story, but over 50 years cover to cover. The *Don't Break My Rice Bowl* project shines a spotlight on the passing of time and the insights gained with age. From Patricia's memoir-style Foreword we can see how her father encouraged her to take in and appreciate the world around her. In many ways, she's 'a chip off the old block' – notice how they both open up at their writing desks. I sense their history of letter writing to each other stretched *her* literary muscles at an early age!

The fragility of life was the late author's parting lesson; however, the words left behind in his manuscript were his ultimate gift. I'm not sure what Bob would have made of this fuss over his work and life, but I believe he would have been humbled, revealing a warm smile to show amazed appreciation.

It has felt like a greater force moved this project along as it got better and better, and we were swept up in the 'working with the words', as Patricia calls it. Shall we swap 'great' for 'swell', shall we switch 'beautiful' to 'radiant'? (Both of which we did, by the way.) However, there comes a time to say this book is ready for its readers; when you 'stop your story', close the laptop, and declare this book complete.

Beth

Beth on the Great Lakes camping trip, 1981
Photo by Robert Dodd

APPENDIX

A Vietnam Vet's Book Review

'Sometimes I had an urge to look down at my shoes to see if I had mud on them!'
—Jim Hubbard

I served in Vietnam from late 1967 through late 1968. During that period, I had occasion to work in and travel through the areas described in this book. The author has, in this autobiographical novel, absolutely captured the smells, the sights, the people, the culture, and the landscapes present during the US misadventure in Vietnam. While my daily duties were entirely different from those of the American civilians involved with the local Vietnamese authorities and villagers, I did have some of the same contacts though on different issues.

Through Robert Dodd's descriptions, I was taken back some 50+ years. His portrayal of village life, of the role of the village farmers, the sometimes blundering of US Army units, the arrogance of ARVN commanders and their soldiers, the passive nature of local villagers who only wanted to be left alone, and the secretive nature of the local Viet Cong cadre are spot on. I have been to Tu Do Street and stayed in an American-occupied hotel in Cho Lon. The narratives and descriptions of what transpired there on a daily basis brought back memories both good and bad. Dodd's description of his utter disgust and frustration with the administration and implementation of some US programmes offers tough lessons for any future US involvement elsewhere. This book deserves a place in the libraries of those who would seek to understand what America did right and, more importantly, what it did wrong over the course of its involvement in that beautiful country.

As I was reading, I smelled the smells, relived the experiences, re-wended my way through Saigon traffic, ate local food, shared tea with a village chief, and drank the local beer. Sometimes I had an urge to look down at my shoes to see if I had mud on them!

Jim Hubbard
January 2022

Jim is co-author of *From Michigan to Mekong: Letters on Life, Learning, Love and War (1961–1968)*

Email to Patricia, July 2022

I see 'Love Song' as the tragic end to the mission of a man attempting to do good OR a man, back home, suffering from a serious episode of post-traumatic stress syndrome. The text of 'Love Song' is not at all clear on this and that is the beauty of it.

Jim

Character List

Eddie, International Agricultural Advisor, from New Hampshire
Jean, Eddie's wife, New Hampshire
Ted, International Agricultural Advisor, from Pennsylvania
Carl, Reporter for a US newspaper, Eddie's older brother
Dr Leitz, Psychologist, The State Department, Washington, DC
Shoop, International Agricultural Advisor, from New York
Stubbs, Senior Training Officer, IRRI, Manila
Warren, Rural Development Specialist, Manila
Divinia, Bargirl, Manila
Rosita, Bargirl, Manila
Colonel Horst, Colonel, US Army and Eddie's boss, Gia Dinh Province
Henry, American Education Advisor, Gia Dinh Province
George, Agricultural Officer, AID, Saigon
Howard, Chief of the Agricultural Division, AID, Saigon
Mr Tam, Director-General of Agriculture, Saigon
Major Harry Keene, US Army Supply Officer, Gia Dinh Province
Sister Claire, Nun at the orphanage, Gia Dinh Province
Linh, Orphanage and Refugee Officer, Mr Sang's niece, Gia Dinh Province
Bob, US Soldier and Security Guard, Saigon docks, from Ohio
Mr Phu, Senior Agriculturalist, Advisory Team, Gia Dinh Province
Mr Sang, Senior Farmer, Linh's uncle, Gia Dinh Province
Tu, Student and Hostess, Saigon
Will, Rice Programme Chief, AID, Saigon
Clem, Credit Advisor, AID, Saigon
Lou, Irrigation Specialist, AID, Saigon
Dr Tommy Chang, Director, Taiwan Agricultural Group, Saigon

Dung (nicknamed Zoom), Agricultural Fieldman, Gia Dinh Province
Miss Cynthia Leggit, Journalist, from North Carolina
Reverend Glen Olsen, Minister, from Minnesota
Mr Ngoc, Head of Livestock, Gia Dinh Province
Lena (nicknamed Marshmallow), Bargirl, Saigon
Lena's friend (nicknamed Cricket), Bargirl, Saigon
Sergeant Beach, Sergeant, US Army, Gia Dinh Province
Turner, Soldier, US Army, Gia Dinh Province

Writer Inspiration

Photos by Robert Dodd (1967 to 1970)

The Philippines

1

2

Is that 'Stubbs' with his arms akimbo?

IRRI, near Manila (photos 1 - 2)

Vietnam

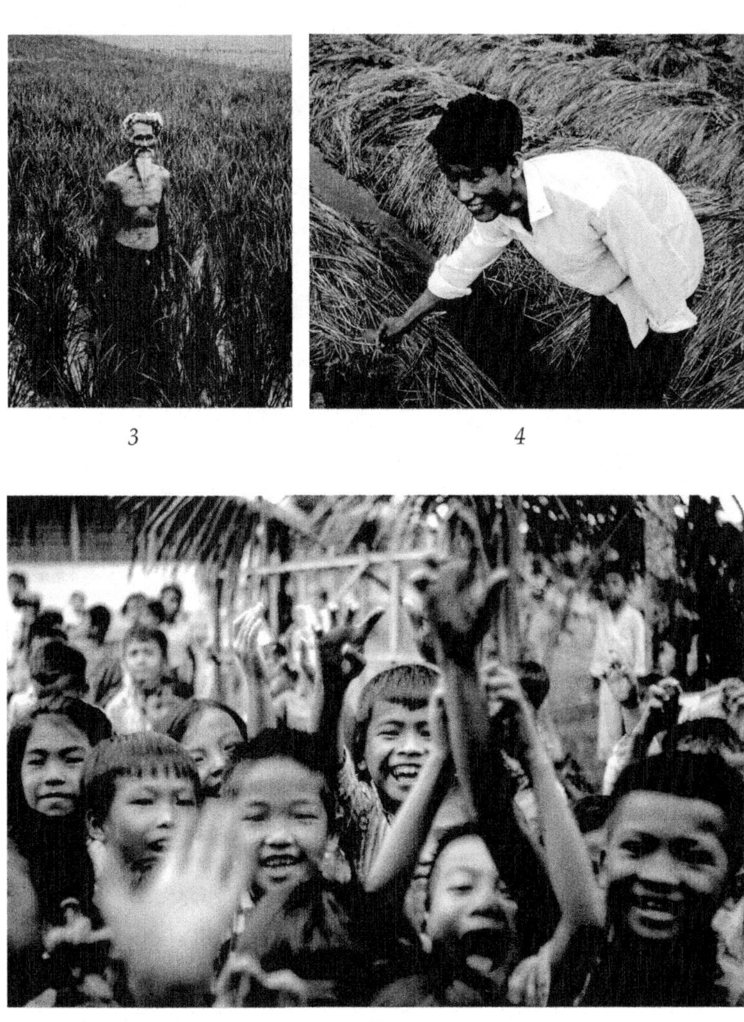

3

4

5

Village Farmers & Community Life (photos 3 - 7)

6

7

8

Saigon

9

Rice Picker in the Rice Production Programme, 1970

Robert H. Dodd, Overseas Assignment Life

1966–1970	Vietnam: Provincial Rural Development Officer; Chief of Agricultural Extension Section; Chief of Crops Production Division – USDA/USAID
1971–1972	Dominican Republic: Senior Advisor to Ministry of Agriculture and Ministry of Cooperative Development – USDA/USAID
1974–1976	Swaziland (renamed Eswatini in 2018): National Director of Extension and Training, Ministry of Agriculture – USAID
1976–1983	Various consulting assignments: • Indonesia • St Lucia • Jamaica • Thailand • Tanzania • Bahamas
1987	Ethiopia: A trip was planned for May–June 1987, but never happened due to his death

From the Gia Dinh Province to North Andros Island in the Bahamas, Robert worked as a senior advisor on long-term and consulting assignments with USDA/USAID projects in the areas of agronomy and crops, rural credit, livestock, fisheries, cooperatives, irrigation and home economics. In Swaziland, where he developed and administered the national agricultural extension and training programme, he also photographed (and painted) the region's wildlife.

On some assignments he focused on soil erosion (a problem in Tanzania and the hill farms in Jamaica), and improved cropping and marketing systems as well as the economic and social welfare of the farmers by more effectively using a region's natural resources. In Northeast Thailand, for example, he evaluated a village fishpond development project designed to create a year-round source of protein and water for the villagers. And he travelled island to island in the remote provinces in Indonesia, visiting small villages to identify ways to improve the quality of life and livelihoods of the villagers.

In Vietnam, in addition to some of the roles listed above, he was instrumental in establishing the National Rice Production Training Center, where district extension agents received intensive practical training in the culture and management of high-yielding rice varieties being introduced into the country, as well as a three-year rice production programme which achieved the national target of rice self-sufficiency.

On his way to Vietnam, he spent time at IRRI in the Philippines and got muddy in the fields with the 'intractable' carabaos.

Robert (holding the plough) with fellow agriculturalists at IRRI, 'ploughing rice paddy', Philippines, 1967

SCHENECTADY GAZETTE, THURSDAY, JULY 21, 1966

LBJ Hails Montgomery Farm Agent Dodd For Volunteering to Aid Viet Nam Farmers

By ALAN EMORY
Gazette Correspondent

WASHINGTON — President Johnson has hailed Montgomery county Agricultural Agent Robert H. Dodd of Fonda as a new kind of pioneer" for volunteering to teach American farm know-how to Vietnamese farmers.

* * *

Johnson said, "I extend my personal commendation for your bold and patriotic desire to help a courageous people struggling for freedom and human dignity."

The White House announced yesterday that Dodd and seven other young farm workers volunteering to teach American production skills to farmers in Viet Nam had been recruited for service as provincial agricultural advisers.

They will begin specialized training Aug. 1, with at least one in each province. The agriculture department recruited the eight.

In a letter to Dodd, President Johnson said, "As on-the-farm advisers to Vietnamese peasants and agricultural workers you will play an indispensable role in carrying out your country's pledge of aid to Viet Nam in a second-front war on hunger and poverty . . .

"The Vietnamese people in the provinces and villages are eager to modernize their farming methods, to speed up land reform, to build schools for their children and to improve health facilities.

"They need advice and assistance. You and your colleagues will help them to adapt and learn to use U.S. technical and practical farming knowledge and to obtain the supplies and services they need.

"Your work and that of other Americans in the villages and on the farms can contribute in an important way to shortening the war and saving the lives and resources of both Americans and Vietnamese."

In a White House statement, Johnson said, "I am grateful . . . to these agricultural leaders who are volunteering to work in the fields and villages to help the Vietnamese build a productive agriculture."

Dodd's six months of intensive training in the language and culture of South Viet Nam and in tropical agriculture will be conducted in Washington, Florida, the Philippines and Taiwan. About Feb. 1 they will be assigned to work 18 to 24 months alongside Vietnamese leaders in secured provinces.

Dodd is employed by the agriculture department's extension service and will work under the guidance of the agency for international development.

Praise for 'Farm Agent Dodd'

DEPARTMENT OF STATE
AGENCY FOR INTERNATIONAL DEVELOPMENT
WASHINGTON, D. C. 20523

OFFICE OF
THE ADMINISTRATOR

JAN 2 1969

Mr. Robert H. Dodd
Chief, Extension Branch
DP/Ext - (PASA)
USAID/Vietnam
c/o American Embassy
Saigon, Vietnam

Dear Mr. Dodd:

I am very pleased to tell you that the Agency's Meritorious Honor Award has been presented to the Office of Domestic Production, USAID/Vietnam in recognition of the outstanding contributions made in 1968 to the accelerated rice production program in Vietnam by individuals in the Saigon office and in the Provinces.

I have told President Johnson about the accomplishments achieved in the miracle rice program in Vietnam, and the contributions made by able and dedicated individuals on the USAID staff. He asked me to congratulate, on his behalf, each individual in the Mission whose dedication and superior performance made possible the successful results of this remarkable program.

I also send my thanks and appreciation to you for your outstanding dedication to the rice program which is of such vital importance to the Governments of Vietnam and the United States, as well as to the many Vietnamese farmers who are benefiting.

A copy of the citation for the honor award and this letter will be placed in your personnel file.

Best wishes to you for your continued success.

Sincerely yours,

William S. Gaud

William S. Gaud

HYATT
ARYADUTA JAKARTA

RICE HARVESTING

The women go in groups,
Young and old,
Parting the lush tillers,
Stepping lightly
Into the soft earth.

Their wraps are
Muted colors
Against the rich green shoots
And lemon-yellow grain.

They work quietly,
Faces hidden
In the cast shade
Of broad, reed hats.

With a caress,
Each grain-loaded panicle
Is taken by a gentle, female cupping:
A sensuous, intimate in-gathering
Of the seed.

As they slowly move
Along the rows,
No gods, no spirits
Of field or grain
Are offended.

'Rice Harvesting', handwritten by Robert Dodd

Lion portrait by Robert Dodd

Acknowledgements and Thanks

To David Rykiel and Ross Greenlaw, our husbands, for your ongoing support and listening ears during this all-consuming project. We had no idea how absorbing, and thrilling, and sometimes isolating, book creation can be!

To Karen Boren and Paul Greenlaw. Your expertise in the world of writing is clear. Thank you for helping us think we could fulfil Robert's publishing goal during a productive transatlantic Zoom call. And for all your insights and tips along the way, including how to identify and handle 'first-person narrator going into third-person self-address'!

To the BBC's Gareth Mitchell, a busy science communicator and radio presenter, for taking the time to read our story. When you emailed saying you were 'already absorbed' after reading the prologue, that only encouraged us more. It was your World Service radio programme, *Digital Planet*, that reminded Patricia of the importance of archiving lives and preserving data.

To Dr Peter Woolley of Fairleigh Dickinson University (FDU), a war scholar, and the Director of the School of Public and Global Affairs. When Patricia emailed her former Political Science professor with a 'Howdy', a friendly 'Howdy indeed' quickly appeared in her inbox! A few fine-tuning suggestions, a wonderful jacket quote and a top letter grade soon popped up in an email. All very kind! Thank you.

To Vietnam Vets Jim Hubbard and Charles Riley, Sr. It was an honour to have you read and comment on the novel, and reassuring to hear your reactions. Jim, thank you for your book review – it's a valuable addition to this book. Charles, we included the gin rummy detail thanks to you. It was important to us that the book connect with you both, as we hope it will for other veterans and their families.

To Thu Nguyen (who grew up in Vietnam and just happens to have undergraduate and graduate degrees in Political Science!) for also helping us feel reassured with the content. Several Vietnamese names and phrases were altered per your suggestion. You also made some great observations like, 'Had you noticed a few of the characters are described as "stocky"?' We laughed at that one and then made a couple of text changes.

To Anura Samara, you digested and connected with this book so strongly and personally. Thank you for your extra-detailed analysis of the story.

To John Vernon Lord, author and illustrator of *The Giant Jam Sandwich* and much, much more. Thank you for casting your very experienced eyes on Justine's book cover. She was honoured to get your encouragement during the development stage, and delighted by your very complimentary feedback on the final image as well as the chapter 'spot' illustrations. We agree, she certainly is 'versatile'!

To Cameron Rykiel, for asking his mum, 'Why isn't the International Rice Research Institute (IRRI) called RICE?' when Patricia played the manuscript in 'Read Aloud' mode on a family car ride. She took note in the backseat, smiling at this ingenious (kind of obvious) idea.

To Hannah and Julian Wilson, who happily answered Patricia's random questions in WhatsApp, checking certain US words and terms (like tailgate and dress pants) were familiar to a UK reader.

To the Spiffing Covers team, in particular to Liz Bourne and Chris Hancock for your trained eagle eyes, thank you so much.

To all the real-life characters who inspired the writing, and the unidentified people in the 'Writer Inspiration' section, we hope this book finds its way to you one day; you are part of the story.

And a big thanks to our amazing beta readers on both sides of the Atlantic and beyond. Your varied professional and cultural backgrounds provided us with diverse fresh eyes (and thoughtful comments) on our project. It was after your encouragement, particularly from Tom, that we expanded the Appendix. From the coffee/smoothie chats to the fun 'working lunch' with Maureen, hearing you engage with the characters like they were your friends was heartwarming. To see and feel your enthusiasm for the project would have left Robert 'Bob' Dodd at a loss for words.

Gowri Abhiram, India
Desiree Antonacci, USA
Micki Bennett, UK
Tony Bennett, UK
Debbie Dodd, USA
Tom Dufty, UK
Dan Entwisle, USA
Derek Erb, France
Julia Gilmore, USA
Tammy Hedderly, UK
Bernard Hunt, UK
Heather Innocenti, USA
Barbara Malm, USA
Rick Malm, USA
Dick Marshall, UK
Maureen Nevill, UK
Thu Nguyen, UK
Greg Phillips, USA
Paul Rogers, USA
Anura Samara, Australia
Ellen Ward, USA

Book Club Questions

- Who are the protagonists? What role do the periphery characters serve? Who are you rooting for?
- What are the life lessons you think the late author was trying to convey?
- Discuss the book's treatment of war. Do you see any repeating patterns in more recent world conflicts?
- President Johnson had ambitions to win the Vietnamese 'hearts and minds'. Do you think this objective was achieved?
- Discuss whether you think it was deliberate or a coincidence that the late author chose to name his main character Eddie while naming another central character Ted (both a nickname for Edward).
- The tone of the book (and Eddie) changes dramatically from Parts One and Two to Part Three. What might be the reason for this change in tone?
- Patricia mentions the 'red thread' of music running through the novel. What other red threads (themes) stand out?
- Winston Churchill famously said, 'The farther backward you can look, the farther forward you can see'. How important is looking back and the passing of time in the main story as well as in the cover-to-cover element?
- Justine's cover rice bowl has a precariously rounded bottom. Discuss its possible meaning.
- Where would you 'stop the story'?

The DBMRB Team Bios

Robert 'Bob' Dodd (1936–1987)

Robert's early years were spent as a Geordie in South Shields, England, living in poverty on a working class street. World War II broke out when he was three – making him witness to the forceful German bombing campaign overhead. At nine he emigrated to America with his mother. After high school, Robert signed up for three years in the US Navy, closely followed by Cornell University to join the undergraduate 'Aggies' studying Biological & Agricultural Science. After graduation he began his career as a County Agricultural Agent in Upstate New York. From 1966 to 1987, he worked as an International Agricultural Advisor and Consultant. He received the USAID's Meritorious Honour Award for outstanding contributions to the Accelerated Rice Production Programme and the USA Medal of Civilian Service in Vietnam.

Robert in his study, Florida, 1978

Patricia 'Trish' Rykiel

Patricia attended FDU's Florham campus (New Jersey) in the late 80s to early 90s, graduating summa cum laude. Her bachelor's degree major was Political Science. This was followed by a master's degree in Broadcast Journalism at UMD (Maryland). She worked as a computer trainer (Washington, DC) in the 1990s, and has been running her own technology consulting business the last 20 years. She was the UK voice of Avast the antivirus for a time – meaning, she knows how to say 'threat has been detected' with gusto! Patricia was also the creator (and voice) of a technology segment for a syndicated American radio show. She is wife to David and mum to Cameron and Justine. Patricia lived in the US for a year in 1984, and from 1987 to 2000; she moved back to the UK with her family in 2000.

Beth Jackson

Beth has a bachelor's degree from Miami U (Ohio) in International Studies, and master's degrees in Technical Writing (BGSU, Ohio); Special Education (UMaine); and Library & Information Science (USC, South Carolina). She has worked in research and editorial roles, but she most loved her 27 years as an educator in Blue Hill, Maine where she established the K-8 school library and worked with teachers and students to bring learning and an awareness of the larger world alive. She also played tenor in a community steel drum band for 25 years. She and her second husband Ross now live in Arizona where they miss sea kayaking and the Maine woods, but where they enjoy exploring the wonders of the desert and playing banjo and guitar together.

Justine Rykiel

Justine graduated with a First-Class Honours from the UK's Kingston School of Art, BA degree in Illustration Animation in 2021. From illustration to animation to motion design, she brings story and character to life. If she were to appear on the UK quiz show *Mastermind*, her specialist subject would have to be *SpongeBob SquarePants!* Awards: 2015, RBA Scholar; 2021, Creative Conscience Award; 2022, nominated for the Ifan Holweger Student Animation award and animation collaborator in the winning Student Documentary award entry, 'Man Up', at the Learning on Screen Awards.

www.justinerykiel.co.uk

We are on Instagram @dbmrb_book, if you want to learn more about the background and making of *Don't Break My Rice Bowl.*

If you enjoyed the book, please press it into the hands of another.

Patricia and Beth and Justine

Patricia with Robert on a concert night out
London, 1984
Photo by Beth Jackson

Printed in Great Britain
by Amazon